My Ghostly Lover

Judith Ann McDowell

This is a work of fiction. Names, characters, places, and incidents are products of the author's imagination or are used fictitiously and are not to be construed as real. Any resemblance to actual events, locations, organizations, or persons, living or dead, is entirely coincidental.

World Castle Publishing, LLC
Pensacola, Florida
Copyright © Judith Ann McDowell 2021
Paperback ISBN: 9781955086349
eBook ISBN: 9781955086356
First Edition World Castle Publishing, LLC, June 21, 2021
http://www.worldcastlepublishing.com
Licensing Notes
Cover: Karen Fuller

Mother Caulder exposed nothing to the public. But even though the inside sat off-limits to outsiders, the townsfolk knew what happened inside. Her establishment served women in their childbearing years. The women and girls received treatment for a disease, while others might be rushed to the legitimate doctor in town. Married women ridded their pregnancy because their family had enough children. Some Caucasian teenage girls came to visit. Their pregnancy will never stain the blue blood of their family.

Miriam's visited because her father's fiddle player raped her. He left an imprint of that tragic night. The accursed seed will no longer grow inside her. The fetus, would no longer be developing inside her, and she would be left with nothing but a haunting reminder of her stolen innocence. He didn't injure her; but used her as an unwilling toy.

She followed the madam across the dusty floor. Non-living rumored to inhabit the shop, and they wanted respect. The spirits must prefer dirt and dust since mysterious footprints appeared and vanished in the traces of sawdust spread across the floor. She led Miriam to a small room near the rear exit. A large black blanket covered the windows and prevented the light from coming in. Candles illuminated the dim room. Mother made Miriam sit in a chair which she must have gotten from the adjacent barber shop as a throwaway. The chair needed repairs, and when she leaned back in the seat, it tilted way backwards. The barbers next door donated the chair to Mother Caulder in exchange for something not even the shavers acknowledged.

Aromas like lavender and cinnamon saturated the small closet-sized office. These essences mixed in with the pennyroyal provided the spearmint fragrance. Miriam leaned back in the seat and once again jerked backwards. "Sit still pretty girl. Don't ya go hurting yourself. Now I specially made dis pennyroyal tea. Take a whiff of dis shit. Don't it smell like dat chewing gum the whores are always chewin?"

Mother handed Miriam a dirty cup of tea, as the teenage girl still spun a little in the broke-down chair. "Girl, I said sit still. You go moving in some odd direction, these spirits ain't gonna like it, and I am not gonna like it either when I poke you down dere. You needs to keep still, otherwise I might poke something else."

Miriam felt the abortion was better than carrying a rapist's child to term. He had appeared and vanished, like he came out of one of those old Creole folktales.

She wasn't going to tell her children any folk tales. Her child would no longer existed after the procedure today. When she matured, will she be capable of bearing children? Will they listen to her story? At least she'd tell the tale to the child of a dear close friend. Her story started this summer morning.

After a night at the local whore house, where the prostitutes made their meager living off the wages of the shrimpers arriving on shore, Miriam, with legs wobbling, used her arms to pull her petite body vertical. It took effort but once up, she strolled home, as her face grimaced with pain. The transaction had been completed, yet only time would tell if the procedure succeeded or not. Mother Caulder informed her that the termination was done, and the pain in her legs and lower abdomen confirmed everything. The witch gave her a mojo or gris-gris bag and Miriam put it in her pocket and carried the burlap bag charm for protection.

She paid no mind to the drug stores, honky-tonks and juke-joints inside the city limits. One half mile into her walk home, the pain shot through her legs into her groin area. Miriam sat on a bench, and bent her head, her legs stretched in front of her. She sat for hours, with a few blocks to go, as she rested, gathering strength. She lowered her head to pray to whichever God listened.

The pain stabbed her midsection like someone poked her with a machete. Raised Catholic, God didn't approve of abortions; however, she knew for sure He didn't approve of her daddy's band mate raping her behind the woodshed the last two months. The pain subsided enough so she could finish the odyssey home. The journey could last forever—she did not care.

****

The robust musician, her father, held his accordion in his hand as if he carried a small alligator. His left hand held the tail behind the legs to play the bass buttons, while his right hand held the gator by the throat as he pressed the keys. The way this man played the squeezebox reminded people of a young man scoring for the first time squeezing his girl's breasts. Clifton Chenier and countless others received their informal training from Miriam's father.

Beside him on the stoop sat the blind washboard player. A large glass of sweet tea or maybe amber colored whiskey sat adjacent to his worn work boots. He flicked away on the cleaning board with two bottle openers. Sewing thimbles were not masculine enough for him.

Adjacent to the washboard player stood the budding guitarist who possessed every trick in the book.

He played with more flare than anyone Miriam had witnessed, but he wasn't a skilled guitarist. He arrived on the peninsula from East Texas where the people lived and listened to the Blues. His Blues and the Creole music created an evolution in music that many attempted duplicating, and many failed. The kid displayed raw talent and undeniable showmanship, which boosted their live performances.

The shadows hid the fiddle player. Slashed across his face lay an inch-wide scar dashing from his ear lobe to the top of his chin and shaped liked the letter "S". Miriam wondered if the man wore a tattoo and the S, stood for a snake. The fiddler with no peers on fiddle became the greatest in the business. Rumors floated around such as he moonlighted as a professional hit man, a government hired assassin. He came and went as he pleased, disappearing into the unknown, but Miriam's father—who was in this business long enough—waited, determined to make it big. The fiddle player helped the band reach the national audience.

"Keep dat scar faced fiddle player away from me. I don't wanna see him no more," Miriam told her father.

"That man is our fiddle player. I ain't heard anybody play like him, Miri," Her father replied.

"But, but, bu…" Tears fell from Miriam's eyes. They came like the hurricanes which hit the gulf coast. Her father didn't care she gave away something meaningful and more virtuous than her family. She packed a bag and started limping north. Oblivious to his daughter's limp, he squeezed his instrument and the beautiful music rang out. The band soon played as one and perfection echoed throughout the neighborhood. Miriam spun around and smiled as the washboard, accordion, fiddle and guitar became one. The saltwater cascaded from her eyes as she witnessed the rehearsal. She turned her head and continued walking alone in no planned direction.

Miriam yearned to play music like her daddy; however, her daddy's career came before family. He hung six nails on the side of the house and attached baling wire to them. The guitar wasn't the fanciest, but Miriam treasured sliding a butter knife or a switchblade along the baling wire. She swiped the switch from one of her half-brothers.

Her father played with the world-famous Caucasian and Melungeon fiddle player. Folks near and far said ain't no one in the world played like him. The accordionist cared less that the man abused his daughter when the band took their whiskey or sweet tea breaks. Her father remained ignorant to the fact his fifteen-year-old daughter drank a cup of tea with leaves from the pennyroyal plant to force menstruation and cease pregnancy. His daughter also had a wire coat hanger shoved up her uterus terminating a pregnancy in case the tea didn't work. She used a Creole witch to perform the unblessed ceremony. The chances were immense Miriam never would provide her father with a grandchild. Turning the regional Southwestern Louisiana music into a national phenomenon with this fiddle player topped his priority list. Miriam's feelings didn't matter.

She hobbled town carrying a broom handle with a red and black bandana tied to it. The bandana contained a change of overalls, some torn underwear, and a hairbrush. She stole a few dollars from Daddy's coin jar and strolled away from their Morgan City house. She named her destination "anywhere but here," as she ventured towards the closest town or parish with the Blues still resting inside her. The spirit from the unborn child haunted her, as an old spiritual wailed in her head. Barefoot and dressed in overalls and minus undergarments she made her way from the peninsula. Somewhere the young girl heard Louisiana Blues calls the devil to you or they kick him the hell out of your body. Miriam wondered, "what's that poor little spirit gonna do that's hopping around inside me?" She thought about it as her young, sore body hitched her way east out of town.

Miriam caught a ride in the bed of a pickup truck from a lighter-skinned Creole man hauling his chickens to a Lafayette market. Once they crossed into Terrebonne Parish, the young girl noticed a juke joint at the intersection and took her second leap of faith.

Chapter 2
Terrebonne Parish

Miriam hung in jukes in Morgan City when her father played in town. Both her parents told her to stay away from them. A ton of men like her father's fiddler preyed on the young, naive and pretty country girls who may arrive. She walked straight in anyways and meandered her way towards the far end of the large shack.

She got herself a big glass of lemonade, while catfish fried in the cast-iron pans, crawfish boiled in the large pots, while the gumbo simmered. The red beans stewed in the large cast iron pots, mixed with sausage, green peppers and the natural spices which grew in the bayou. Pots of rice also waited for the guests to smother the grains with either the gumbo or red beans. Miriam snuck a few slices of catfish and nabbed a cup of gumbo. She wrapped the cornbread placed inside a napkin and put it inside the top pocket of her overalls. It rested beside her mojo bag and the switchblade knife she used to slide across the strings of her diddley bow.

Her body cramped from the previous day's experience, so she discovered a seat, as an older man played some country Blues on his guitar, his hair matted in dreads. The ancient man wasn't flashy, and his rhythm absent, but Miriam listened as the guitar wept, and she acknowledged the pain in his voice. The blues strangled the man. Miriam didn't smile, but her attention undivided, she focused on this man. The Blues jammed inside her, capable of outplaying this hack.

The crowd arrived as the old man relaxed the

audience for the popular man. This aged man wasn't the greatest player—his old and scratchy voice gave distinct meaning to the music. The troubadour played a little slower than most, but the slow Blues created a certain ambience. He made his dollars riding rails across the country, hopping off and washing dishes for a meal and shacking up in hobo camps, trying to get some rice and beans. On occasion, he opened a show or two in town and moved on. No one wondered if this man guarded the Crossroads. Most people in the area assumed the man was an old drifter playing his brand of country Blues.

After he played a few songs, he acknowledged the crowd. He tipped his hat straight at Miriam. "I goin' to sing a song I heard up in Wes Virginny, about this little house over yonder in Narleans." He hoped he pointed towards the Crescent City.

With a haunting voice resonating like he smoked way too many cigars, puffed way too much on his corncob pipe, and drank way too much rum and whiskey he started into the song, after going through the chords. Miriam recognized the A minor, the C, the D and F chords all in succession. Again, Miriam agreed he played the guitar too slow, even she figured she played better, but the eerie and haunting way he played created enchantment.

Then he sang:

There is a House in New Orleans,
They call the Rising Sun
It's been the ruin of many of poor men
And God I know I'm one.

During his rendition, most of the people gathered

and ate their grub. The audience dropped their spare change for the following performer anyway. Besides most people remained occupied scarfing the catfish, beans and rice and sipping on homemade corn liquor, passed around in jugs and mason jars. Others walked around, conversed with others, and did their damnedest to drown out the nice, old, rat- resonating man who played with passion to entertain the inattentive crowd. Miriam Landry, however nursed her glass of homemade lemonade while she paid attention to the old man. Before he even finished the set, the headliner came rushing on stage with his entourage. She frowned a little, as she desired to applaud the man. The song about the whorehouse in New Orleans stuck in her head.

Spectators sat waiting for the main act and rushed towards the stage and fought to sit in the folding chairs, so they enjoyed their comfort when the man was introduced. Tommie Parker, fresh from leaving his famous female companion, made a name for himself across the South. Acknowledged from East Texas, Louisiana and Mississippi, Tommie Parker, also known as Lightning Bug Parker, slid onto the stage. Known as the firefly, he glimmered in light and disappeared to the unknown. He moved on and off the stage like a firefly skipping through the Louisiana night.

An older dark-skinned Creole man running the juke announced the following act at his joint. He announced it in broken English and broken French since diversity ran amongst the Cajun and Creoles. The French weren't the only folks living here. Blacks and whites called this place home. The tin shack, sitting five miles across the Terrebonne Parish line, masqueraded as the juke joint. Lightning Bug Parker soon reappeared and ran across the stage with his Gibson guitar playing the Blues shuffle. About halfway across the stage he slid in doing the splits without missing a beat. He placed his guitar above his head, as he played his axe behind his noggin. Moving his guitar towards his face, it appeared he gave his lover a wet, sloppy kiss. He opened his mouth, picking the six-string with his incisors. He didn't notice the young woman eyeing him like she craved him. She devoted her entire focus on the man. This man never missed a note, not even using his chompers as the guitar pick.

He started singing about a cheating woman from a back-door romance, as a young lighter-toned Creole man came visiting. Lightning Bug sang partly in French, and the song reverberated loneliness, desperation, and sadness. Strictly the Blues at its purest, and for a fifteen-year-old girl running away from home, Lightning Bug Parker sent her an invitation. Raised around music, this became the initial time Miriam hung out in a juke by herself.

The man mesmerized her. She hadn't seen nothing like him, and her father traveled the country playing his music. The kid, reacting better since her hips moved to the rhythm of the music, her eyes and mouth ajar as her eyes pursued the man's every movement, and his hips moved in ways she never seen. Music from New Orleans, Shreveport, Lafayette and on the boot created a surreal effect on everyone.

"*We growed up way to fast back then,*" Miriam told me. "*Ways to fast. I just wanted to get out of the swamp and live in da city. I thought this old guy was my meal and my bus ticket out of here. I ended up living with him in Texas for a couple of months, before he dropped me off on Fannin Street in Shreveport. By the time that*

20

man was done with me I was ready for that life. He done did me up really good."

I guess the girl didn't care some older man got some cheap thrills from banging some underage girl. If that happened today, the man would be cuffed and sent away.

"Sara, you know I was a virgin."

"You were a virgin once?" I chuckled.

"Yes Sara, I was once a virgin and I would have taken yours if I was able too." The dark-skinned girl smiled at me as we talked on the shores of Sabine Lake near Lake Charles in Southwest Louisiana. This is where I welcomed the rest of her story.

Chapter 3
Tommie Parker

The modern and shiny 1936 coupe departed Terrebonne Parish in a hurry, and for once no hellhounds, law enforcement or mad as hell Creole men chased Lightning Bug. The car held two people and one passenger as it sped towards an adjacent parish in the middle of the night. Tommie Parker drove the Caddy. The rider, a naïve country girl by the name of Miriam Landry, sat beside him in the passenger seat, willing and waiting for anything. They headed for a little farm in Northeast Texas which Lightning Bug Parker owned. The little farm stood northwest of Shreveport and across the state line in the sleepy village of Omaha, Texas. Miriam wasn't sure what chores she'd perform in Texas. She hoped she'd play guitar and sing duets with the wizard. Miriam didn't wait until they got to Texas to discover her main chore. Her tender, young body wasn't ready for what stood in store for her. Miriam soon discovered all the reasons why he received the nickname Lightning.

"Why we stopping so soon, sir? We not in Texas yet."

"You such a pretty little thang. I'm taking you home and making you my new wife. I gotta divorce my current old lady first. You ready to get broke in?" The eyes weren't the only organs protruding from the bluesman.

Her body still bled, and for sure she wasn't ready yet. She wasn't more than thirty-six hours from having a spell, a cup of tea, and a wire hanger removing the rapist's fetus. Miriam wasn't ready for penetration. "No, no Lightning, I'm so sore down dere." Upon deaf ears Miriam pleaded with the man, about the pain in her lower abdomen, but her begs hushed, and a few miles northwest of Lafayette, Lightning Bug Parker took an unwilling Miriam in the backseat of his Caddy. Thirty-six hours earlier a coat hanger poked inside her, destroying a child conceived by a fiddle player's rape. Two hours later the coupe pulled off the muddy road. Miriam still found the sex painful, she still bled but she started to enjoy the act. He demanded another sexual favor to satisfy him. The oral pleasing performed on his farm the following morning and nowhere as painful.

"I could still taste my blood on his thing."

"Ew. What did you do?"

"I done did what I had to do. I took all of him."

Miriam stayed with the man in his Omaha, Texas farm home. The shack sat on a small piece of land his family owned, since they became free some seventy years earlier. It became Miriam and Mr. Parker's home. The small house sat in the middle of the three acres he owned. No plumbing inside the shanty, but five rooms occupied the structure, and on the outside an outhouse stood about one hundred yards away. Every time she used the toilet, Miriam pulled off a slice of the peeling paint from the walls of the outside of the restroom. Lightning Bug also raised chickens. He used them for eggs, and to slaughter and cook the birds when he arrived home. The chicken coop stood behind the outhouse and was twice its size.

The five rooms inside the house consisted of a kitchen, two bedrooms, a parlor room, adjacent to a small living room. In one bedroom sat a small horse tank, where they bathed. They ate in the parlor room and practiced in the living room. Miriam made her initial mistake by tossing her bindle stick on Tommie's bed.

"You don't frow your fucking shit on my bed. Dis ain't your bed bitch. Take that cheap ass back, and stuff it in your room. Da little one with da cot and tub in it. Now bitch. Get da..." Miriam started leaving the room, but Tommie kept yapping. "Don't you walk away when I'm talking to you." The man raised a fist at her. Miriam held her breath while noticing the blue veins protruding from his neck, however God intervened since she escaped getting beat-down.

Between tears, and after a loud and large swallow, Miriam responded. "I's sorry Lightning Bug. I doesn't know your rules yet. I thoughts we sharing your bed since I gonna be your new wife."

The Blues singer shook his head and said to himself. "This girl can't be that dumb." He noticed Miriam's big brown eyes and noticed the moisture coming out of them. "Nah, she ain't dumb, she ignorant." He collected his thoughts and gleamed straight into her eyes. "You are going to be my new wife, once I divorce my current wife. You're in Texas now. We need to be divorced before I marry someone else. Dis ain't Weesiana." He walked away shaking his head. He attempted speaking under his breath, but Miriam made out his muttering. "What da fuck you get you self into Tommie Parker?" He soon kicked a wall with the steel toed boot he wore.

Miriam sat on the edge of the cot. "I's sorry for throwing my stuff in your room."

Mr. Parker reentered the room all cool and breathing normal. He acted as suave as the initial time she noticed him. "You be fine, just do what I say. You gonna be a good wife to me. Now come into my room, and I'm gonna show you something I really like for ya to do to me."

After they finished, she licked her chops and made the man a tasty chicken dinner. Miriam already made great meals. She held her own in the kitchen creating mouthwatering meals, cooking chicken, critters and crawfish for her Mama. At her father's place she made crawfish pie and turtle soup. She caught the reptiles and crustaceans. Often, she shared the food with both parents, if possible.

Lightning did not demand too much of Miriam, sex, sex, more sex and meals. He expected her to clean-up after herself, and him too, even though he wasn't a sloppy guy. He desired a woman who satisfied him, and Miriam became his little whore. She started to enjoy the consensual pounding he gave her. She also assisted him with some of the farm chores, gathering eggs the hens laid, and taking care of him in bed, or wherever he chose his onslaught.

"Hey beautiful lady. I knows you wants to play the guitar, and I got dis old Stella that I won it from some fool, in a game a dice. Caught him playing with loaded ones, and it was his guitar or his life. I told dat mudder fucker dat since dem dice is loaded, dis gun is too." He got his handgun out of his pants and pointed it straight at her. Then he pointed it away from her towards the wall, pulling the trigger. The gun remained empty, but Miriam stood unaware of the fact. Nothing happened, but the young lady came close to peeing her pants. "Scared ya didn't I? Well I was pointing it like this, and dat was over in Jasper. Real bad place for a black man. I got dat boy's guitar and got the fuck out of there before them white hellhounds started chasing me. Not sure of what happened to da cheater. Could care less, but no one, no one cheats on Tommie Parker. I mean no one cheats on me, ya hear me?" The gun still rested in his hand, and still pointed somewhere near the girl, while she gaped at him, frightened, but with star-struck eyes. The older musician fascinated her, as her big brown, doe-like eyes focused on the way he moved his body when he moved and played his guitar.

He entered the parlor, sat beside her on the davenport and continued, "You know you can play it when I'm around and we're relaxing. We do that Spanish tuning. Here lets me tune it up for ya." Tommie plopped on the couch with the guitar and spun the tuning knobs on the end of the guitar. He tuned the bottom two and the high E string, resulting in strumming a perfect G-chord without using the left hand. "Now this is what they call Spanish tuning baby. Now's lets me find a slide that works on that purdy little finger." The man gave her ring finger on her left hand a kiss, then stuck it in his mouth and gave it a wet and passionate suck. When finished he kissed her fingernail. Miriam shut her eyes and grinned. A warm rush of desire filled her body. The legend soon walked to the kitchen. "God dammit bitch. Where da fuck is da slide?"

"I don't know Lightning. I hadn't touched your stuff." She recognized the noise of a loud crack and glass shattering. The musician returned with a full glass of beer and a broken Jax bottle. He came towards Miriam quicker than she liked. With the cracked edges pointed straight at her, fear soon replaced loving feelings she craved for the man. She peered at him, and her body trembled as if she skated on a frozen pond in the north. However, in Texas, and in August, one does not get cold. The glass of beer went on the table beside the davenport. He grabbed her finger again and placed the bottle neck on her finger, as if they got married. "Be careful of da jagged edge. Can't be cutting oneself. I can sand this down later, but first things first pretty gal we're gonna learn the slide."

She gazed deep in her man's eyes and smiled and started shredding the guitar strings. Miriam played the slide on her didley bow her father made for her, since she turned eight. She didn't demand lessons, she displayed natural ability, but she loved it when Lightning took the time to teach her. She wanted Tommie Parker to show her. It made her desirable and when nurtured and craved, Miriam relished returning favors.

Her feet tapped to the rhythm, as she thumped the bass string with her thumb, while she slid the broken Jax bottle from the fifth to the seventh fret, and all the way to the twelfth, back to the fifth and returning to the twelfth again. On the twelfth fret she shook her left hand on the strings inducing the vibrato. She smiled at her tutor with batting eyelashes.

Her brown eyes shone brighter than ever. She exposed her teeth for one of the rare times. They weren't a pearl white. In fact, her teeth displayed a pale white, almost yellow due to her smoking, and they protruded at angles, with small gaps between them. One incisor vanished due a string and door following decay, but to Tommie (Lightning Bug) Parker, and anybody else privileged enough to witness her grin, observed the most beautiful smile in the world. "Damn girl. You is good. I was looking to sit down and teach you some stuff. You might not need me too."

She reached out her hand to his and took his middle finger and pulled it to her mouth, and placed it inside, and repeated the kissing, licking and sucking action performed on her. "You can still teach me stuff." She repeated the suction on his fingers. The guitar lessons waited, until after he sanded and polished the bottleneck, and after she finished polishing. That night, sleep was intermittent, and he made her a large country breakfast in the morning. Biscuits with gravy, eggs and sausage, and following a repeat performance, they limped towards the chicken coop.

"I am gonna show you how to catch and clean up some chickens."

"Lightning, I already know how to cook and clean dem. Show me which one you want." Lightning showed her a rooster, and Miriam entered, intending to grab the bird by the legs. The rooster ran, but Miriam dove like a football player at Grambling, attempting to save her team from giving up the winning touchdown against Southern and grabbed the cock by its legs. She held it upside down as the blood rushed to the bird's head, giving it a euphoric high like the bird smoked some of Lightning Bug's most potent reefer. For a brief period, the bird squawked, clucked, and flapped its large wings trying to escape. Miriam, an expert in this, took the bird to the chopping block. One quick slash with the hatchet and blood spurted everywhere.

Miriam tossed the headless rooster into some boiling water. Feathering the bird was an easy chore, like sweeping the floor for her. With the feathers all plucked, she ripped out the organs of the dead bird and rinsed the poultry off. She got another knife and chopped the cock, like a scar faced fiddle player and soon tossed the pieces in a bowl of salt-water. She grinned again and brushed her hands back and forth together, then washed and dried them. *"Mrs. Parker?"* Miriam imagined someone saying. She'd accept Tommy's proposal. It didn't matter to her if another Mrs. Parker existed. It didn't matter if there were two or even three Mrs. Parkers scattered about.

Tommie Parker stood impressed. He smiled at her, aware the girl had bride potential, plus she's young and gullible enough to go along for the ride. Miriam wondered if she's the one for Lightning Bug, but he didn't apprehend. One woman demanding a lifetime became too much to ask of him anyway. He received what he craved from her—well it made him a happy and content man.

The sweet fragrance of mesquite freshened the Texas air, as fire burned in the pit. The logs burnt enough for Miriam to throw the chicken and some potatoes on the grill and she made her and Lightning Bug exquisite dinners. She satisfied him in several ways, and Mr. Parker never complained. They continued strong for a few weeks until he traveled North for some shows. He packed his coupe and gave Miriam a kiss goodbye. "I'm gonna write you every day my Louisiana gal. The place is all yours, make sure to keep da coop clean, but slaughter what you want."

"I'll be thinking of ya every night." He went out the door and the Caddy departed, spitting out gravel behind the rear wheels, as he busted out towards the highway. *He didn't seem in a hurry the night before,* Miriam wondered, and figured she over-studied the situation. She completed the chores; cleaned the chicken coup, gathered the eggs, and slaughtered herself a rooster, and fried the bird.

His Stella guitar remained at home and in Spanish tuning. Miriam practiced the slide techniques he taught her. She played guitar first-rate, but the girl sat alone surviving in East Texas by herself. She didn't crave a lot to get by. Miriam desired food and guitars. Not much else mattered to her, except her man lay elsewhere, and not next to her. She knew without a doubt he'd return, but since he made no contact, she sat alone, clueless about his arrival.

Lightning told Miriam he'd return in three weeks, however the initial letter she got from him stated extra shows were added in New York. He'd perform at the Apollo. About the same time a neighbor from nearby came by checking on her. The man, younger than Tommie in his early twenties checked Miriam out. His eyes went from the top of her head down to her little bottom, and he smiled and told her, "So you're alone. Heard you damn good on dat guitar, and you makes a mean chicken dinner also. Minds if I stays a bit and listens?"

"Sir, I don't even knows ya. Lightning says no visitors."

"He ain't here, is he? Ain't he on the road again? You gots to be lonely." He moved his hips a little and the focus of Miriam's eyes went with the swaying motion.

She eyed the visitor from head to toe, stopping her vision near the middle. The stranger appeared, younger, taller, darker and stronger than Lightning. Something about him exuded sexuality. He wore blue jeans and a white sleeveless tee shirt. One quick glance at his exposed biceps glistening in the sun, proved this man worked the land for a living. The droplets of perspiration added to Miriam's gleam, and he kept smiling at her.

"I'm his girl. I needs to be faithful to him, so I can't let nobody in." She tried to shut the door, but she couldn't and not because the young man prevented her from closing it in his face. Like a deer hunter who witnessed a beautiful buck, she couldn't pull the trigger. "Well I suppose you can come in, but we ain't doing nutting. I'm just going to give you some sweet tea and some leftover food and plays you a couple of songs."

"Dat's all I want. I knows whose gal you are, but don't ya think he's doing every lady from here to Chicago?"

She gawked into his eyes, gave him a total glance. She smiled at him, taking in a deep breath. "I don't cares about dat. As long I'm his, I'm staying faithful."

"Damn girl. Just feed me and play me some music. Dat's all I want. Nobody talked about me getting stuff from you until you did." Blushing, and squinting, Miriam shook her head and walked away, she grabbed some food for the young man as they sat in the parlor room of Lightning's little shanty.

He took a bite of the chicken. "Mmm girl, you make some mighty fine chicken. Now lets me hear your best chops."

"Wacha wanna hear?"

"Do some man cheating on me song."

"I don't knows any."

"Make one up. Dat's what most Blues guys do around here. Just make one up on da spot."

Miriam started doing the twelve-bar shuffle on the Stella. She didn't like playing the shuffle in Spanish tuning, she preferred standard when she flat picked the guitar, so she adjusted the tuners. She fiddled with the knobs and tuned it, and she smiled at the man. She kept strumming, waiting for the correct part to start singing. The younger man tapped his stinky dogs to the rhythm of her playing.

Since My Baby's Gone
Don't mean it's time to play
Since that man is gone
Don't mean it's time to play
Dat man been gone for several days.

My baby's gone
Don't need nobody else
My man be gone
Don't need no one else.
Coochie all wet, but it stays up on the shelf

My baby's gone
Don't mean it's time to play.
My man is gone
Don't mean it's time to play
Got things to do, even when he's away.

My baby's gone
Don't need no one else
Dat man be gone
Don't need no one else
Da coochie all wet
Just take care of it by myself.

Miriam finished the song and put the spare guitar in the guitar stand. "You got to leave now sir."

"Pretty lady, you talking and singing about you hoochie coochie, make me feel a little mean right nows. I can't leave ya feeling dis way." The man didn't focus on Miriam, instead he eyed the grandfather clock which stood tall in the parlor. He glanced out the window. "Damn baby, I got to leave ya here. Don't like leaving a woman waiting for shit, but I's gotta run." He bolted out the door. Miriam exhaled all the air out of her lungs. Remaining faithful to Lightning remained a dream, but she also desired a tumble with this man. She relaxed for a minute. The front door burst open again, as Miriam's jump escalated her from the davenport.

"Lightning Bug, what you doing here? You tell me you're going to New York for two more shows."

"Who da fuck was over here. I sees me an extra glass of tea and an extra plate. You got a man over here? You be fucking someone? Where da fuck is he?" Each screaming question got louder and louder. Miriam squeezed the arm of the couch trying to relieve some of the new-found tension in her body. She sat her ass on the davenport, tapping her toes, with eyes wide open, but with the rest of her face void of expression. She told him the truth, since she did nothing wrong.

"Dis man stopped by. I told him I can't have no company."

"Then what da fuck is dis glass of half drank tea doing here?" He raised the glass and threw it near Miriam's head. It cracked on the wall behind her. "Now you is gonna clean dat up. Now what da fuck is dis plate doing here? Half eaten piece of chicken on it." The drumstick crossed the floor as he threw it at her. She deflected it with her guitar picking hand, and he flipped the plate at her too. It came soaring at her but missed. It shattered behind her, close to where the glass lay in pieces. "Now you is cleaning all dis shit up."

33

The guitar stored out of place, and of course he noticed. He used the stand for his Fender. "I let you use da Stella, but bitch you need to put it back in da right place. Damn girl, I leave for a few weeks, and you fucking some guy, and messing up da place. I know whats I gots to do with ya."

"Lightning dis guy came over. I didn't invites him. I told him to leave, but he didn't. I fixed him a plate and glass of tea, and just played him a song. Dat's all, and then he left like dat fox dat raids the chicken coup. I didn't fuck him or nutting. I told him I'm your gal, and ain't want him. I told hims to leave many times." She grabbed a broom, and a dustpan, bent over and started sweeping the shattered pieces of glass.

He glared at her, with scrunched eyes and a scowl on his face. His lips protruded outwards. Even louder than before he screamed, "Did you want to fuck him?"

"No!" Miriam screamed her reply. "I just wants you." Still shaking like the leaves on a pecan tree, she swept the large pieces of glass, also getting the small slivers. She bent over showing Tommie Parker her butt, and the man decided he no longer desired Miriam Landry. He kicked her hard with his steel toed boots he wore. He kicked her in the crack of her ass. She went flying into the kitchen face first and landed on her nose.

"Now get in da car. We is going for a ride. Taking you to a place where whores like you hangs out. Get a move on bitch."

She packed her small bag. Her wardrobe tripled in size since she moved in with Tommie Parker. Everything still fit into her little bindle stick. Strolling at a turtle's pace by Tommie's Stella guitar, her eyes roamed all around its curves and she wondered if she'd

34

pack the Stella. After all he let her play it. She kept drooling over the guitar, like she admired the man earlier. She longed to hold it, like she desired to caress him. If a partner accuses you of cheating, and the accuser won't even take a half of a second to listen, maybe Miriam should have dropped her pants, and let him fuck her. She carried the guitar towards the car.

"What da fuck, you ain't taking my guitar either bitch. Set it down, before I cracks you over da head with it." He paused, took a deep breath. Clear as day the uneducated East Texas accent disappeared as he said, "Fucking retard. Stupid bitch." Miriam dropped the six-string, not caring if his worn guitar received another scratch, and ran out the door towards his car. Her whole body shook as she plopped in the passenger seat. She no longer desired to change her name to Mrs. Tommie Parker. Living another day mattered to her.

He came out to the car, a relaxed man. "Baby you just gonna leave like dat? Don't you love me anymore? I'm just testing you. I know you didn't fuck dat man. I told him to come over. You failed parts of da test but passed da other part. You can still stay with me."

She glared back at him. Her eyes clueless on how to respond, and her mouth remained shut tight. Aware, her response wrong, whichever way she answered. After she took a deep breath and she exhaled loud enough for her man to witness. "You talk shit to me, and I don't need none of that. Take me to wherever you're gonna take me. I'm done with dis shit."

"But I is sorry." He put his arm around her and tried to kiss Miriam. His eyes big and bright enveloped her. His long and lean body also released a pleasant fragrance.

She twitched her nose as she inhaled his essence. She lowered her head, gathering courage or praying. "You ain't sorry, besides you're gonna hit me with something you throw and knock me out. I want out of here." Miriam exhaled, folded her arms, sat upright and peered straight ahead waiting for the man to drive her anywhere. She sat and waited and waited. The sun started setting in the western sky, and neither the car nor the girl budged.

"Baby, when I was on da road, I only think about ya. I want you to be my wife. I'm sorry for the way I acted." He didn't get on his knee to propose; or even give her a ring. However, the man planted a soft kiss on her forehead, his lips brushing her below her hairline. Snatching her hand, he led her inside his house. Tommie made her dinner and they made love. The man still couldn't satisfy her, but in Miriam's mind, she felt complete.

The following day the future legend ran some errands in Dallas. He might have been with another wife, searching for wife six, or buying some smack, or selling reefer. Miriam didn't know or care. She lounged home alone all day long, her chores completed, wondering what to do. She always admired the Gibson guitar he played. The craftsmanship, the woodwork, the body, the guitar radiated beauty. Miriam lifted his Gibson guitar and wondered about the differences among his National resonator guitar, the Stella, and the Gibson. She played better in Spanish tuning, so she tuned downed the Gibson. Striking the strings open in Spanish tuning makes a perfect G chord, and it's also perfect for the slide. She grabbed the knife she used for a slide. The Gibson performed much quieter, since two cones lay inside the

National to increase the volume. The National was an electric guitar, before the great Bluesmen invented electricity. She placed the guitar in the stand without changing the tuning to standard.

When Lightning Bug Parker went away from home visiting his wife or lovers, buying or selling some pharmaceuticals, or working the land somewhere or playing an impromptu show for neighbors, Miriam picked up his Gibson guitar, and started strumming in a down, down, up, slam the thumb on the bass and repeat the pattern. She changed chords in the traditional I, IV and V patterns. The progression played the same she used on the porch with her father, the blind washboard player, who played with bottle openers instead of sewing thimbles, because sewing thimbles were not masculine. Sometimes the white fiddle player with a scar across his cheek played along.

She missed the sweet zydeco songs from the peninsula, but once she slowed the tempo a notch, she made her guitar cry and sing, and she fell in love with the Blues, and soon wrote one of her first songs. A smile came to her face as she wrote a song about a fifteen-year-old sex slave to a future national treasure.

After completing her song, she smiled, feeling a purpose to her life evolved. She didn't count her impromptu song she created when Lightning tried to catch her cheating. That ditty she performed for giggles. She relaxed on the davenport with his custom-made Gibson. "I'm ready to shows the world who I am." Miriam said to no one in particular.

Unfortunately for Miriam, her initial lover also became her audience for her debut performance. She ached to surprise him on his custom-made Gibson.

Tommie Parker once again came home hours early. The Gibson guitar sat strings down, resting on the sofa. The Stella stood at attention in their bedroom placed in the stand reserved for his Gibson. Miriam grabbed the Gibson and started to show her man what she figured out today. She wasn't met with applause; however, the bluesman still used his hands and fists to communicate.

"You ain't never touching my Gibson again." The frustrated man shook his fists. His fists shook near her beautiful but broken face. He hadn't struck her, yet. Spewing from his mouth loud and vicious yelling, but the words were tame compared to what followed. She discovered his knuckles which connected the fingers to the hands hit harder than the ones dividing the fingers in half. At least, Miriam received the slap on her cheek as she received the backhand from her man. His steel toed boots inflicted pain on her thin, petite body when he booted her from a raised porch and she fell into the thorny rose bushes lining the house. Miriam struggled to her feet, hanging on to anything she grasped, forcing her body to stand. She realized what she needed to do.

She brushed the tears away from her innocent face and wiped her eyes dry with the palm of her hands. The innocence on her face disappeared and was replaced with a sight the Blues legend must have been familiar with. Miriam's sweet innocent face burnt with fire in her eyes. If looks could kill. "I'm running home," she told him as she walked past the man.

"Miriam I'm sorry, but I thought I told you no one touches the Gibson. You can always use da Stella. Hell, bitch I was gonna trash it at my next show. I'll give that to you, but no one ever touches that Gibson." The man pointed to his beautiful crafted guitar. "You ain't running home neither. You too pretty to be wandering around East Texas and Louisiana by yourself. Lots of mean peoples out there. I know. I am one of dem."

"I'm sorry Lightning Bug. I just wanted to play you a song, and I can play every bits as good as you, but I can't do da fancy moves and stuff. Do you want to hear me play?"

He grabbed her little hand and fondled her fingers. "Your fingers are much too small to play my Gibson anyway." He reached up and kissed her hand like a gentleman. His whiskers tickled the back of her hand and the legend sped away towards the house. He came out with his Stella guitar. "We going to practice for a couple days. I know of a few places in Shreveport you can play."

Miriam didn't recognize the sarcasm in his voice or the sarcastic gleam in his eye. Blinded by the fame and blinded by the East Texas legend, Miriam didn't leave. She anticipated something special between the two of them.

"Here's the song I's gonna play for you. I wrote it myself." Miss Landry started the shuffle with the Stella guitar, Mr. Parker let her play, the young gal started singing to her man and mentor.

> *You got a wife and another one on the side,*
> *You got a wife and another two on the side....*

"No, little gal, dat ain't no Blues. You doing it all wrong. Plus, baby, your voice is much too sweet for the Blues. You need to get sad and angry. Grit dem yella chompers when you sing." He smacked her in the stomach. "Sing from here girl, sing from here."

"Let me keep trying." She wrote a better opening

39

phrase and started again.

You didn't save me; I came here on my own.
You're not a savior, I came up on my own
I am just fifteen when I ran away from home.

This girl ain't a dog, you keeps on a chain.
I ain't a dog…

Again, the man interrupted the girl. "Fucking retarded girl. You never going to be doing it right. How many fucking times have I told you to play behind the beat? Most of your stuff is good, but also write lyrics dat ain't so obvious. I can see the talent. Damn it girl, you still ain't hold the guitar right. Bend your wrist a little more." He grabbed it harder than he intended, leaving a bruise. "You ain't ever going to get it are you?"

Endless attacks, endless sex for Miriam and Lightning Bug went on for the following two weeks. The sex didn't matter to her. She desired playing the Blues and since she lived them, she stayed bound and determined to play them. She was not letting let some future legend get in her way. Lightning Bug Parker grinned, oblivious to Miriam's inspiration.

"Takes me to some juke-joint so, I can play at a show."

"I got a better idea. Pack your stuff and hop in. We are going for a ride. I know a place in Shreveport where you can play sumfin I know you is good at."

She played before twenty drunken black men in a club near St. Paul Bottoms on Fannin Street in Shreveport. "You played terrible little bitch. I'm gonna show you everything you need to know after we get home."

She played some of Lightning's songs, the couple she wrote, and she played a couple she observed in various jukes. She played the song from that drifter in Terrebonne Parish. Miriam couldn't remember all the words, so she created her own.

There is a house in New Orleans
They call the Rising Sun
And it's been the ruin of many a poor girl
And God I know I'm one,

My mother she worked the land,
growing them old Red beans,
My father played accordion
South of New Orleans.

Now the only thing a rambler needs
is a suitcase and a trunk,
The only time she is satisfied
Is when she's on the hunt
Mama, don't tell all your other
To do what I have done,
Lay your life in misery
In the House of The Rising Sun.

A well-documented fact stated the legendary singer Leadbelly used to roam Fannin Street in Shreveport. He still frequented the area. Also, it was a fact Leadbelly had published recordings of him singing, The House of the Rising Sun." Where he picked up the song no one knew for sure. When Miriam played the jukes and street corners in the poorest section of town the infamous Leadbelly also visited the area.

Tommie Parker no longer gave Miriam guitar lessons. He decided Miriam's talents suited for different pleasurable activities. They returned to Shreveport after another week and visited an old friend of his. He shoved her in the door without the Stella or any guitar. She possessed only the clothes on her back. The coupe pulled away into the Shreveport night while Miriam stood at the door of the shanty, disguised as a whorehouse. She turned her head over her shoulder as she witnessed Lightning Bug's coupe drive away from Fannin Street. Spinning around she noticed her unfamiliar employer, an overweight Negro woman in her mid-forties.

"Come in Miss Landry. I was expecting you." The woman whom Miriam would address as Madam called to an younger woman, not much older than nineteen and the girl led Miriam to her room. Miriam studied her co-workers' every move.

Chapter 4
Felicia

"Am I a whore now?"

"We're whores. We live in dis whorehouse and Madam treat us pretty good. We got us a bed to sleep in and foods to eat. Better than some girls living down in the swamps where I came from, or out in da mean and dirty streets."

"I don't want to be no whore. I want to play music. Dat mean ole man took his guitar back from me, but I can play real good."

"Well maybe if we whore good, someone will get us out of Madam's house, and we can be live ins. Cook and clean dey house for dem, as well as screw dem."

"I's don't want to screw no one else. Lightning Bug says I's gonna be his wife someday."

Felicia, the older girl, glared at Miriam, rolled her eyes, and spat on the floor of their shared room. The room they shared possessed small beds for each of them, and a flimsy curtain separated them, enabling little privacy while the men received their entertainment. Felicia stood taller and a little thicker than Miriam. Some guys preferred thickness. Others liked Miriam's thinner, petite body. To most men it didn't matter. They craved satisfaction. "You say you was engaged to Lightning Bug Parker? I was engaged to him too. We gonna be married last summer. Then suddenly, he dragged me here. I like my life much better that wid dat foo."

"You're lying. He loved me, and Lightning will be back. I know it." Felicia spat on the floor again.

"Miriam Landry you da foo. Next time when dat

motherfucker will be back is when he drops off his next girl. I promise ya."

"Den he's gonna take me back." Miriam said trying to convince herself, even though she understood the answer. Felicia gawked at her, shook her head, and spat into the bucket again. The girls used the bucket for mopping the wood floors.

"Lets me shows you around Miriam. Follow me. There's not too much. Ain't no toilet. You need to go to da toilet you walk down da street. Dere are outhouses across the lot. We do needs to bathe every day. Some white folks want to screw us, so we need to be clean for dem. Now some of these mudder fuckers are rich. Had some girl get hired by a rich lawyer. She's working as a maid in da white parts of town now. Dat's who you just replaced. The tub is right there." She pointed to a metal pool; the girls bathed in. The four girls dat live here s'pose to bathe together, unless we're busy. There are men dat likes to join in too. They pay Madam extra money to takes baths wid da four of us."

"I needs me a bath."

"Me too Miriam. I's had me a busy day already. I needs to get this scum out of me. We can take one together." Felicia eyed Miriam like there were no finer slices of crawfish pie in Louisiana. She walked towards her and lifted Miriam's dress off her, pulling it above her head. Miriam wore no undergarments and soon she stood naked. Felicia hugged Miriam's naked body and whispered into her ear. "Welcome to being a whore. Dis is the only time we get to enjoy it." She kissed Miriam on the neck, and Miriam squeezed her mentor back. They held hands as they got into the bathtub together.

The nineteen-year-old took Miriam under her

44

wing, and Miriam grew to adore her mentor. Felicia wasn't her real name. She changed it when she went into business. She liked the name since it resembled her specialty.

The men loved Felicia so much, they even gave her a nickname—they called her Slurpy. Felicia became an expert at performing certain pleasurable tasks with her clients and always left the customers satisfied. A lot of the men preferred oral sex anyway, especially the married clientele; whose wives refused to perform it on them.

Felicia and Miriam became close and shared their bed during break time. Also, men requested both together and sharing never became a problem, if it involved no bizarre fetishes. Both girls enjoyed sharing each other's intimacy. Miriam never questioned her sexuality. Whether she's a lesbian, bisexual or something else, she never identified herself. Miriam, always Miriam, and who attracted her never mattered. Felicia became the initial woman in Miriam's life and gave Miriam her first orgasm. Lightning Bug Parker never gave her pleasure. She trusted Felicia but admitted she did not love her. Miriam and Felicia became great friends who protected one another. They resided in an area of town which claimed heavy drug usage, and a high murder and crime rates. Inside the house, petty theft ran rampant, and the girls protected one another. For the girls, as the saying goes when you got nothing, you got nothing to lose.

On Fannin Street near the St. Paul's Bottom, drugs ran amuck all around the area. Madam Lavell's, no exception. One discovered everything from heroin, cocaine and reefer. The girls used it to ease their pain of the job. Madam Lavell encouraged the use and supplied it to her workers if they desired it. The heroin created the euphoric relief the girls craved through the day. The cocaine made it possible to service the client load. They serviced more than twenty clients a day to make a living. The reefer they smoked calmed their nerves. A lot of the girls got hooked after a few months.

Through the grace of God Miriam Landry never indulged in the narcotics. She survived, as she chose to abstain from even the reefer. Felicia didn't do drugs either and wasn't a junkie by any means. Miriam didn't buy into the rumor that Felicia supplied the girls with the smack. Possibly, she received dope from Madam at the meetings she attended with the boss. Felicia didn't tell Miriam until much later. Once she got them hooked on the smack, the girls resisted leaving.

Miriam enjoyed the younger clients. The young guys sought their initial screw, hoping to lose their virginity, so they could claim experience when their time came to deflower their girl. Due to segregation laws, most of the clientele was black. However the men creating the laws, the white power brokers of the city, also frequented the establishment.

Miriam preferred the older men. She didn't like the rich and powerful, "I-own-you" men, but the desperate, "we-need-someone-to-talk-to" men she could relate to. Most of the time these men desired companionship, not sex. A woman to kiss their forehead. A woman to laugh at their lame jokes. They craved companionship. Sometimes a kiss on the cheek, a neck rub or simple conversation was all they required. They craved the love they lost when their spouse died or departed. Being with the girls allowed them to procure the love they never got, if only for an hour or two. These men occasionally even paid higher since sometimes a man craves affection, and the one hour became the grandest time of the week for him. Of course, most men desired fucking.

Making the men feel loved became her specialty. Most men didn't miss the sexual release. She radiated guilt in taking their fifty cents to a dollar, but Miriam needed to eat. Evolving into a whore in one of Shreveport's seediest houses had not been her a long-term plan. Survival was. Little did she realize, she gathered power for her lifelong ambition.

She serviced everyone; men arrived she despised. Younger professional white men. The men with the plantation mentality of seventy years earlier. These men arrived with fetishes. One of the fetishes involved possessing a colored woman. She reserved her disdain also for the older professionals and the Shreveport elite who acted like they owned the woman. The prejudiced white men bought and paid for her services and performed anything they desired on her. The plantation mentality involved raping the woman, taking her into a back alley and fucking her behind the woodshed, but they wouldn't be caught dead taking a black girl to dinner or the picture shows. Of course, these same men battled integration. These men stood behind the discrimination laws called Jim Crow.

Chapter 5
Judge Paul Mitchell

Judge Paul Mitchell, a regular client at Madam Lavell's house and Felicia, the girl who served him when Miriam began her employment at Madam's—an unlikely pair. The Judge at first didn't fit Miriam's stereotypes of the rich and powerful. A playful and friendly man, he desired fun with the girls, laughed a boisterous laugh like the bearded man who came calling every Christmas Eve. Like Santa, The Judge stood heavy set, with a full beard, and often wore suspenders.

He made Miriam laugh even though the jokes he told degraded people of color and women. He performed the storytelling, in a certain harmless way, telling his racist and risqué jokes, but his laughter was more humorous than his jokes. The laugh started rumbling in his oversized belly and finished with snot shooting out his nose. Miriam laughed, not at the jokes, but at his method of orating the tales, or it might have been receiving the tips, which were twice as much as her regular clients.

The elite of Shreveport were mostly clients the girls disdained, however Judge Mitchell displayed redeeming qualities. The man spent his money at will, and always appeared on the lookout for a housekeeper, a whore's dream. Get out of the slums, take care of the house, cook meals for the family, and fuck him when requested, making twice the salary.

Miriam became acquainted with several girls from the Bottoms who received similar employment with lawyers, executives and city councilmen. A whore's dream to get out of the shanty and live in a mansion with a wrap-around porch, a white picket fence and a white family. The white elite of Shreveport loved showing off their possessions. A black or dark-skinned Creole housekeeper wasn't human, nothing but property, a possession. She wasn't even an employee. The dogs, cats, and the mice what roamed behind the large mahogany desks received greater respect than the colored housekeeper. Since the powerful man paid her, his logic concluded he owned her, and he did what he pleased.

Miriam fit all the requirements of a housekeeper. She cooked, cleaned and was trustworthy. Unaware life's changes would soon arrive. Miriam Landry could never be prepared. No girl in the Bottoms could.

Judge Mitchell became popular in Madam Lavell's house. All the girls fought to get with him since he tipped higher, and entertained the girls, making everyone laugh. Felicia serviced him and never hinted at anything peculiar in his behavior with her before Miriam and her blessed soul arrived at the whorehouse.

A short time after Miriam got dumped at the shanty, the judge approved a law on a landmark case for tighter discrimination laws in Louisiana. With the bribe money he received, he arrived at the shanty with a fatter wallet and fatter stomach. His intentions at the black whorehouse revolved around Felicia's specialty which the judge, like many other men craved, and with the extra money burning a hole in his wallet, he figured two whores were better than one. Miriam had already caught his eye, the man asked Madam about Miriam. He paid Madam the price to obtain entertainment from both, and Miriam and Felicia did not object to sharing a man. It gave them a chance to play with one another, and both Miriam and

Felicia agreed, the playtime between them became their favorite part of the job.

The inaugural night Miriam received payment from Judge Mitchell, he kept his fat paws off the girls. He spent the opening half sipping some homemade whiskey brought in from a moonshiner, north of town. The man engaged in his raucous and racist humor with them, before the three of them went into their room, where the horse tank sat. Judge Mitchell studied Miriam and Felicia as they undressed one another, kissed and made love. All the while he took care of himself. The following visits, the routine remained the same. The girls never objected, and he even paid them a little extra, because he enjoyed the soft moans of pleasure they evoked. It got him off.

After a few weeks he joined them, and he preferred Miriam's technique to her partner's. Something she did he preferred, so when Madam cracked the whip about the threesomes, the fat judge chose Miriam. Alone with her in the beginning, he never asked for sex. The two talked about his home life, how he made it to the top of his profession, but even though he told his racist jokes she still laughed. She told him parts of her story; however, she omitted the part about the Early Greene raping and her subsequent abortion.

"I can't have kids. Something happened to me months ago, and now I can't have none."

"Well, Miriam. Do you want to tell me about it?"

"When I'm good and ready. I just told one person, and dat's the guy dat drop me off here. I don't want dat to happen to me again."

"Well I'm sorry and not sorry about that." Customers are always conscious about leaving something behind. "Once we start it, then I don't have to worry now do I?" He laughed, and his belly shook. He enveloped Miriam in a large hug, making an interesting contrast. Miriam not even one-hundred pounds swallowed up by the three-hundred-pound man.

He reappeared the following day and they started their relationship. He visited her every Tuesday afternoon, even rearranged court proceedings to spend time with her. Sometimes, mere small talk, sometimes small talk and straight sex, and he also arrived for a needed blow job. Nothing indicated anything peculiar about the man. No abnormal fetishes, no outward violent behavior. Yes, he recited racist jokes, but again, a rich white man living in Louisiana in 1937 tells racist jokes. There was nothing out of the ordinary.

The Judge's lifestyle made him desire to keep pace with Shreveport's high society. Having a housekeeper meant you staked your claim in the social scene. The Mitchells fired the last girl who worked for them, another prostitute from the same house where Miriam solicited.

"I got something to ask you Miri." The judge adjusted his suspenders when they went back to her room. "It's a big step for you."

"What is it?"

"Now I want you to think this over carefully. This opportunity I am presenting you may not come again, and it will be a way to help you get that guitar you said you want."

A small-time prostitute in the shanties of Shreveport's biggest slums, living in a two-story house with a white picket fence, and a wraparound porch—most of the whores on Fannin owned this fantasy.

The fantasy never entered her mind. Becoming

51

property, she never desired. Miriam fancied sharing her life with someone, and maturing and developing herself as a young woman, a musician, and a person. At the time leaving the ghetto of the bottoms for a white picket fence life never entered her mind.

"Sara, I should have refused that pig. I was fine hooking dem streets."

"Miri, don't ya know, dat every step you took back then led you to the person you are now? Maybe dere was a reason why you did, and it wasn't just to get out, maybe you sought a lesson."

Miriam looked at me. She pondered my statement. Ah, and then she smiled.

Chapter 6
House Maid Miriam

He waited for an answer. She still pondered the opportunity as the conversation came to an abrupt stop. "Miriam?" She gazed at the fat man. "What do you want to do? I don't think anyone wants to live this life. So, what are your goals?"

She eyed him with caution. Every methodical move the fat man made she took notice. His hand movement, the suspender stretching, the tipping of his cap, she noticed. Sexual activities were not happening today. They talked for an hour. He paid her double since he orated some risqué jokes and stories about Negroes, but Miriam gave him a genuine laugh. Miriam played with herself, but for five dollars and giving herself an orgasm, she tolerated his racist humor. "Judge, you know I wants to play da blues, trying to work enough to gets me a good guitar, and hopes to finds me a man to teaches me how to play better."

"I can get you a job at my place. You seem like a hard worker, clean, seem to be trustworthy and all. Now I know not all these girls are like you. I heard about some of the stealing that goes on, but there is something about your face." He took her chin by his fingertip and petted her like a kitten. "I mean there is just something about it." He hesitated for a couple minutes. "How would you like to work for me, in my house watching my boy since the girls left home, you'll clean up after him, and cook and clean for us? I pay you twice as much as you make here, plus you get room and board. Again, watch the boy, clean and cook. Oh, plus we need our time too." He scratched her chin again, as she purred a little. "You will have your guitar in no time. I will even give you time to practice." She purred longer.

Miriam pondered the offer for about ten seconds. Most of the girls craved becoming a live-in maid and whore. Working for some rich man in a safer neighborhood. Most of the hookers on Fannin ran around high, so never were they trustworthy. Miriam never shared this dream, but opportunities like this may never come by again, and the stories of the streetwalkers on Fannin who disappeared, haunted her. She jumped at the chance, and Miriam strutted around the shanty, gave Felicia a hug, and ran out the door. For a bonus she flipped Madam Lavell off, as she ran to Judge Paul Mitchell's Caddy.

The Mitchell's bore three children, two girls who had moved out, and one boy, fourteen. They seemed like the perfect Southern couple portrayed in the Hollywood movies, and in the glorious Southern literature. The couple met when he worked as a burgeoning lawyer in Shreveport. Mrs. Mitchell's father, a business tycoon in Monroe. She grew up with money and society, so the woman disdained taking care of a mansion. She craved someone to cook and clean for the family, since the college-aged girls moved away. Their younger son refused to help. He played football and rumors floated around he raped some Negro girls from the Bottoms. The boy's destiny had always been following his father's footsteps. Miriam often seemed lost in the Mitchell home. The environment never made her feel comfortable, often hiding in her room.

Her room stood on the top floor of the two-story

house, adjacent to the daughters' shared, vacant bedroom. The boy's room sat downstairs across the hall from the parents' master suite. In Miriam's room, there sat a twin bed, with a small wooden dresser. Judge Mitchell bought her some clothes, so she didn't wear the dress on her back and wash it every other day.

Besides caring for the boy, she cooked and cleaned the house and whitewashed the picket fence twice a year. Miriam didn't stick around long enough to wash it twice. The seedy part of Judge Mitchell began showing itself. This change arrived slowly and gradually like a male losing his hair.

The judge approached fifty years old, while his wife approached forty-five. Younger in years, but after giving birth to their three children she put on several extra pounds. Mrs. Mitchell no longer craved the sex. His attention to Fannin Street and the black prostitutes came right after her refusals became automatic.

When the Judge visited Madam Lavell at her house in Shreveport, there wasn't a finer gentleman in the place. He consumed a beverage or two in the lounge, with the rest of the clientele, and talked and danced with the ladies. It wasn't an indecent place if nothing else happened. Even with the main function of the whorehouse, it wasn't the worst thing in the world. Ninety nine percent of the time when a married man entered, his wife refused to give him that special something, or a wife refused any sex with her man, for whatever the reason. Sex, or receiving love became the reason why men came to Fannin, including Judge Paul Mitchell.

Miriam never complained about her job. She serviced her boss and followed orders. Her Mama once told her, "Miriam, dere are only three ways for you to get out of the swamp. Be a whore, get a job for a white man as a servant, and whore yourself to him, or play da blues." She played the Blues and became serious about the guitar. Several girls and woman became destroyed by men once they got out of the swamp. She witnessed several and developed perseverance and inner strength to survive.

Chapter 7
Fried Alligator

For Judge Mitchell's fiftieth birthday party, his family took him to Cross Lake, Northwest of Shreveport. Miriam went along, since the several guests attending the gala event also were too lazy to help. Unable to handle the load Mrs. Mitchell called on Miriam. "Miriam darling, can you be a dear and help a little for Paul's birthday. We'll need you to prepare just a few things. We'll pay you a little extra. I can't do it all myself." She displayed a beautiful Southern white woman's societal voice.

Miriam, aware she couldn't handle much of anything overheard, her say, "only a little Nigrah could do the work for this party."

"Of course, wacha want me to do?"

"Just cook the gumbo and jambalaya for Master Mitchell. We're also roasting a pig, so if you can maintain that too. I guess we will need just a little extra help serving the guests. Don't worry hon, I'll be there to help you." She hugged Miriam, but not to close. At least six inches remained between them.

Miriam smiled as she walked out of the kitchen. When the wife remained in the parlor Miriam said beneath her breath. *"You ain't gonna help no one. Your fat ass will be sitting drinking champagne, why I do all de work."* She ascended the steps to her room.

The gumbo and jambalaya grilled on the open fire. Crawfish boiled in the Dutch oven, and the pig roasted on the spit on a fire. The band there played several marches, as well as classical tunes. There weren't any Blues or zydeco, and Miriam, the sole person of color there, took care of all the cooking and kept the wine and champagne of the thirty or forty guests who attended the outdoor gala full. The Judge preferred a bootlegger's homemade whiskey. The man lived in a juke-joint a few miles north of town.

Paul Mitchell's kids also attended. His two daughters hob-knobbed with some rich attorneys twice their age, while the boy hung out with some of his societal friends. They played football across the way in a vacant area, with short trimmed grass, and the trees cleared with the stumps burnt out. Adjacent to the lot lay Cross Lake. The boy, entering high school, went with some of his team-mates as they tossed the pigskin around. Miriam continued her hostess duties while the all white guests roamed around, talking about politics, the happenings in Europe, and assorted white folks' adult conversations. The champagne, wine and brandy flowed, as the adults gulped them, while, in a flash, Miriam refilled the glasses. The crowd yelled loudly, but they weren't raucous. They laughed often, but no one said anything humorous. The women talked about fashion on one side of the pig, while the men talked politics and lynching across the roasting animal. The daughters stayed beside the men. Miriam remained busy cooking, and spinning the cooked pig on the spit, while racing to and fro between the two pots stirring the gumbo and jambalaya. She returned to watching the barbequing sow.

"Daddy, Daddy. Help." The screaming came from the Mitchell boy.

"What is it boy?" His head didn't even turn towards him. Stretching back in his chair with his feet elevated smoking a fat cigar, and nursing a glass of wine, he asked his boy again. "What's da matta boy?" On your birthday party you desired relaxation.

"A gator daddy, It's a big long gator over by the water." The discombobulated boy ran all catawampus towards the rest of the party. His small group of friends lollygagged their way to the party at the pace of a slow-moving snapper, while Judge Mitchell's son showed the speed of a halfback on the football team, even though he played left tackle.

"Daddy, Daddy, there's a big old gator. I think I saw one."

"Malarkey son, besides you are interrupting my party, boy. Should have never brought you kids." The fat man muttered beneath his breath. The party proceeded unphased as they alternated taking drinks and gawking at the young maid working her magic on the drinks, gumbo, jambalaya and the spinning pig.

"Miriam?" The boy called his father's maid. "Can you kill this big bad gator?" His breath heaved as he spoke. The sweat poured from his face, even though the temperatures hadn't risen far. "I know you from da Southern part of the state, and you caught these for dinner. I know you Nigrah Creoles like your gator."

Miriam rolled her eyes and sighed. She walked to the spot where she chopped the firewood and grabbed the hatchet, she used to produce the kindling. Nobody bothered to gather any firewood for the party. She gathered a couple of knives and followed the bravest of the boys to the clearing. It stretched about three feet long. The gator wasn't big, but if hungry, chomping on a petite sixteen-year-old girl can happen. The ancient reptile's eyes shut tight as Miriam wandered towards it, while the brave boy stopped in his tracks when he noticed the gator, but Miriam continued. In her hands she clasped the weapons required. Killing gators wasn't a hobby for her when she lived on the boot, but she did it out of necessity, when a neighbor toddler came too close, or if families nearby starved, or a someone desired a new pair of boots or belt, she'd capture one.

Sleeping in the sunshine in the peak of the afternoon sun, the gator wallowed in solitude on the shore. What it dreamt about no one knew, but Miriam wondered. The time of day was perfect to spot one since the little gator slept. Like humans, gators ate in the evening.

Miriam eyed the reptile, snickering a little as she wondered how these big brave football players got frightened by a small gator like this one. Killing gators at a family picnic was something she didn't contract for, but the repetitive chores she needed to perform. Killing the gator at least provided food, and the skin could transform into a belt, boots, or even a nice purse for Mrs. Mitchell.

Miriam Landry needed to accomplish her job, and she got rid of the large hatchling. Not treated like an employee by the Mitchells, but as a slave, she'd never refuse a request. She despised accepting every directive.

She retreated into the woods and came out with a large log she tore the branches off and strolled towards the gator. Oblivious to Miriam, the gator didn't budge. She decided she didn't have to conk it on the head first, so she tossed the log and reached for the Bowie knife she borrowed from the Mitchells. One quick stab to the top of the head, in the soft spot, right behind the eyes finished the hatchling. and to make sure Miriam stabbed it several times, twisted the knife around and pulled the bloody knife out. She rinsed the blood off the killing utensils, and rinsed herself in Cross Lake, and rubbed her hands together.

She grabbed it by the tail and dragged it towards the party. After all, where Miriam came, she had just caught dinner for a week. Miriam came from the country and in the southern part of the state, killing the ancient reptiles became customary. For those born into society and from the northern part of the state, living in the city, hauling a gator home presented an anomaly.

The Judge stopped her in her tracks. "Miriam, why did you bring that huge thing back? Don't ya know it gonna attract more gators?"

"I'm hoping to take it back and skin and chop it up so we can have some food. Don't want to throw it out. Wasting an animal like this is bad. If you're gonna kill it, use the meat for food, and the skin for boots, belts, or make a new purse for Madam Mitchell. I know how to skin one. Creoles never threw nuttin out. We use everything."

"Miriam. Don't you talk back to me. You know what happens when you talk back. Just take that thing back and toss it in the lake."

"But…"

"No buts, you know what will happen. You are interrupting my party."

"I can make use a nice belt for your birthday."

"Drag it back and toss it in the lake. You gonna give me my present later. Ya hear?" Judge Mitchell peered around at his guests. He laughed his deep laugh, reminding his friends of the roar of an adult gator bellowing. "Can't argue with idiots." The rest of the party laughed at him and at the young colored girl.

61

She rolled her eyes after she departed and walked away. "You got that right." She said to herself hoping no one witnessed her mumble, as she took the dead critter across the clearing to the lake and kicked it in the water. Miriam never did anything she desired. Skinning and cooking the gator would have provided her with an occupation which kept the fat slob off her for a while. The skin with the correct tanning, transformed into new boots, a belt or wallet, for the man's birthday.

They returned to the plantation style two-story home with the picket fence and the wrap around porch in the early evening. Miriam put all the food away and returned to her room. The time was getting close to eight pm, when the judge made his routine visit. Sometimes he desired straight sex, sometimes he preferred to pee on her, but tonight was his birthday. He hungered for something special. Miriam wondered what he lusted for.

She took a deep breath as she glared at the creep. On rare occasions Miriam asked for favors, but she already realized the outcome. This time she got brave. If you don't ask, the answer always would be no. "Sir, before we start, can I get some extra money for killing dat gator? I never knowed I had to kill a gator for da family. I'm glad I knowed how, and it was a smaller one, but you never says I needs to kill me one. I think I went over da call of duty." She sighed after finishing the question. She tapped her feet while squeezing the mattress.

"You don't get any extra money from me bitch. Nincompoop, I pay you plenty. I'm sure you make more than the other maids around here. Hell, I could head back to Fannin, and pick me up another two-bit whore to replace you. Now nigger, when is the last time you peed. It's my birthday. I want your pee. That will be my present from you."

She took him with her mouth, while sitting on his chest. When she relieved herself, the Judge released. The man smiled at her as he got dressed and elevated himself. He stomped away, departing her room. Miriam spat his goo onto the floor.

Miriam started to plot her escape. In her spare time, she made herself a cigar box guitar from one of Master Mitchell's cigar boxes he threw out. He let her use the discarded box and found some fishing line for the strings. Miriam made the little three string herself. She went to the hardware store and bought herself a two by four and a few screws. At an early age she taught herself how to survive.

She practiced her little three-string in her limited free time, and she hoped to get herself a pawned Stella guitar one day. She saved her tiny income to buy one. Miriam got stuck working there longer. She couldn't stay another night, but she stayed another season's worth.

Chapter 8

Sylvester

The younger attorney visited from Monroe one Saturday afternoon. He came unannounced and Judge Mitchell hated it when folks dropped by without warning, but he accommodated the younger aristocrat attorney. They lit cigars and Miriam made them both whiskey and water as they sat in the parlor room. The man dressed in coat and tails, a little overdressed in the sultry heat. He wore a stove top hat reminding people of a famous president Southerners disliked.

"We need to discuss some business before we talk about pleasure Paul." The man doffed his hat and sat on the wooden chair in the Judge's office. "Now we are talking about the total outlawing of homosexuality." It appeared Sylvester winked at the Judge, as the Judge returned the gleam. Sylvester took a deep breath before he finished his statement. He tapped his fingers on the mahogany conference table. "I I..." he stuttered, "got some constituents that would like dem queers have rights like the rest of us. Not sure what this world is coming too. They queer and abnormal. Your honor, I just want to make sure where you stand on this? I think all them queers need locked up in jail or in da asylum."

The judge raised his lip as he smirked, and wiped his brow. "Dem Jews are behind this you know. It is all because Hitler driving them here. We need to do better and keep dem Jews out of da States and especially out of Louisiana, den dere would be less queers. Luckily dere aren't no queers up here. If there are, they are all locked

64

up in the asylum, or drugged up on Fannin, which is fine by me. Don't worry, Judge Paul Mitchell wants this to be a clean state. I know who gonna have rights in this state, and it ain't no queers, or no Niggers or Jews."

"I figured as much, Paul. I know how you think. Now the rest of my visit is all pleasure." Once again, his smile proved a little suggestive. He flashed a smile a man doesn't give another man, but it reminded Miriam of a debutante, smiling at a suitor.

Sylvester downed another shot of whiskey and took a big puff off his cigar. The smoke circled around the judge. "Mighty fine hooch there. Where did you get it?"

Judge Mitchell smiled. "I can't really tell ya that. Let's just say I know a man that knows someone, and their family owes me favors." He took a swallow of the whiskey, slammed the shot glass on the table and smiled. "Wacha doing in town? I'm sure you don't want to talk about queers."

"Hell no, I don't like talking about no queers. They give me da creeps anyway. I'm looking to hear some music."

"Well the symphony is in town. Mrs. Mitchell and I must make an appearance tonight. Ya know I don't want to go, but sometimes we just have to."

The guest, dressed formally in his suit, continued puffing his cigar as Miriam brought him another shot of the home-made whiskey. "Paul, that ain't what I am talking about. I don't want to hear that classic stuff. I wanna hang with the other half. In fact, I want to hear some coon music."

The judge rotated his head away from his guest, and focused his gaze straight at Miriam, but not long enough where she was required to wait on him. The fat man didn't fancy her attention but remained focused on his younger guest. "I don't know where they play the coon music here. It is not a place I would frequent."

In the shadows of the room, Miriam held her hand over her mouth, but unable to contain herself, released a quiet snicker. Totally aware the fat pig frequented the bottoms, and knowledgeable about where he ventured for fun, she realized another big fat lie came from an obese man, desperate to keep a clean identity before his high society friend. Miriam stifled her giggling, so the two men did not notice.

"Like I said Sylvester, I don't know much about this Nigger music you be talking about."

"Well they play much better than us white folk. Must be their genetics or something. Dey learned dem songs in prison, or on the plantations back when slavery was; and should still be legal. You see dem hands on these spades. Their hands are bigger, so they can play the guitar a little better. It makes it easier to reach across the strings. I try to play a little. You don't gotcha self a guitar here do ya? I want to play ya something."

"Nah, we don't got none of them dirty sinner instruments here." The judge glanced at Miriam, who hid in the shadows. He did not search for her but glanced in her direction. Miriam in the meantime started her ascent towards her room, where she kept her little cigar box guitar she made. Her three-string homemade guitar, best played with a slide, whether the slide was constructed from a pipe, bottleneck, prescription bottle or a knife. She was also aware of a place where white folks could listen to the music, and come out in one piece, and with all their money. However, in the Bottoms sat places a white man

66

entered, and never to be heard from again. Miriam played these places with Lightning, and she wished to send the Judge there several times.

Miriam descended the spiral staircase with her little three string guitar made from a cigar box, scraps of wood, and some fishing line. She walked into the parlor room playing some zydeco music on it. The guest lifted his head and glanced towards her, smiling, anticipating Miriam's charms, as she walked into the room, slower than a snail and uninvited. "Sir," she stuttered a little. It was obvious, Miriam's nerves stood on edge. Her hands shook a bit and her leg twitched. "I know a place you can go see some folks plays stuff like this." She played a quick little number and the man started tapping his feet a little.

"Oh, I don't want to go to the Bottoms. I want to come out alive and with most of my money."

"Oh no sir. This place ain't at the Bottoms or near Fannin. Is close to downtown though, but across dem trolley tracks. I been reading about it in da paper." She peeked at the judge who never gives Miriam the time to talk that much. However, he gave her the penetrating glare she dreaded. He grabbed his cane by the brass handle and stood at attention. Groans echoed around the parlor room as he stood. He cleared his throat, and everyone in the room turned at him.

"Excuse me Sylvester, I need to talk to my maid about boundaries."

"It's okay, she might be talking about a place I…"

"Sylvester." The judge exhaled and pointed the cane at his guest. "This is my house and my rules. I do not care who you have in your pocket and how many senators and congressmen you own. This is my house, my rules and that is my maid. She doesn't come in here like that. It's her job to keep our drinks full, and to bring us our sandwiches." He shook his head towards the area where Miriam stood. Grunting again he pointed his cane at Miriam. From experience, she realized what the judge meant. Miriam took three steps backwards.

The judge continued, "Miriam, you have added nothing to this conversation except for interruption." He flicked the ashes from his cigar into the marble ashtray. "You keep your nose out of my bidness."

"But…"

Judge Mitchell replaced his cane with an umbrella. "No more talking and skedaddle back to your room. Now. One more response and we know what we will do with this umbrella. Ya hear." He pushed it forward as if penetrating a woman with the umbrella. This wasn't the initial time Miriam received the umbrella, but it needed finalization. Grabbing the umbrella evolved into a warning to keep her trap shut. He also got gratification from using whatever thick instruments lay scattered throughout the house.

"Paul, I was interested in hearing some good music, whether it be from da coons, or even the crackers. Believe it or not, I like the country hillbilly sound."

"Sylvester, if I said it once, I said it a thousand times. You can't argue with idiots." He glared straight at Miriam, who already backed away, rolling her eyes in search of escape. She glanced at Sylvester for help, and he sat speechless with his mouth agape. "I'd let Miriam show you out, but she is all mine, and I don't trust you, and I don't trust her. I certainly do not trust the two of you together. I know I'm going to have to get up and show you out myself. Then I must take care of my maid."

Miriam ran up the flights of steps, as Judge Mitchell escorted his partner out the door. She lay in her bed, beneath her blanket shivering, even though Aprils in Shreveport aren't cold. It's the month where the heat and humidity escalate. The umbrella, cane, or golf club could never enter her body again. She hated Judge Mitchell's golden rain showers, however she soon received one. The Judge stomped into her room.

"Mastah Mitchell. I wants to go sees my mama."

"I can't let you go now darling. We need you up here, especially this week. We are hosting a big party for those right-minded people here in Shreveport. I'm going to need your help all week long and during the party too. Ya know what I mean."

"Yes sir." The small smile disappeared from her face. The frown she often wore replaced her grin as her eyes got enormous. She felt as low as a toad in a dry well.

The judge interrupted again. This time he spoke with greater volume, and at a quicker pace. He reminded her of a Yankee. I pay you an outstanding salary to cook and clean here and entertain our guests. I mean I pay you several dollars more than the rest of the servants in the area."

At the end of April in 1938; the temperatures already steamed. Life relaxed a bit. The girls never came home, and the boy roamed around trying to make it with some girl or playing football with his buddies. The Judge ran off during the day for a few hours, and Miriam pondered on what her future held. She also felt upset about her wages. Judge Mitchell cut them by a few dollars a week. "You ain't whitewashed the fence yet. Once you finish dat, I will give you extra. Plus, you not serving me like you used too."

"I should get me extra every time you piss on me." Miriam didn't mean to say it out loud. It wasn't the most intelligent thing to say to your employer, however a street whore lived a better life. She waited for him to respond as her lips got pouty, and her eyes focused on the fat freak.

Silence prevailed in the room, as both parties glared at one another. It was reminiscent of a shootout in a Western movie. He contemplated his move. He adjusted his pants, glanced at the cane and umbrella stand and smiled. His smiled reminded Miriam of a mad scientist, and the man snickered and forced an evil laugh. "I pay you plenty little girl. You want more money you need to do more for me, and my family." He poked her with the umbrella down towards her privates. He pulled his pants down and showed his flaccid dick. "You're getting both next time." He turned and walked away.

With wages lower than a snake's belly in a wagon rut, she craved to sit outside on the porch and play music to calm her nerves. He let her play her home-made guitar at nights on the porch, before he fucked her. She grabbed her glass of iced tea. Miriam preferred tea with lemon rather than the sweet tea with extra sugar Mrs. Mitchell made her brew. The Mitchell's at least considered her preference in tea, while allowing her to put the two slices of lemon in her glass. She grabbed her glass and started heading to her room to get her little three string.

"Where you going with dat glass young lady?"

Miriam, petrified, resembled one of the whitetail deer which lined the exterior of the glass she carried. She gaped at her employer-raper and wondered why he talked like he did. She had completed all her chores, supper was done, and all the dishes placed in the wooden cabinets.

Miriam's glass of tea was still half-full, and she wanted to top it off before she went out on the porch and practiced the slide on her cheap little homemade guitar.

"I'm taking it up to my room to get my guitar and practice. You always say it's okay."

"Leave the glass down here. I wouldn't be surprised to see ya collecting them in your room. I noticed there were a couple glasses missing. I'm sure you have a nice little collection up there. Your people are always stealing stuff from us. Now I remember as a boy a couple of you folks snuck into my Daddy's grocery store. There was a reason we didn't allow them in there, but they snuck in, stole a few loaves of bread and ran out before Pa Mitchell could shoot 'em. I ran after them but you folks just way too fast. Anyway, they got caught, and the Judge gave them five to ten and they deserved it. That was the moment I decided to become a judge, so I could put thieves like you away. Ya hear me Miriam?"

"I ain't take nothing. I forgot once and washed it in the morning one time."

"I'm coming with you, now you understand me?" She pleaded with right at him with her big brown eyes. His belly rolled across his trousers. He loosened his suspenders as they headed upstairs on the extra wide spiral staircase. The stairs reminded people of the staircases in the picture shows, which Miriam never attended. The movies of the aristocrats, the ones Miriam imagined in fairy tales, of the maid and the wicked stepmothers. She took the long ascent towards her room, with the fat judge closing fast on her. He grabbed an umbrella out of the rack, as he followed her. "Miriam, you are being disobedient to me. You know what that means?"

71

Her climbing pace quickened, but she tripped on the final step. The judge caught her and shouted at the youngster. "Let's go to your room, young girl. Ya know the room in my house, which I pay for. You hear?" With her mouth open, she shook like she was frozen in the Louisiana Springtime. Unable to stand, and when she tried, she stood like a newborn foal. She started crawling on all fours. The judge smiled, acknowledging full well Miriam knelt in the correct position for him. He held the umbrella, pointing it at her ass and strolled into her room with the closed umbrella pressed against her butt. The man pulled it away, opened it, and snapped it shut. The sick judge repeated the action.

"On the bed and everything off ya hear me?" I ain't even gonna fuck ya. If you keep protesting me, I'm gonna open this brella inside ya." He released the umbrella behind her spread legs and snapped it as fast as it opened.

Miriam required being an obedient slave, but in actions and not in heart. She soon removed everything and squinted as the judge removed his suspenders and removed his pants. He held the rain protector firm in his grip, while his left hand gripped the maker of yellow rain. Miriam knelt on the bed face first, butt high in the air, the crack smiling at the fat judge. It was close to a year since she lived with the Mitchell's and the poor girl had become used to the torture. However, this session stood as the worst. He poked inside her with the umbrella, as she received the warm downpour of his golden shower on her body. The judge walked away relieved and spun around.

"Now there, sweetheart. You be disobedient again; you be getting the umbrella opened again. Ya hear?"

She lay drenched in his piss on the bed. She longed to move but couldn't. Judge Mitchell gave his final performance, his last hurrah. She'd rather hook on Fannin than go through this humiliation. The girl she saw in the *Shreveport Times* seemed better off than her, and that girl hung lifeless from the tree.

The young, dark-skinned girl plotted her escape from the fat judge. Judge Mitchell had raped her for the last time. Miriam Landry took the knife she used for slicing the pork roast and slid it between the sheets of her writing pad. She stuffed the pad under her black apron and retreated to her quarters. The honorable Paul Mitchell would no longer receive his depraved sexual satisfaction from the tiny, dark-skinned servant. The girl lay waiting for him.

Later in the evening Miriam prepared her ambush for the judge. She always stretched out attentively when he climbed the stairs. The footsteps echoed noticeably throughout the house. Fat judges possessed fat feet, and their homes boasted wooden floors. Fat men, fat feet, and wooden floors were not an ideal combination for the judge to sneak around the house to visit his servant and rape her, since the creaks echoed everywhere.

Miriam wondered about jumping out the window and cascading into the beautiful shrubbery surrounding Judge Paul Mitchell's home. Tying the bed sheets together and making a rope, became another solution. At least she could lower herself from the window and walk away towards her escape. Miriam, a skinny, runty little girl weighing about one-hundred pounds soaking wet could depart the bedroom door, descend the two flights of steps and walk out the door, since solid wood floors protected petite little Creole gals like Miriam. Walking away, way too easy and after her rapes and golden showers, the girl craved to go out in style.

You couldn't blame her if she stabbed the judge, however for Miriam revenge never became motivation. The judge deserved a filet knife attack and to be gutted like a catfish, or stabbed in the head like the baby gator, but she refused to become a murderer. She longed for a chance to prove herself. She desired to show the world her talent. Redemption became her motivation.

She raised the window and crawled out. She took the plunge with the knife and a few changes of clothes packed in her bindle sack. The small cigar box guitar didn't even fit, and it remained behind. She dove into the shrubbery and started walking once she got her balance. She sought to go anywhere but there.

Part II
Chapter 9
The Barnums
August 1938

Bo Barnum dropped off his kids at his father's juke north of Shreveport, en route to a farm in Western Mississippi and picked up a load. The farmer only wanted hooch from Grandpa Cecil Barnum himself, but would honor a delivery from Cecil's kin. Bo dumped the shine off at the old man's place. Wandering back to his jalopy, he noticed a beat-up guitar, and Bo, a decent musician who loved to play, admired it like a lost lover. He caressed the body, the neck and plucked the strings. He peeked around once, then twice and never saw anyone. He threw it in the back of the car, returned to his father's that afternoon and picked up his two children, before returning to their Zwolle home.

Smack dab in the middle of Creole country and approaching the Cane River Bridge near Natchez, Louisiana, Bo Barnum spotted Miriam. The girl stood on the far side of the bridge as Barnum's 1934 Ford coupe came to a stop. The girl peered over the edge of the bridge, while she dropped stones into the river. Barnum glanced at her, and the girl kept her focus on the river. The family wondered if she pondered jumping.

Louisiana Highway 1 sliced the Pelican state in half diagonally. It started Northwest of Shreveport and meandered to Bayou Rigaud on Grand Isle. Traveling with his family somewhere near Natchitoches, Bo

Barnum spotted a young hitchhiker. A few years earlier Barnum lost his wife and struggled as a single father raising his two children, a fifteen-year-old daughter Sara, and his twelve-year-old son, Tomas.

Barnum ran a little-bit-of-everything shop near the Sabine River. They sold bait and tackle and ran boat rentals. A juke-joint also sat adjacent to it. The place masqueraded as a whorehouse, so Bo entertained the grand folks of Louisiana and East Texas.

Besides the music, Barnum's family made the finest moonshine in the three-state area. Bo ran his place like his father would, and hired a few prostitutes to work in the juke, since musicians and guests required entertainment.

He pulled the Ford over on the bridge. "Where ya going?" The father asked the young Creole girl.

She didn't answer, or even acknowledge the man. He asked her again.

"Do ya need a ride? We're going to the state line."

The girl turned her head, and glanced at the Barnums. Dressed in ripped overalls and a straw hat, carrying a red plaid tucker-bag, her straightened hair splayed past her shoulders. Bo Barnum thought she couldn't be any older than fifteen, the same age as his daughter, Sara. She moseyed towards the coupe at the pace of a painted turtle and gazed straight at the man.

"I needs to cross the state line. Can you take me dere?"

"Hop in. We going almost dat far." The father opened his door and scooched forward as the girl climbed in the seat behind him. She kept quiet as the coupe made its way west.

Sara sat in her spot in the front seat, her permanent

spot since her mother vacated the family, while her little brother occupied the rear seat behind her. Miriam took over the seat behind Mr. Barnum, but for longer than a bull snake stretched out on the road, she peered out the rear window, as if the cicadas on a bald cypress tree required counting.

The man introduced himself as Bo Barnum, his daughter Sara, and son Tomas Barnum. He seemed harmless enough, and for a young woman searching for a male suitor, something seemed attractive about a man traveling alone with his children. The young woman revealed her story to Mr. Barnum. "My name is Miriam Landry, and I's running away. I got to get me anywhere but where I comes from."

Miriam wasn't sure what to expect of the Barnum family. Tomas sat beside her. Little Tomas eyed Miriam like he planned on marrying her. The boy at twelve had just entered puberty. At that moment he thought discovered his future wife. Tomas was already blessed with a sexy smile, but at his tender age, he remained clueless on how to use it to his advantage. He eyed Miriam up and down, and constantly except when she peeked at him. The lightest-complexioned Barnum shifted his head, as if the kid possessed a crick in his neck and peered out the window. Miriam glanced away and glanced out her window. Tomas checked her out again, eyeing her legs, and small breasts. Miriam peeked again at the boy, and this time he kept eye-contact. The brother attempted a sexy face but failed. He portrayed a twelve-year old funny face. He stuck out his tongue, and a small smile lit Miriam's face. In Tomas's eyes, ecstasy awaited him.

The daughter, Sara, regarded Miriam with

mistrust. She glared at her with scrunched up eyes and wondered to herself. *"Who was she? Was she going to replace her Mami? Was she going to replace herself?"* Sara Barnum, a daddy's girl all the way. Her Papi taught her how to play guitar and blow harp. He hopped freights with her. He also taught her how to trap and fish and he taught her how to chew and smoke tobacco. Sara always wanted to remain number one, and wouldn't allow any competition, unless their mother returned. Sara despised the hitchhiker at the beginning and refused to make any eye contact with Miriam.

Miriam approached eighteen years of age, and in her own eyes, she was a woman. Plus, she had lived a fuller life than most people she encountered, and that happened in the last two years.

Miriam, a woman at the age of consent, hoped the father was single. She always desired a wonderful family man, one who worked hard, brought home the paycheck, and worked the garden. She longed to cook his meals and present them when he returned from the fields, or whatever his job involved. The house would stay spotless also.

Miriam shared most of her story about the judge and working as a house cleaner to the judge. He reassured her, raping and taking advantage of a woman was against his nature. Besides, he pondered, Sara and her appeared similar ages, and something's wrong with messing with a girl his daughter's age. However, Miriam dreamed one day soon people would call her "Mrs. Barnum." A small Louisiana church would perform the ceremony. If possible, they'd make children of their own, as beautiful as his two.

Much to her dismay, Bo Barnum never made a

move on her. His wife's disappearance forever haunted the man, and he'd been with no one else since Lydia. He hired Miriam to take care of the children and to cook and clean the house, while he brewed the whiskey, farmed the land and put on late-night shows. He also ran a whorehouse and employed Miriam at the same time he hired the whores, but Bo never let her work the shows. No one else could caress her, so she wondered if he loved her. Bo had no desire to be compared to her previous employer, and refused to use her as a sex slave. The men, different from anyone she had previously met, made Miriam impatient.

Chapter 10
The Couple

Miriam often walked towards Bo and smiled at him, twirling her hair around her index finger. She'd bend over right in front of him, showing her backside. Sara noticed her, and wondered, *is the little maid trying to steal my daddy away from me?* The daughter often gave the maid a scowl and scrunched her eyes at Miriam.

Miriam tried to find her wedge, and she realized the Barnum family cared about music, whiskey and parties. She realized changing her approach might catch the man. However, Bo still thought of Miriam Landry as a kid of merely fifteen or sixteen. Too young for a man of thirty-three to mess with.

"Miriam, why didn't you tell him you were eighteen?"

"He never asked."

She continued to work hard, making sure the meals got cooked, and the place cleaned, and the kids kept out of trouble. Tomas helped her with chores, followed her everywhere, and did everything she said. Sara, well Sara, a free thinker, developed a mind of her own. Sara never listened to a thing Miriam said.

It took a few seasons, but Bo noticed Miriam. One humid morning in the sweltering Western Louisiana heat, he let her sleep in, while he made breakfast for the entire household. Bo scooped the flour out and added the milk and baked the biscuits. In the pan, he added additional pinches of cayenne pepper. Grabbing a grinder, he cranked his wrist, the same way he opened a jar of jam,

80

pulverizing the black peppercorn. The black spots filled the gravy, as the flour darkened with the spice. He figured he'd add an extra kick or two to the gravy. He hoped he made the gravy like Miriam. She seasoned the food the way the children and father liked it. Subtle, adding the spices, she added a couple shakes more than required. Her food always arrived with that little extra shebang. One extra flick of the wrist worked. Bo added two extra shakes … maybe five.

While Bo hovered above the hot stove, Miriam, Sara and Tomas came to the table and took their seats. Sara sat closest to her father on his left side while Tomas sat beside her. Miriam sat across from the two siblings.

"Mastah Barnum, are you ok? Looks like you was out in a snowstorm. You gots that flour all over you. You need some help there, sir?"

"No Miriam. I gots it. Just sits yourself down there." Bo acted nervous as he dropped the measuring cup into the cast iron pan. He reached in the pan for it, and hitting the pan and he came close to knocking it off the stove. Bo burnt his hand on the edge of the iron skillet grabbling the scoop out of the simmering gravy. He shook his burnt hand, and soaked it in water.

The young girl sitting across from Bo's children laughed while she sat at the table. "What's so funny?" Sara asked.

"Look at your daddy. He all covered in flour. Dat man look like a ghost. And now he shaking his hand."

"Go help him, I think he wants ya to help."

"You never said that you didn't want me hooking up with your daddy."

"I wanted Papi happy, and I noticed the two of you looking at each other."

"You hated me at first."

"I didn't hate you Miri, I just, didn't want to know you, but I started liking you in time. You grew on me. Oh Miri, you know Papi was a good cook. His gravy was always good." I winked at Miri.

The astonished children couldn't recall when she had laughed out loud. Like a jack-in-the-box she rose to her feet, pushed her chair in and walked towards Mr. Barnum. The kids were not used to her standing so close. She rubbed her privates against his hip and brushed against his arm with her hand. Their father stayed put and smiled at her, not walking away. "Let me show you how Mastah Barnum." Her petite body came close to straddling his, grinding into his hips. Both parties kept their eyes clapped right on one another.

She grabbed the wooden spoon, which sat in the pan, and raised it to her lips. She kissed the gravy and spoon as she sampled the sauce. Miriam made a face as her face scrunched like she got a whiff of animal crap. She spit Bo's gravy into the sink. With her right hand, she wiped the gravy off her face, glanced towards Bo and smiled. "Mastah Barnum. Hard for me to say this but you putting too much pepper in da gravy."

"Well Miriam, I think I'm overcompensating. My ma, she couldn't cook at all. Hell, she was whiter than a virgin bride in a Nebraska blizzard. Pa told me he married her, so he could bleach his kids up, giving them a fighting chance in life. She didn't want us to run shine but guess what we did. We ran da shine, all three of us. My oldest brother, I am not sure what happened to him, and my other brother, well he joined the Klan. I guess someone dumped too much bleach in him. I'm the only one that kept my Creole roots."

Miriam started the gravy over. She kept bumping into Mister Barnum. Her hips once again brushed his, and she rubbed his bicep. They spun and faced each another. "Let's me show you how. We're gonna make da gravy together." When the man went to spice the bubbling liquid Miriam grabbed his hand as he shook the cayenne pepper out. She stood close as she ground the black peppercorn. They even held hands a little and exchanged winks. "Dat's how you spice da gravy, Mastah Barnum." She walked away smiling and rubbing her hands together. She had hooked another man, she desired that he reel her in.

Miriam helped him clean the kitchen, and he gave her the day off, so Miriam took off and disappeared that day. Hiding behind the juke with Bo's cheapest guitar, she played some of the sweet songs she learned from her father on the peninsula. She lost the blues, since the music coming from the guitar resonated sweeter than molasses, music whose origins came with the same Blues formations. Porch music, picking and grinning music, like what Bo played.

Saturdays Bo gave Sara guitar lessons, but his daughter played much better than her father. Sara had become a superb player on the guitar and everyone wondered who gave whom the lessons. Both played the scales going faster and faster each time through. The metal of their switchblades snapped open as Bo taught his daughter the slide, so she created those swampy tones. Bo noticed a guitar missing from his collection. He owned four guitars: the Kalamazoo, Stella, a Regal, a Montgomery Ward's catalogue guitar, but his favorite instrument was always the banjo. Bo abandoned his daughter and went outside with the five-string, wondering if he discerned some music. He peeked around the yard and the buildings and spotted nothing. He walked to the corner of the house. Nothing.

Around the corner sat Miriam, studying his every move. When Bo went to one corner, she dashed around the joint, giggling while she sat on a bench and played and sang. The songs ran upbeat, with origins in South Louisiana, and Bo tapped his feet while seeking the jangle. He dashed and danced towards the portion of the building Miriam haunted with his five-string strapped over his shoulder. Miriam, cackled, sped off towards an adjacent corner, sat on a hay bale and strummed and sang a quick little ditty enticing the man. She understood the music captured Bo, and she set the trap. The kitten purred a Robert Johnson song, "Come on in My Kitchen." It was one of Bo's favorites.

He wandered across the lot to the juke joint, and still couldn't locate anybody playing. He followed the music, as his ears led the way. The sweet Southern music got louder and louder. Tired of playing cat and mouse, Miriam set the trap and permitted herself to be conquered. He strolled around the corner of the juke joint but failed to notice anybody. After crossing the entrance of the joint his eyes rested on Miriam. The sweet songs of the Creole reached his ears. She played the songs of the peninsula as Bo cranked his picking hand—she called it "Lala de Creole." Bo picked the banjo in time with Miriam's guitar playing. They created an impromptu love song, with Miriam singing the initial verse and Bo singing the second.

Don't you go messing with my mojo.
Don't you touch me above the knee.

Don't be messing with my mojo
And keep your hands off my gris-gris.

I don't want your mojo,
It's not your mojo that I want.
I'm not after your mojo
Mwen vle fè sèks avèk ou.

Miriam stopped playing for a second. She missed a beat on her guitar, gleamed straight at the man, smiled and laughed, and nothing else mattered. Once she gives a man her irresistible smile, he's hooked.

Baby don't you mess with my mojo,
You touched me above my knees,
That's mess up my mojo,
But keep your hands off my gris-gris.

Baby, don't you mess with my mojo,
You know I've had plenty of dat.
Oh baby, don't you go messing with my
mojo,
Eske ou vle danse?

This time Bo stopped. He noticed Miriam covering her face, holding her giggles in. She held in her laughter, covering her mouth with dainty hands.

Bo started laughing with his friend. "What … what … what's that mean?"

Miriam peered deep into his eyes, and he returned the gleam. The eye contact shattered his remaining restraint. They both acknowledged the mutual lust, and both knew the expectations coming, however they longed to finish the song.

Miriam responded. "I don't know what dat means." Laughter came out of her as she fell on the grass and rolled on her butt. Still on the ground with her legs spread, guitar on her chest, she focused again on Bo. "I think it means 'you wanna dance.'"

"Of course, Miri, I'll dance wid ya." He grabbed her hand and he danced a little two step with his right arm around her waist, while his left arm extended out as they held hands and he twirled her around. "Let's finish the song." He changed the rhythm a bit.

What if I'm that man
That you are supposed to see
What if that little red mojo bag?
That you call gris-gris.

Now red is the color of love
Maybe we is meant to be
This comes from the lord above
And that bag you call gris-gris.

Miriam continued the last verse. She sang it a little slower and repeated the verse three times.

Baby, you mess with my mojo,
Touch me above my knees.
Baby you can have my mojo,
Thank you for my gris-gris.

She kissed her mojo bag and licked her lips as she devoured the new man in her life with her eyes. Her large brown orbs became browner and more seductive than ever. He took her by the hand, and they departed towards a vacant bedroom in the juke.

"So, you play the Creole on the banjo?" He asked her as they walked hand in hand towards the juke.

"Mastah Barnum, you can do anything you want." She smiled at him as she tilted her head sideways and winked at him. They settled in the nicest bedroom, the room with the largest brass bed, quilts home-made by the former residents of the whorehouse.

She glanced around the room, noticing the fancy blue paint, the handcrafted mahogany furniture, and she plopped her little ass on the brass bed. She gleamed her smile wider than the Sabine at the man. "Dis is a nice room, lots nicer than yours or mine."

"This is the star's room when we put on some shows." He inched closer to her, while his legs trembled.

"So, am I the star? Miriam eyes continued their gleam, while she flipped her hair back behind her head.

He continued inching forward and reached out his hands toward her. Miriam stretched her arms out and Bo grasped her hands, lifting her up and pulling her toward him. She stumbled and fell face-first into him. He held her to protect her from falling onto the wooden floors. Instead her noggin planted into Bo's chest, while he wrapped his arms around her, preventing her from a further tumble.

Miriam regained her balance, and she lingered in Bo's embrace. Soon their lips were inches apart. Both parties were eager, and afraid to move closer. At last Bo reached out and caressed Miriam's face, then put his hand behind her neck to move her closer. Their lips brushed against one another's and they savored their first kiss together. The kiss lasted all afternoon and all night.

Neither wanted to stop the physical contact, as hands roamed, clothes were tossed, and fluids exchanged. Miriam slept on Bo's chest, and played with his chest hair as they drifted off together.

Waking up in the wee hours even before another round, Miriam told Bo, "Dat was a first for me, Bobo. Ain't no man made me feel dat good." She laid her head on the hairy chest and ran her fingers through them.

"It's been a long time for me, Pumpkin. I ain't been with no one since Lydia disappeared." He gave her a gentle little swat on her butt.

They left the nicest room in the juke. He turned towards her and gave his new love a kiss. Their lips melted together for a brief second. When Miriam broke the kiss, she asked him, "Why didn't you do something before? I wanted you to make a move."

"I'll be honest, Pumpkin. I didn't want to be like dat fat judge. Plus I thought you was just sixteen. I'd be a crappy father, if I started courting a gal the same age as Sara."

"Bobo, I'm eighteen now. I'm all woman." She smiled at him as they strolled towards the house hand-in-hand. They went into his room and curled next to each other for the rest of the night. He held her tight, arms wrapped around her, like a real man.

The daughter and son never spotted their father or Miriam the rest of the day. They discovered them together making breakfast for the family the following morning. Both smiled and stood way to close to one another for the children's comfort. "Bobo, dat's much better with da pepper. You're getting it. You gonna cook like me." The father grinned like a little boy when she called him Bobo.

"Thank you, Pumpkin, but no one cooks like you do. You are da best." He scratched beneath her chin like he would pet a kitten. Miriam smiled. She possessed a beautiful smile, but the kids didn't see it.

Disgusted by their father's interaction with the house cleaner. The daughter's lips curled up, and she drooped her eyes when she witnessed them together. She departed the parlor room and slammed the door.

One day she confronted her father. "I don't like her. She is not my Mami," she snapped at her old man.

"I know she is not Mami, but Mami left us. She was kidnapped, killed or just ran da hell off. Hell, I don't know since it has been years since we have heard from her." Bo sighed and reached out to Sara, brushing her hair with his fingers. "I need someone in my life that will take care of us and me. She's cute and I like her. I think she's for me; however, she will never replace Mami."

"I don't care. I don't like her and never will," replied the daughter. She stomped her feet as she walked away. Miriam and Bo listened to Sara's bedroom door slamming shut. The house shook like a fall cyclone hit it. They witnessed Sara calling the train home, as she wailed on her harmonica. The daughter got the guitar going and she ripped the Blues on it.

"Dat girl sure can play." Miriam told Bo as they lay naked in each other's arms.

"I taught her damn good." Bo said smiling. He held Miriam close and made love to her again.

Bo Barnum hadn't been the greatest father to Sara and her little brother, but Bo taught his daughter an invaluable lesson. He taught her how to play the Blues and feel the Blues.

"Bo was the only guy ever that made me hit that

blue note. You know the note that make your fingers and toes curl up. The note that makes you scream in pleasure. The note that makes you want to cuddle up with him and give him his special reward in the morning. That was Bo Barnum. He knew how to bend my strings to hit that note, and if used his slide, he played right above my frets."

"Miri, do you think I want to hear that about Papi?"

Miriam took a glass of lemonade, chugged the glass empty, and spit some out and continued her story. I hung on every word, even though I remembered these days well. I noticed things from her perspective.

Miriam soon vacated the maid's quarters as she and Bo were no longer employee and employer. She moved her scant but growing wardrobe into his room. Miriam became Bo's lover after his wife's disappearance, and the two never separated.

Miriam taught Bo the nuances of her Creole music. The rhythms and subtleties came from the swamps of Southwest Louisiana. Most folks inherited the talent to play the chords and notes but to master the Blues or zydeco you had to live it. It required mileage. Miriam made Bo Barnum return to his Creole roots through the music—the roots his family tried to shred.

Bo Barnum gave her the love she sought in all her eighteen years. The Blues man she ran away with never loved her. She never received his love. She absorbed his body, from the hand across her face, to the daily forceful slams into her. Even at the tender age of sixteen, she realized Tommie Parker was not making love to her. Once she experienced Bo Barnum, she figured out the connection between love and sex.

Bo took his pumpkin to visit her family in Morgan

City. There, they met her father and played a whole lot of zydeco music. Miriam's father respected Bo and earned his mutual respect.

Miriam's father hired a different fiddle player. One not running around across the country and raping his music partner's daughter.

Bo Barnum, a man who got along with everyone. It's part of his Creole heritage. He's both a white man and a black man—folk music and Blues played with equal skill. For Bo Barnum music was not about the talent, but about the passion you played with, and how it brought people together.

The following weekend Miriam's father drove up to the Barnum's place in his 1938 Chevy pick-up truck. Out popped the replacement fiddle player, whose face wasn't slashed up, but he was nowhere as good as the previous man.

A boy younger than Sara, but who looked older, jumped from the bed of the pick-up with his guitar in hand. He failed to gather the other traveler's gear and went straight for Sara. Out came the blind washboard player, who carried his bottle openers on his hands, and refused to play with thimbles, since they were not manly. Miriam hugged her father and the washboard player while all the time the young guitar player talked to Sara and played her little ditties on the guitar.

Miriam glanced around. "Where dat other fiddle player at, Daddy?"

"We had to replace him, gone too much, says he has important business to take care of. Dat man always roaming around. Damn, dat guy can play, but this cat ain't bad."

The boy broke free from Sara's charms and came

over to greet Miriam. "Hey sis, glad your friend is here." He put the guitar behind his head and started a solo, running up and down the fretboard like a master, showing off to his older sister. "I bet you can't play like that."

"Don't need to. I always be able to outplay you." She eyed his guitar, then scowled at it. "Sara, where's dat Stella dat Bobo brought you?" I wants to show my baby bro something."

"Dat your brother?" Sara's eyes got even wider. She rushed off to get her and Miriam's favorite guitar, the used Stella Bo picked up on a moonshine run to Mississippi right before they picked Miriam up. Miriam never knew where they got the guitar.

Sara came back with the guitar as fast as a duck on a June bug. She rested the instrument in Miriam's arms, while peering and smiling at the boy, and ignoring her friend.

Miriam never once played behind her back at least in public. She gave the guitar a couple of strums. "I don't like standard tuning." She fiddled with the pegs, strummed the guitar again, and smiled at Sara, who still paid her no mind, and then Miriam glanced over at her brother, whose focus remained on Sara.

Miriam ripped into an old Blues song from a few years earlier, regarding Hellhounds. She played the song to perfection, almost like the writer himself taught her the song. Once finished, she put the guitar down, wiped her hands clean and smiled that crooked, tobacco stained smile of hers. Sara and Miriam's brother, both gawked at her, then returned to their state of transfixed puppy love.

Bo returned after talking to the men about the two scheduled shows and rehearsals. Sara took off running once she saw her father stalking about. Miriam raced off towards her younger rival as Sara sped up the stairs to her room. Miriam went to the kitchen to peel the crawfish for the pie she'd be cooking for dinner, as well as chopping up some onions and peppers, and kneading the flour for the crust. The guests went up to the juke while Bo strutted in looking for his daughter. Tomas sat near the still shucking corn for the corn liquor, singing his little song he sang.

> *Tommy cracked corn, Daddy don't care*
> *Tommy cracked corn, Daddy don't care*
> *Tommy cracked corn, mi Papi don't' care.*
> *Tommy's going away.*
>
> *Tomas cracked corn, Sara don't care*
> *Tomas cracked corn, Sara don't care*
> *Tomas cracked corn, mi hermana don't*

care

> *It will be mine one day.*
>
> *Tommy cracked corn, Miriam don't care*
> *Tommy cracked corn, Miriam don't care*
> *Tommy cracked corn; Miri don't care.*
> *She'll be mine one day.*

"Miri baby, have you seen Sara? We gonna rehearse for a bit. You coming over also?"

"Sara ran up to her room. I think she's nervous about the boy coming up. Dat's my baby brother, da guy she was kissing down home.

Bo's lip protruded, as he rolled his eyes a little. He knew it became time to act like a father. "Yeah, I know, I'm not sure how to handle this. I'll just keep dem away from each other. You and Sara be on da left sharing a mic, while dat boy and I will be on da right of your ol' man, and me in between. He ain't gonna try nutting while I'm here. I already gave him looks dat kill."

Miriam studied Bo's face. She felt disappointed. Miriam always was a sweet young woman, but sharing was never her best attribute. She craved being the only girl for Bo, even if he split his attention with his daughter, as he gave her fatherly love. She watched him proceed towards the staircase and march up to his daughter's room to lay down the law. Miriam kept chopping and peeling.

Soon the three made their way across the yard and into the juke. The Morgan City crew were playing already. Miriam's father had the accordion moving, while her brother did things on the guitar that most people twice his age couldn't. The fiddle player was no Early Greene, but he played his part, and the blind washboard player, kept tapping them bottle openers on the ridges in rhythm.

Soon Bo, Miriam and Sara would join the combo, while Tomas continued to shuck corn and work the still. The three walked into the juke together, Sara standing behind the couple and proceeded to follow her father towards the boy. "Sara," Bo told her. "You and Miri go over there, and tune up. What kind of tunings do ya use? Standard or open?"

"Do da open G. My boy likes standard, but I know Miri like her open G." Miriam's dad replied. Bo, you and da girls follow along. We needs to do some old standards. Dese are ones folks in New York City been listening too." The blind washboard player banged the bottle openers together with a clicking noise to get the rhythm going. Her father hit the squeezebox, while the kid strummed the G chord to get the song started. The chord progressions were consistent with what Bo and Sara played, just different rhythms. Bo messed up several times in the timing while Sara and Miriam played flawlessly.

"Damn man, if you can't keep up, just let da girls play."

Bo retorted. "It was good Sir. Music ain't supposed to be perfect. It's passion and energy. Dat's what we played with."

"Mr. Barnum, all due respect, you pass for a white man. You can get away with shit. I'm a black man playing in a white man's world. It gots to be perfect each time. Figure dis out or sit and listen to perfection."

Bo took a song break, sat listened, learned the nuances, and continued. They rocked the rehearsal with Miriam's dad leading the way. They were ready for the next two nights.

Folks came from all over the Pelican State, and others crossed the river by boat, bridge or ferry to see Miriam's father. The Barnum juke grew packed, as the whores served the band and the crowd. Bo kept a close watch on his daughter, as well as Miriam. Sara never got the chance to sneak off the first two nights. Her father made sure of it, however when the music is right, the chemistry can explode.

Sara inched forward, peeked at the boy. Bo often checked the where the boy's eyes were directed, and they switched from a couple of the hookers working the room, over to Bo's daughter. A smirk flashed upon his face when he peeked at Sara. The Barnum girl smiled back at Miriam's man-child brother, swished her hair in the smoky juke. The boy danced his duckwalk, with knees bent. Sara smiled, cracked up laughing and missed a beat, then botched a chord change. Bo quit playing altogether, while Miriam never missed a beat. Bo and Sara didn't play the following night.

After the second night's show, Sara snuck out of her room to join the boy. She found him with two of the older hookers. The tears streaked her face like a levee broke on the Sabine as she ran across the swampy fields between the two buildings. Her bare feet squished in the mud, but only she knew what happened. She opened the door, and the it creaked loudly enough to awaken the occupants. The creaks even stirred the gators. The creaking door also called out to the spirits roaming the bayou who were a part of Louisiana folklore.

Sara soon reached the steps, and easily snuck up them in silence. She never realized when a teenager tries to sneak in and out of the house, the quieter she tries, the louder she becomes. Bo Barnum noticed the creaks of the wooden floors. He witnessed the tears of his daughter flowing. The time was right for Bo to act like a father his daughter, instead of loving Miriam. He unwrapped his arms from around Miriam and went to Sara's room, and when he left she was close to smiling.

"Sara, why you talking about dat? Dat's your story, not mine."

"Miri, it's important, since it talks about you always being second to me with Papi."

Miriam, sighed, "I think you rolled your eyes at me."

Miriam slept beside Bo, while he placed a plan in motion, a gradual change in the family's lifestyle, eliminating the house shows and the prostitution on his property. Raising children in a whorehouse and juke-joint wasn't the ideal lifestyle. It took a while, but the house shows which had been running three times a week were reduced to one, or maybe two shows a month. The whores got let go, but Bo Barnum, in the goodness of his heart, still allowed the hookers to work the shows. The Chitlin Circuit always stopped at Bo's. He developed into a major player.

Miriam stayed since she had become Bo's gal, but she wasn't ready for a domestic life. Becoming his girlfriend seemed very suitable for her, a housekeeper, again no problem, but evolving into a stepmother confused her. Miriam felt comfortable with the house shows, the parties and the musicians screwing with the whores in the juke, but she refused to go to church with the family. However, getting himself and his family Christianized became Bo's number one priority. Miriam Landry completed his life, and he sought matrimony.

As Miriam and Bo grew together, the children became comfortable with her. She mopped the floors, made some incredible food, and kept everything in order. She cared for the kids when Bo helped some Yankee navigate the Sabine for the greatest fishing. Always a scrapper, Bo Barnum did the dirty jobs as the work required. Most of Bo's businesses were legal—farming, fishing guide—however the profitable part wasn't. His inheritance came from the successful moonshine business started by Bo Barnum's grandmother, and improved by his father, Cecil Barnum.

Tomas Barnum took an interest in continuing the whiskey business, while his father and grandfather worked on ways of keeping the legacy alive.

Sara Barnum coveted no part in the family business. She wished to get rid of the whiskey altogether, and she didn't desire making, distributing, or even drinking it. People wondered if the girl, who now attended a Baptist church, became holier-than-thou, since she took no part of the business which clothed and fed her. She longed to become a lawyer and fight for civil rights, another Barnum legacy which she craved to live up too. Her father fought for civil rights while living in Nebraska, before he moved his family back to Dixie. In Nebraska everything he owned was burned to the ground.

The family attended Zwolle Baptist Church every Sunday. The church faithful looked down their noses at the Barnum clan. The Barnum family often came in their Sunday best, overalls and torn shirts. The town folks were aware of Bo as a known bootlegger, a pimp and an early freedom fighter, and the respectable Black folk of the rural South couldn't handle him.

Miriam Landry, a young passionate woman, craved success. She loved the Barnum family, and they became family to her, but the children weren't hers. Also, her Bobo gave greater attention to his children than to her. After six months of their relationship she got the itch. The Blues itch, the itch what gave a true man or woman the blues.

Chapter 11
Lucas Turner

Lucas Turner, a promising young Blues singer from East Texas, arrived. Bo booked him to play a house show at his juke. The whores he let go returned for entertainment. Big Lucas Turner stood about six foot three—sleek, athletic, and familiar. The man, a protege of Lightning Bug Parker, and maybe related to an old troubadour, arrived with all the moves. He duck walked like the original, played his axe with his teeth, and behind his head. Tall and lean, his physique drove the women crazy. His clothes were stylish, and there on his belt loop, sat the solid gold money clip. If the talent didn't attract the women, the physical features made them toss their panties, and if his looks failed, the money attracted young women from the swamp. The rumors making the rounds on the Chitlin Circuit said he made a deal with someone. She never asked.

At present Miriam wasn't playing second fiddle to Mr. Barnum's children. She loved turning into his pumpkin, but he was required to treat her like his pumpkin, and not like some ordinary squash. Miriam often wondered why Bo Barnum treated her third behind Sara and Tomas Barnum, his children.

The family went to church together, while Miriam stayed home. Miriam had been raised Catholicism, but she refused to practice, while the Barnums made futile attempts at being Baptists.

Tomas received whiskey-making lessons from his father and grandfather. Cecil and Bo showed him the proper brewing methods, when to remove it from the fire and how to cook it. Sara, her daddy's favorite learned everything else. The daughter, already an incredible guitarist, played on-stage with the likes of Lucas Turner—against Bo Barnum's better judgment. Sara Barnum with all her talents, was under her father's watchful eye. Miriam watched Sara to. She figured Sara, now sixteen, and ripe and ready and may slip off with a gunslinger one day.

"I never thought dat for a moment. Besides you're just a kid."

"Oh, come on Miri, I was the same age you were when you ran off."

"Why you making this 'bout you anyway?"

"I don't know what you mean." Sara swished her hair and continued. Miriam sighed, recalling the events.

The three musicians in the house jammed with Lucas Turner. Bo enjoyed this night, although the closest neighbors may have debated its quality, as they contacted Deputy Bourgeois about the ruckus. The place rocked, and on the river, gators grunted their ummmm. Young gators grunt when they're happy, and these reptiles wandering on the banks of the Sabine liked the music coming from Barnum Manor.

All but Tomas squeezed into the juke joint, as it filled beyond capacity. Meanwhile Tomas stretched out in the barn cooking the whiskey. As usual Tomas presided over clusters of corn, and had his pocket-knife out, slicing the kernels of corn off the cobs.

After shucking and cracking corn, the young Master Barnum dumped the maize into the grinder, crushed it into gruel and mixed it in a copper pot with sugar and water.

Meanwhile Bo, Sara, Miriam, Lucas, and his

entourage entertained the folks following Lucas Turner from Nacogdoches, in East Texas, a city with an incredible Blues following. A lot of the best music which echoed in the halls of Barnum Manor came from across the river. Bo tried to end the Texas jinx haunting his family. The origin of the jinx he hadn't a clue about, except like an old ball glove or a pair of overalls, he inherited it.

Inside the juke joint Lucas Turner and the musical portion of the family cooked, like the whiskey Tomas brewed, and nothing seemed different. Sara went to her room, while Miriam and Bo went to bed together. Lucas Turner took two whores with him, and they spent time in the motel rooms above the juke. Bo and Miriam made love and vowed never to part.

The following morning Sara made breakfast for the family. Bo Barnum slept in. When he opened the curtain, he witnessed Lucas Turner's Cadillac leaving Barnum Manor. There she sat in the passenger seat, a young and restless Miriam Landry. Peace and harmony came into her life, and at long last she received treatment like a human. But the domestic lifestyle wasn't her cup of tea, and she caught an itch. She decided it was time to hit the road with another gunslinger. Clothes tossed out the rear of the Cadillac convertible, and goodbyes remained unspoken as the car bounced along the bumpy mud road.

The father seen it all throughout his life. His boyhood Texarkana home disappeared in flames before he moved north. The ashes of his Omaha home lay scattered at his feet on a return trip back home. Lydia, his beloved wife, kidnapped at knifepoint while she sang in San Antonio. Not much phased Bo Barnum anymore.

Miriam Landry leaving his ass never affected the man. Bo Barnum expected this event and glanced at his two children as he shook his head side to side and kicked the mud below his feet. Bo vanished into the his house.

"I should have never left your daddy. He was da best. I guess we all makes mistakes."

"Are you going to tell me what happened in Texas? I know some of it. Some of it I pieced together. Remember I'm a lawyer."

"Sara, I know. I told you something. Somes of it I just made up. I'm telling you everything now. Da real truth."

"Ya, as opposed to the truth you told me before? Do you even know the truth Miri?"

"I just didn't want to hurt you or Bobo. Sometimes a little lie ain't that bad."

Chapter 12
The Weight

Miriam and the Blues singer sped from the Zwolle home towards the bridge about fifteen miles north of the Barnum residence and crossed the Sabine into Texas. Something about Texas Bo and his father disdained. The reason, never explained, however tall tales disclosed a family named Bourgeois, who controlled a large area near Huntsville and San Antonio. The Bourgeois' and Barnums were rumored to be close cousins in the 1800s and early 1900s. One rumor stated the Bourgeois family changed their name from Barnum. The Barnums clung to their Creole roots, while the Bourgeois gang claimed to be Caucasian. Bourgeois terrorized Barnums for years. Some even joined the Klan. At least this became the conspiracy theory the Barnum family spun. Bo Barnum lost his wife in Texas. Maybe there was truth to the rumors. Maybe not.

Lucas Turner came from Nacogdoches. His young wife and three beautiful children lived there but he didn't inform Miriam about them, until she settled into his second residence in Palestine. He wanted her to stay put, a better option if she knew about the wife and kids who remained in another city. He never informed her, she never asked. Miriam didn't desire being another notch in this man's belt. Palestine, like similar cities with biblical names, became a perfect location for his concubines, and Miriam soon lived with three new women. The harem she lived with were all below the age of twenty-two, and like

Miriam, scratched the itch of containing the charismatic Blues man. They comprised a triad of sexy young women who hoped and prayed Mr. Turner would choose one of them. Maybe they'd have to settle being one of the several whores who catered to Lucas Turner. Although Miriam Landry knew she was the latter, deep in her heart her motivation was to become his one and only. The opportunity came once, or maybe twice, in her life and she blew it.

All she craved in life was sharing the spotlight with a powerful man, both on stage and at home. She wailed the blues—after all she carried them inside her. And she hadn't the foggiest idea how to get them out. She made people happy playing the blues. Most of all, the Blues put a smile on her face when she hit the blue note. Playing music was the gift God had given her, so she desired to give it to others. The gris-gris bag she still held told her so. At least she imagined it did.

Miriam's pants flew off by the time they got out of Shelby County Texas. Shelby County sat on the West Bank of the Sabine, across the river from the Barnum's place. The county where Bo Barnum aimed his shot gun, while sitting on the east bank. The Texas curse, whether real or not, passed down to him and there was nothing he'd ever do about it.

Miriam removed Lucas Turner's pants near San Augustine, a mere twenty miles from the Barnum property in Zwolle. They finished their encore performance in Palestine. "Baby you going to be my number one gal. I am taking you on the road and treating you right. I ain't going to treat you like that Barnum guy, or da others. We might even get married."

By the time we got to Palestine, we were as tired

as can be.

We stopped several times, cause that man kept wanting me.

We just pulled that car over, there was no bed in sight

When we go to Palestine, he smiled in the moonlight.

Lucas Turner kept most of his promises. Well at least he took her on the road. They performed in East Texas, and he let her play. In fact, the girl outplayed her latest lover, but Miriam still lacked showmanship. She stood behind and concentrated on her axe and sang her parts. She lacked experience playing before an audience. Lucas Turner gave her the opportunity.

She became the lone girl the two months they traveled. The man who messed around with at least five women, eliminated all but one, plus his wife. "Tell me you loves me Lucas."

"You know I do, sweet thang, since you is the best girl I got."

"You gonna leave your wife?"

"Sugar, I can't leave her. She raising my kids."

"Then what's am I to you? I gots to be more than a guitar player and singer?"

"Oh, baby you much more to me than that." You keep me going when we on da road."

"What about when we done touring Lucas? What's am I too you den?"

"I heard you like girls. You can play with your friends, until I get back to you. I got nicknames for all of you. I calling you Fanny, cause of your nice little fanny."

He grabbed a handful, and he gave it a quick swat. Miriam smiled at him. Go sit in that chair over there and make yourself comfortable Little Miss Fannie. He gave her another loving spank and they hurried in the house to relax. The rest of the harem was nowhere to be seen in his small home. Miriam noticed this as Lucas grabbed her a glass of lemonade.

"Where are da other girls and what are dere names?"

"Well there is Annie, I don't have no nickname for her, and then there is Chester…"

"Chester?" Miriam question him. "Dat's a boy's name." Then her laughter filled the room."

Lucas laughed with her. He attempted to control the outburst, but the laughter spurted from his mouth like a volcano, he endured an impossible time containing himself. "Well when you see her you gonna know why I call her Chester." They both burst out laughing. "Den I call da one Moses, cause she thinks she can walk on water, all perfect and that. She also thinks she gonna be the only one. Annie and Chester like each other too. Hopefully, you gonna like dem. Moses, I ready to send her packing."

She tilted her head and shook it side to side as if she attended a fancy tennis match. "So, sir. What if I want to be your only girl?"

He laughed in her face. Saliva came shooting out of his mouth and missed her. "I gots me a wife and her name is Carmen. She part Mexican, and me and her roam around a lot. Half my home time is spent here, but da other half is there. Don't ya go looking for us, cause when I'm with her, we walk hand in hand, like lovers s'pose to do."

Miriam soon wondered what she got herself into. She missed Bo, but the notion of going out on the road with this man intrigued her. They relaxed for the rest of the day. Annie, Chester and Moses joined them in the evening, and they stayed together the rest of the week. Lucas joined his family and stayed there the following week, leaving Miriam alone with the concubines. She enjoyed herself with them and spent nights with Chester.

She had her bag packed, and ready for the road.
A few changes of clothes, a brand-new guitar in tow.
Then she saw Carmen, walking with her man outside.
He gave her a kiss, left her waiting, taking Miriam
for a ride.

"So dat's your wife?" She questioned him as they went out on the road. Lucas Turner drove the Cadillac towards Tyler, Texas as they traveled for their show. "I want to be the only one. Me and you gonna take Texas and Louisiana by storm."

Lucas said nothing as he drove dive to Tyler. Miriam wondered if he had any notions about leaving his wife . They walked towards the juke where they scheduled themselves to play. Hand-in-hand they walked.

"Ha, ha, ha." His laugh bellowed across the East Texas forest. He resonated like Santa. "One woman ain't enough for Lucas Turner. You and me on da road all da time, I can't get with these locals. I go home to see my wife and kids. I need to get me some relaxin'." Lucas sat on the ground against an elm tree, stretched out and put his hand on the bulge in his worn blue jeans. Miriam paid no attention as she hiked towards the juke joint. a few blocks away, on the edge of the thick forest.

The joint sat on the edge of Tyler. Still mad, Miriam wasn't in the mood to play. She sat behind the stage pouting, with her lips protruding, her eyes almost closed and enjoyed listening to Big Luke play his opening set alone. During intermission he talked to some of the local whores trying to get with him. Damn hooker climbed on top of him and rubbed his pants. Lucas smiled, and he peered straight at Miriam and said, "This could be all yours if you obey." Raised to obey, Lucas was still Miriam's man, she came out for the second set.

She got to her feet, joined him onstage and played her guitar and sang her songs and the duets. The special chemistry between them enhanced their performance and intoxicated the crowd. The man, a master of seduction, turned her on, with music and in other ways. Miriam ripped her switch across the strings, calling all the creatures from the forest and even from the swamps in the state adjacent to them. The man strutted around her as she performed her solos, shaking his junk at her. He even laid on his ass, with knees spread and playing his guitar while she continued to solo. Without missing a note, he rose to his feet, duck walked around and finished his extended solo. Miriam loved it and forgave the man. The crowd loved the two, and soon Miriam and Lucas planned on bigger and better things. Sweet Home Chicago sat off Lake Michigan. The Windy City awaited.

After the performance they walked towards a Negro hotel. With a bankroll of money stuffed in his pockets, Lucas Turner wondered about Miriam, and what a wonderful little partner she developed into. He made plans of giving her something special. Mr. and Mrs. Turner would become permanent partners up north.

Chapter 13
Billy the Kid Bourgeois

Young Billy the Kid Bourgeois arrived in town from Huntsville. Little Billy, the son of Judge Bourgeois and the nephew of the warden, came from the most feared family in East Texas. However, Billy displayed a learning disability, making him different than the rest of the Bourgeois clan. Some people never mature as an adult. The kid, not named after the famous outlaw, received his nickname at the ripe age of twenty-two. Some folks called him crazy. Other folks called the boy additional derogatory names.

He strolled past the rose-lined sidewalks of Tyler, Texas in the evening. He took his beagle for a walk. Yellow and red roses filled the parks as he strolled closer to the section of town where roses don't grow. The Tyler Negroes never witnessed the beautiful flowers sprouting from the ground like oil wells. Instead, they witnessed rusty water fountains and dandelion weeds which at least bloomed a yellow flower.

Big Lucas Turner and his companion, the young and pretty Miriam Landry, hiked along the road in the black part of town, from the juke-joint where they performed. They walked along the railroad tracks towards a little barbecue spot, so they might rustle up some grub, before they returned to their chicken shack of a Negro-only motel.

Crossing the field of yellow flowers, Miriam and

Lucas Turner witnessed a man spying on them. The man carried a long scabbard meant to hold a sword. He stood average height and weight. He bordered on the scrawny side, and even in the dark Texas evening, they observed his light complexion.

During their stroll Miriam and Lucas sang a song about Chicago. "They all moving on up there. Lots of them, all going up like geese in da springtime. Migrating on up. You, me—going on up". He started slapping the wood on his guitar and sang. "You, me, leaving Carmen behind. Just you and me, leaving Carmen behind. I gots My Miriam, Chicago on my mind."

Miriam sang her own version, subbing Lucas for her name. They talked and sang about moving there and getting away from the awful segregation they experienced while on the road.

"What if I leaves my wife and all those others in Palestine, and I moves both of us up there? Lots of others are going up there."

"I'll go with you. As long as I'm your one and only like you promise."

Big Lucas Turner laughed his bellowing laugh. "I never said you will be one and only. I just leaving these other bitches behind. That includes my wife." He laughed again, and slapped Miriam on her bottom.

"I'm going," She smiled at him.

Kissing and fondling one another, and ignoring the mysterious stranger, they soon came across the man. He stood on a wooden footbridge which crossed the murky swamp setting in the poor section of town.

Billy the Kid Bourgeois went after Lucas first, his initial mistake, making the attempt with a homemade sling-blade. His custom device consisted of a Bowie knife strapped on to a baseball bat, which he harnessed in his worn homemade sheath. Billy the Kid didn't spend quality time on the baseball diamond as a child. His initial attempt at mugging the couple went awry.

The knife struck Lucas Turner's thick bushy beard and managed to slice off a piece. The curly whiskers fell to the ground. Miriam's eyes followed the pubic-looking patch of whiskers to the surface of the wooden. Did he miss on purpose and wished to attack the girl?

Miriam stormed after Billy, but he stood ready as he took out another knife. The blade glistened beneath the gas lamp, the lone light near the bridge. Billy the Kid Bourgeois held the knife to her throat with his right hand. His left arm engulfed her chest.

"This purdy little thing is coming with me," Billy said with a thick Texas drawl, escalated by the undiagnosed mental illness he suffered from. "Fallow me," he continued, the knife pressed against Miriam's throat as he dragged her.

Lucas watched the slow-witted man struggling to drag her away, as he replaced his homemade sling blade in the homemade sheath. Big Lucas Turner stood helpless, doing nothing. Shooting the kidnapper seemed a rotten idea, since he wasn't an accurate shooter, and might shoot Miriam instead, or the knife might cut her once the bullet impacted.

Lucas was fully aware a colored man in East Texas wouldn't get a fair trial or a trial at all. He also pondered the idea of Miriam Landry as a replaceable piece of flesh, although a talented one., but maybe this man didn't care if she lived or died. Back in Palestine sat a plethora of whores to go to Chicago with. Plus, the man

111

already had a family.

But Miriam offered something most potential whores didn't. The girl played a mean axe. A couple act may turn into his bus ticket out of the South. However, folks came to admire him. He watched Miriam struggle, aware that by their next destination she might be roadkill, like the armadillos on the side of the road.

Miriam scrunched her face. Her lips puckered, but not as if to kiss someone. Her eyes squinted, and she prepared for battle. She stuck her left leg back further than expected and tripped the man. Billy the Kid went sprawling backwards. His left arm swung back, as did his right, and the man dropped the knife and fell on his ass. Miriam grabbed the black handle of the knife, and standing above him, whipped his homemade sling blade from his homemade sheath. She placed the Bowie knife in her pocket, as she raised the blade above her head. Ready to attack she took a deep breath, bending her arm forward, cocking the blade to gain extra momentum. In her mind, his destination was hell like the boll weevil in the song.

"Wait m-m-ma-ma'am," the mugger said stuttering. "I just wanted to know you and get some money."

"Dat's not how you get a girl, by attacking me. You got to talk with a gal." She studied his face. Perspiration dripped from his face as his scrawny chest heaved, like a bullfrog stuck in his shirt. She noticed his higher cheekbones, wider nose and his complexion, darker than most Caucasians. He was Creole.

The man scratched an itch three times. Her last lover, Bo Barnum always scratched his itches three times before he stopped scratching. The man also shook his neck to the right, an annoying habit he shared with Bo. With a similar facial resemblance, she soon realized this man, Billy Bourgeois, one of those Texas relatives Bo Barnum hoped he'd never meet. "You look like someone I know," Miriam continued.

Still shaking and breathing heavy, he scratched three times again. "How do I do it then?"

"I'm taken anyways. Dis man over dere and me are moving to Chicago." Miriam peeked over her shoulder and smiled at Lucas.

Billy the Kid gave his rebuttal. "No, you are coming with me." He tried to move but Miriam held the sling blade cocked and ready to slice. In a flash, shots rang out as Big Lucas Turner deciding on rescuing her. Blood popped out of the challenged man, and the human liquid stained Miriam, as she and the sling blade disappeared into the Texas forest.

Lucas and Miriam both were arrested for the murder of William Bourgeois, nephew of the warden of the State Prison where Lucas Turner and Miriam Landry would soon reside. The father of Billy the Kid Bourgeois sentenced the pair.

Billy Bourgeois shot dead, four times in the chest.
Lucas Turner and Miriam Landry, they both faced arrest.

Ten to twenty years, down on the prison farm.
Killing a Bourgeois in East Texas shouldn't do any harm.

Chapter 14
The Great Escape

The tall folklorist stood above the lanky young black man. He made a habit of visiting prisons throughout the South, seeking songs of the working people—the trains songs, and more important the prison songs. He wore a nice suit, with his tie loosened at his neck, and a tan cowboy hat topped his head. A hint of a goatee bordered his face. The bluesman wore black and white horizontally striped clothing.

"You gotta get me outta here sir. I hear ya got Huddie out of Angola, and dat place is tougher dan here. Plus, my pappy taught Huddie how to play. My pappy taught everyone to play."

"I'll see what I can do, Mister…"

"Turner, Big Lucas Turner, I can outplay anyone, I mean anyone under the table. I cut heads wid all. Only person dat plays as good is da girl I hooked up with. We need to get her out too. She didn't do nuttin', anyway."

The folklorist tried to sooth him. Lucas was aware a Lomax got Leadbelly—Huddie—out of jail before. He begged the folklorist, he realized his influence, although Lucas may or may not have known about the jailbreak conspiracy. After talking to the warden, the man returned. "Mr. Turner, your release has been scheduled. I don't have a date yet, but the warden will deliver your instructions."

"Thank you, kind sir."

"I didn't have anything to do with it, Mr. Turner. Don't thank me."

Being a talented Blues singer created advantages for Miriam also. Goree Prison was renowned for its string band. The world-famous band played on the radio all the way to Nashville and even New York City. Folks listened to the convicts serenade the country from Nashville to New Orleans and even Omaha.

The lead singer of the band was the pretty and talented former Lydia Fuentes Barnum. Mrs. Barnum got the fame she craved, and never got with her marriage to Bo Barnum. Miriam Landry got tossed in the cell, oblivious of her cellmate. One glance at the beautiful, older Hispanic woman's face soon changed everything. She resembled a picture hung in the Barnum's parlor. A photograph of Lydia Barnum stood in the pantry, with the family photos. There sat Bo's former wife, and the mother of Sara and Tomas Barnum, on the bench of the prison cell. Miriam recognized her right away, unaware Lydia knew Miriam fucked her husband.

Judge Lynden Bourgeois divorced Lydia Barnum from her husband Bo, so she married the judge's brother, the warden of Goree. The marriage, a total sham, as Lydia spent a lot of time incarcerated, but allotted her certain privileges. Home-cooked meals and sex with the warden, her husband, were only two of the favors.

In her marriage to Bo Barnum, he received all the attention. Lydia desired more, and in Goree, the woman evolved into the guitarist and singer of the band. She loved the accolades so much, she'd never leave.

Used and brainwashed, the money Lydia earned for the prison went straight to the warden and the judge. The Bourgeois controlled vast territory in The Lone Star State, and another Barnum sat out there who required elimination. This one hunkered across the river, the only

115

heir aware of the family recipe. The trap was now in place as the Bourgeois used both women to lure Bo. One knew about it; the younger naive Miriam, remained oblivious to all this.

Lydia got to know about her cell mate living in Sabine Parish. The Bourgeois family stretched into Western Louisiana, in the form of a cousin, the deputy of Sabine Parish. He kept his eye on the Barnum Family. The Bourgeois family had total knowledge of the whiskey and whores, and they sure recognized Miriam Landry as the woman Bo Barnum slept with.

While awaiting Miriam's arrival, her husband came and got her. She cooked dinner for him, serviced the pig. As they lay in bed together, he asked. "Lydia, if your former husband knew you were alive, what do you think he would do?"

Lydia answered her current spouse. "I know he would try to rescue me. Bo isn't very bright, but he has a good heart. Sometimes too big."

The warden smiled at her. "Do you think he would help you escape?"

Lydia smiled at her mate. She peered at him as her eyes focused. "Bo would do anything for me. That includes breaking me out of here."

"Do you want to leave with him?"

"No. I want to stay here so I can be the star. You know that is what I always wanted, and that is what I have now."

"I'm not saying you will stay with him, but I have a plan."

"It better be a good one, since I know Bo will follow me forever."

"It's a good one. We both know someone who

will take care of it. Then I will be all yours." Smiling, the warden escorted his bride back to jail. He let her back in the cell she shared with Miriam Landry.

Miriam and Lydia took to one another like a match to kerosene. Lydia, aware Miriam lived with Bo, assured herself they lived as a couple and fucked her husband. Lydia also recognized her cell mate Miriam played guitar better than Lydia, but her voice, while not as pure, sounded more passionate. Lydia screamed at the guard. "Why is this little bitch my cell-mate? She won't be the star, will she?"

The cell they shared was atypical of a normal jail cell. Guitars weren't allowed inside the locked walls of the prison. Shoved into her quarters she shared with Lydia; she noticed the Regal guitar. Before she introduced the person, she soon called bitch, she grabbed the instrument and played, "Hellhounds on my Trail."

Lydia followed her by playing a Mexican folk song she wrote.

"Should we cut heads?" Miriam asked her as she kept her fingers loose doing the shuffle.

"Not with you." Miriam was, without a doubt, capable of shredding this bitch to pieces on guitar. Bo told her she played and accompanied herself, but no one ever accused Lydia of selling herself at an intersection in Mississippi with her guitar playing. Miriam plopped next to the older woman, stretched out on her cot and eyed her competition. Lydia kept smiling at her, dreaming of the future ambush in place.

Lydia sucked Miriam into the Bourgeois scheme. Miriam, a naive country girl raised in the swamps, had never been part of a political scheme or raised by political revolutionaries. Her mother, a prostitute, bedded her father at Guidry's. Her father, a touring musician. Women dropped everything when they witnessed him play, including their skirts. Miriam hadn't even met several of her siblings.

Miriam swum like a tadpole to a snapping turtle as she soon fell into the Bourgeois trap. Unknown to her, another person had already been enticed into the con. In fact, conspiracy theorists later debated whether Lucas Turner came to the Barnums for one reason. The daring escape from the Men's farm already prearranged with the Bourgeois, his job was simple—grab Miriam Landry and aide her escape. Whether Lucas Turner knew the escape was a predetermined trap was anyone's guess. The folklorist never interviewed Lucas Turner again.

Lucas Turner arrived around midnight at the Huntsville women's prison farm. He waited in the forest a few hundred yards from the train track carrying the Texas-Louisiana railroad. The rails headed East by the sleepy Louisiana town called Zwolle, sitting East of the Sabine River, and where the Barnums called their home. Deputy Bourgeois also lived in Zwolle.

Miriam had been locked behind prison walls for about six months, tolerating her part time cellmate, playing and singing in the prison band, but she craved freedom. "When would Lucas going to rescue me," she often wondered? Around six in the morning on a Saturday in the fall, she walked by the edge of the fence. The sun already rose in the Eastern sky, and Miriam took her morning stroll. Alone all morning, Lydia had not returned from the wardens, Miriam noticed Lucas Turner lying by the edge of the prison grounds. She walked towards him, and noticing some loose leaves, she kicked at them, and she stumbled. She got on her hands and knees and found a tunnel. Thanking whichever God she prayed to, she went to crawling, and had soon slid under the fence and was free. Walking through the front gate, would have been a much simpler task, then but how would she realize the escape sat pre-arranged? The Bourgeois empire wanted her oblivious to the notion they had set up her release.

Lucas Turner grabbed her, and they hopped the freight. They took the damn train the wrong direction. The train took them deep in the heart of Texas going towards San Antonio.

"We needs to be heading east. Gets us back to Louisiana."

"Das what we be doing, but dat's what they be spectin'. You know dem damn Rangers and guards will be searching all over da forest for us and stopping dat Eastbound. I got us a plan." The singer screamed, since riding in a box car isn't a conversation-friendly location.

Riding the rails, going to come on home to you
Hopping a freight, cause that what you want me to
do.
Heading towards Louisiana, I want you back in my
life
I gotta find Bo Barnum, so I can be his wife.

The car hopped along the rails for at least an hour or two. Lucas put his arm around Miriam, like a lover should. The cuddling began nice and comfortable. He put a move on her and started rubbing her breast and kissing her. C'mon baby, it's been months since we've done it. C'mon baby, we alone on dis train." It made sense he desired her, and craved sex with her, but Miriam wasn't having any of it. She no longer desired Lucas. She didn't like the way he rescued her. He shot Billy Bourgeois, after she relaxed him, so he never saved her. Billy, now, nothing more than a crazy man murdered in cold blood, so instead of becoming a hero, Big Lucas Turner evolved into another cold-blooded murderer.

Besides she missed the Barnum kids, but she missed and loved Bo. Lucas made a move on her, but she pushed him away, and she took the leap of faith. The train moved about fifteen to twenty miles an hour she figured, but she still jumped out and rolled near the town of LaGrange. Lucas Turner did not follow her.

The young woman hoped and prayed she had freed herself from the singer. She longed to be in Bo's arms and bed. She hitched along the railroad tracks towards the sun. She hiked East, while mesquite trees lined the tracks, and the cars driving on the highway rolled close by. She hoped the train would pass any minute, before the police or Lucas Turner spotted her.

Gazing straight ahead, her placed her focus on the vanishing point the railroad tracks provided. Startled by the car's horn, Miriam's head jolted, and she noticed a shiny Caddy parked beside the road. The tall black man stepped out of the Caddy. "Hop in." Lucas Turner called to her. "I is sorry, Let's get going." He opened the door for her and tired of walking, she climbed in. The mystical powers of the man drew her inside the car. Soon, they sped eastbound towards Louisiana, but they required driving some distance before they got there. "I borrowed dis car from someone in LaGrange. Dey was visiting dat big whorehouse. I figured dey would be dere for-a while." Lucas smiled as if he told the biggest lie in the biggest state, since everything is bigger in Texas. The man waited for Miriam to return his smile, but she never did, as they cruised East Texas in the stolen coupe. About fifteen miles into their journey, he glanced at Miriam again. He kept the same expression on his face. "I was wrong. Dat man came out when I was in his car, so I hads to shoot him."

She gazed straight ahead as the car sped across the highway, soon it went past Huntsville. "Now we is gonna head to Chicago. You is coming with me. If nots I'm dropping you off right back where you belong at da farm."

"I wanna go back to Bo, and I is returnin' to him. I love him, not you." Her focus shifted as she peered out the passenger window counting billboard signs to herself.

"We going to Chicago." They sped past the prison farm and continued to head east.

A few miles past Lufkin, Miriam took another leap of faith. She already took several too many, and still at the tender age of eighteen. The car slowed to a stop to let some longhorn cattle cross the road. He didn't plow the herd into ground beef and grab any steaks for the rest of the trip, instead he stopped. Once the car came to a halt, she jumped and fled into the forest towards the railroad tracks. She knew where the rails led, and they headed towards the man Miriam confessed she loved. She ran as fast as her scrawny legs carried her. Lucas Turner, also aware of where she headed, caught her five miles from the river. Close to freedom, she recognized Bo's home, as the sun descended behind her.

"You coming with me." One fist hit her cheek. He followed it with a combination Joe Louis would have been proud of. Soon she laid on the ground and he ripped off her clothes—some removed with expertise, others ripped, torn, and tossed in the field. Lucas Turner made a fatal mistake as he dropped his pants. The handgun came tumbling from its spot. Miriam grabbed it. She pointed it. She fired. The explosion rocked the Sabine Valley, and soon she sprinted towards the river. She remembered where she hid the skiffs. She required another hour before she nestled safe at Bo's.

Chapter 15
Call and Response

Some folks living in the South say a harmonica calls the train home. Bo and Sara Barnum, and Miriam Landry acknowledged this myth as fact. After a day of avoiding the female suitors, Bo Barnum strolled to the picnic table, a few hundred yards from the banks of the Sabine River. Texas sat across the river.

Bo sat on the edge of the picnic table playing a few Blues songs he taught himself. His harmonica snuggled so comfortable in the harmonica holder while he picked the Blues shuffle and called the train home on the harp. Exhaling out on the one, two three holes a few times, a quick in on the three, four and five, and a long exhale on the three, four and five, doing a vibrant hand tremolo. Bo shook his hand as if he acted nervous or cold. Soon he got in the zone, the musician's zone, where everything he tried became incredible. Bo Barnum walked along the alligator infested shoreline, picking the guitar and tooting the harmonica. The gators didn't mind. They coexisted with the Barnum family. When the gators got a little frisky, Bo and Sara trapped the reptiles and the family ate dinner for a while. They even fed the neighbors, and Bo, Tomas, Sara and Miriam owned lots of different boots and belts.

Off in the distance he heard a scream, followed by a gunshot. He was aware the blast came from across the river where gunshots belonged. For Bo, Louisiana meant safety. However, across the river in Texas told another story. He figured the killing, nothing but another senseless Texas murder, and the shooting didn't bother him at all. Hell, to him they'd knock each other off.

Bo continued to prance around the riverside, playing in rhythm to the rushing river. The guitar cranked; the harp blew. He walked towards the house, but curiosity got to him. He set the guitar on the porch, but he kept on wailing Blues riffs on the harp. Blowing a harmonica calls the train home. They also call mysterious strangers across the river.

> *He called the train again.*
> *The paddles splashed the water.*
> *Bo blew another riff.*
> *Paddles cut through the water.*
> *He called the train.*
> *Someone found a skiff.*
> *He blew another riff.*
> *The splashing got louder.*
> *He kept playing, he kept dancing on the riverside.*
> *Voices heard in the distance—he heard his name.*

This continued for about twenty minutes. Long enough for someone to paddle across the Sabine. Bo Barnum buried skiffs on both sides of the river in case someone needed to engineer an escape. He soon got an incredible rush about the mysterious stranger. Again, he overthought the situation. *"Could this be my lovely wife coming home? She doesn't know where we live now, but it could be her. Could this be Miriam? She knows about the skiffs. In fact, she was the one that hid them."*

Miriam wondered about telling Bo Barnum the

news. She met Lydia and they became cellmates at Huntsville. Miriam still loved Bo and regretted leaving him, but she had a murder rap on her head, and now she was an escaped convict. Miriam, always ridden with guilt about leaving Bo, realized fleeing her home in Louisiana was wrong, but she also wasn't contented with her lifestyle. If she stayed put, Lydia became a memory for the Barnum family, and not in the picture. She considered Sara and Tomas, for whom their mother lived and breathed. Lucas Turner, now a memory for her, a dead memory, a man she captured life from. He would soon turn into a haunting memory for her. She'd apologize to Bo, he'd forgive her, and they'd marry.

Bo took her inside the house, where he drew a warm bubble bath for her. They both got in and shared the tub. Sex at this moment, forbidden, but the intimacy shared replaced the lack of physical sex. He observed Miriam's body and noticed the bruises on Miriam's arms, legs and face. Her soft naked body soaked in front of him and she never imagined feeling closer to any man, ever. Sometimes making love isn't having sex but sharing your most intimate moments—becoming vulnerable to your lover and sharing yourself. The night of her return, she fell in love with Bo Barnum, as his arms wrapped around her, and the white bubbles cascaded off her dark body. It made for an intimate contact. Bo held her tight to him. After the bath he helped her dry off. They walked hand in hand, returning to the bed they once shared. He laid behind her and they slept in bliss. He spooned her with his arms draped around her. Still naked, he held her all night, with no physical sex.

Baby just take a load off your feet,

125

Come on and lay with me.
You don't have to do nothing,
Just lay with me.

In the morning Miriam peered at Bo. Her eyes penetrated his soul as words remained absent, however actions took control. She desired, lusted and craved him more than ever. He became that drug that she depended on. She climbed on top of him, straddled him, and peered deep in his eyes, while bouncing up and down on his body. The pleasure fulfilled them as the house shook like the shanty huts on the bayou, and in the slums of Shreveport, where the poorest of poorest folks lived.

Bo and Miriam came downstairs holding hands. The looks on their faces told it all. If a man and woman appeared ashamed, accomplished and exhilarated at the same time; Miriam and Bo portrayed that image. "Sara looks like you need to make an extra biscuit or two. Plus, make more gravy."

"Papi, I know. I already have."

Sara made an exquisite breakfast of biscuits and gravy, grits and some sausage. She had become an incredible cook in Miriam's nine-month absence. Bo and Miriam walked to the table together. Tomas had already taken his seat in his usual spot, beside his father. Tomas, fourteen, already returned to the table with his second serving. The creamy gravy speckled with black and red pepper swirled above the golden-brown biscuits. He liked gravy on his sausage also. He hardly noticed Miriam when he glanced at her, as he scarfed his breakfast. As usual, he slept through the previous night's commotion.

After they finished breakfast, Tomas cleared the table, returned and took his seat. Miriam addressed the

Barnum family. She decided on doing the honorable thing hoping Bo no longer desired his wife. "Bobo, remember I told you last night, that there was something else? This is important."

"What is it Miri?" He asked her as he gazed in her direction.

Both kid's eyes also focused on the Creole woman. Miriam stood and walked towards the dark brown Mahogany cabinet, where some of the better bowls and plates sat—the dishes the Barnums use on holidays and special occasions. They never used their finest china. Also on the cabinet stood a row of photographs. About ten pictures lined the shelf, but the display consisted of family photos before they met Miriam, and a few photos of her and some of the shows the family hosted. She kept glancing at the pictures, debating if doing the honorable thing stood as her wisest option.

She was aware righteous people told the truth, and if Bo ever found out she kept a gigantic secret from him, the initial creatures finding her tied body would be the alligators. Bo taught Sara how to hunt and trap wildlife. They stored traps near the river, and Miriam might place a foot in one. On the other hand, if Bo Barnum found out his wife still lived, he'd try to rescue her and bust her off the Texas farm where Miriam herself escaped from. Useless to the Barnum family, and once again with no purpose in her life, she'd venture out with some Blues singer to beat her, use her and take her on the road. For a quick second she wondered if gator bait became the number one option. The family's eyes focused on her as she exhaled.

She'd never been a righteous person, but not an

evil one either. She glanced at the photo, glanced at the family. Like a pendulum, Miriam moved her head to and fro, peering at the photo, and then took one last peek at the family. She grabbed the photograph. Her hands shook as she glared at it. She accidentally knocked several photos over. Miriam failed to replace them while she nabbed the photo of Lydia playing guitar on Grandpa Cecil's dock on the Black Bayou singing the Mexican folk song she loved so much. The song of the cockroach, "La Cucaracha." The image had been taken a few days before the Barnum family departed for Texas and a few days before Lydia disappeared. Bo never moved it.

Miriam's initial glance was towards Tomas. He leered at her tiny frame, eyes studying every curve. She peeked at his sister, and last, gazed deep into Bo's eyes, yearning for the love she received last night and in the morning. Expressionless. she returned her gaze towards the children, her eyes retreated to Bo and she refused to take her eyes off him. She came to the table and stood by her lover.

Tomas resembled a snapping turtle as he stretched out his neck attempting to get a glimpse of the image Miriam carried. Sara peeked at Miriam, aware the image she possessed was of her mother. "Why else would she go there? We just visited Grandpa Cecil and his woman." The only photographs were of family and a few musicians.

Miriam sighed a gigantic sigh and she glanced at the picture. All the Barnums gave her their full attention and wondered whose picture she clasped. The pressure built, but it all on centered Bo in one minute. She realized Bo's answer would reveal how much he loved her.

After what seemed like an eternity Miriam

reached the head of the table, the picture of Lydia playing guitar pressed firm against her stomach. She snuck one last peak at the photo and realized she did a bit of jackassing by getting the picture. She knew Bo needed the photo. Her fingers held it tight, and she refused to release it, even though she figured the family, sat aware of her secret. She showed Bo the photo.

"I met her when I was on a farm in Texas. She was my cell mate and we played in da prison band together. Dey got dis band dat's world famous and Lydia is da lead singer, and she sang real purdy. We was all over da radio. I was playing guitar too." Miriam held her breath waiting for Bo's response.

Bo covered his face with his hands, hiding his tears from Miriam and his children, or maybe hiding the elation on his face, since his true love still breathed. Bo Barnum prayed for the correct answer. Only the heaving of deep breaths became audible, the one noise everyone witnessed. Even the gators remained quiet.

The spotlight shone on him, and him alone. Like a lone wolf, Bo stood in the moonlight. He glanced at his audience, his family, and girlfriend, as they devoured every move he made. As a man of principle and integrity he earned respect as a stand-up-person, but it also got him in trouble. The searchlight still shone on him as he returned Lydia's photo to the cabinet. He placed it in its spot and stood the fallen photos upright.

Bo searched diligently for the correct words. Those words became as elusive as a cottonmouth swimming across the Sabine. He soon spoke, and the correct words may have remained lodged in his throat, while he ejected miscalculated ones. He peered at Miriam. "Pumpkin, are you sure?"

"Yes Bobo. Da warden said her name was Lydia Fuentes Bourgeois. Plus, she sang real pretty. Dat was her, all right."

His eyes glanced back and forth across the room as he ignored the fact Miri mentioned the last name Bourgeois. "You escaped off the farm Miri? We could go get her. It wouldn't be too hard, I think."

Miri glared towards Bo, and to the wooden floors in their kitchen. Sniffles resonated around the dining room and teardrops fell as Miriam thought about running towards the stairs, and into their room.

She swallowed her pride, and gathered her courage, while remaining seated. "Dat Blues man and I escaped. There are tunnels under da fences, and dey by the railroad tracks, Da tracks cross over here by dat trestle up north. Lucas and I followed dem once he dumped the car he stole."

Bo eyed his kids, Miriam and returned to Sara and Tomas. "We need to get your mother. We will go visit tomorrow, but I need to talk to Pa first."

The answer wasn't the one Miriam sought, but again she received treatment much worse in her short life. This obstacle stood as one of the smallest in her lifetime.

They planned to visit her, and Miriam accepted the Barnum's idea. Sara and Tomas owned every right to visit their mother. She became incarcerated through no fault of her own. She acknowledged Bo had converted into the most confused person in the household. Before last night he assumed Lydia dead, so she forgave his poor judgement.

Bo devised a plan, but Grandpa Cecil's help became essential, so they sought his help to complete the task. Cecil'd always been an incredible father to Bo, but

130

a more devious man. His youngest son lacked the sinister side. Cecil, in his twenties, aided a cousin's escape from Angola. Rumors spread about his father, the son of Legba. Trains, boats and the car were required. They started phase one as the family strolled to the river.

The Sabine River displayed its eerie powers in the early afternoon. The river's voice loud, haunting but the Barnums liked the river's spooky tones. Bo glanced at the skiff, the little dugout canoe he owned, and the motorboat. He tossed the twigs off the craft with its Evinrude mounted at the aft, and they camouflaged the skiff Miriam took across the river the previous evening. He climbed in while the kids and Miriam pushed it into the river.

With the full moon rising and the wind velocity increasing, different noises in the bayou increased. Sara and Bo started smiling—they loved days like this. The girls both said, "See ya soon."

Tomas replied. "Papi going motorboating." Tommy sat there with no expression on his face. Sara busted a gut laughing, as she fell on her butt. Miriam kneeled above her to aide Sara to her feet, her limited cleavage exposed to the young girl. stretching out her hand. Sara glanced at the flat chested Miriam while she laughing on as snot shot out her nose.

"He ain't motorboating with you." She laughed at her inside joke. Miriam laughed too, while poor Tommy, hadn't a clue what he said that was so funny. All three of them walked towards the jalopy parked beside the house and drove to meet their father by the trestle. Sara and Miriam still laughed, slapping their hands on their hips, and falling into the mud, when Sara started the car. She kept pounding on the steering wheel, giggling at Tomas's unintended joke.

Bo cranked the Evinrude and went up the river towards the trestle a few miles north of town. According to Miriam, the same tracks which skirted around the town of Huntsville rolled across the trestle north of their homestead. Bo landed the boat on the western bank of the river and hid it in a dug-out cypress in the bayou. He climbed the trestle, crossed it and met Miriam and the kids in the jalopy.

Bo drove the back roads to his father's house towards Black Bayou. He kept a low profile lately since Early Greene sightings became frequent the past month. His former friend, one of the potential kidnappers of his wife, and the father of Miriam's aborted child, stalked Bo's house. Who wondered whom Early sought? Miriam imagined it was her, while Bo worried Early stalked him.

Mr. Barnum feared for his life. Miriam replaced Sara once again in the front seat as Bo took the wheel. They soon arrived in Shreveport and headed north to the Black Bayou. At Cecil Barnum's they developed their plan.

The following morning, they drove to Huntsville and went to the prison. Miriam hid inside the trunk of the car. Inside the prison Bo tried to coax his wife to escape. On his own, Bo failed in convincing his wife. He called in the cavalry. Sara, as the future lawyer could be the most persuasive, but she still failed. Sitting in the wing with his grandfather hid Bo's secret weapon, little Mama's boy Tomas Barnum. Lydia loved the little guy, and once she noticed him, she cracked. Tears fell from her eyes like Louisiana rain, and she told Bo to meet her at the fence by the edge of the farm in either of the following two days.

Cecil returned with Tomas to his home in the bayou, while Sara, Miriam and Bo waited in the forest near the fence. In between lay the railroad tracks crossing the Sabine less than one mile from Bo's home. Underneath the trestle sat the boat Bo hid earlier in the cypress trees.

Miriam, Sara and Bo crouched on all fours digging tunnels into the ground, burrowing a large enough hole which would cover all four of them. Once the small cavern was dug out, it had an impeccable view of the prison fence. They took turns eyeing the prison yard for Lydia, careful not to be discovered by the search light. After a day and a half, a woman appeared by the fence. Lydia stood in the shadows, and Bo sprinted away to retrieve her. She used the tunnel Miriam used to wiggle below the gate. Bo wondered how many other women used this tunnel. They hurried to the cave. One train passed by as Bo and his ladies timed it. It chugged along, slowly enough past the prison to hop it.

"There is another train in two hours we need to take that one."

"You know we live in Louisiana, right across the river. This train will get us there."

Lydia eyed her former husband with excitement. It became the first time she smiled. "You mean I could have run a long time ago?"

Sara interjected. "Yeah Mami, but you didn't know we lived there."

"That's true, mi hija."

Lydia glared at Miriam. Her big beautiful brown eyes became red. "What is she doing here?" Miriam retreated into the cave she finished digging.

"She is helping us. She knows the land. We

133

don't."

Lydia still glared at Miriam. "She tried to steal my gig, and she's stealing my man too. I'm not coming."

"Mami, you have to. Miriam is our maid. She helps Tomas and me."

"Where is my baby?"

"He's with Cecil. Damn, I hear the train coming. Let's run up there."

The four of them ran towards the train tracks and hid behind the trees stretching along the fence like a picket fence surrounding a house. They waited for the engine to pass. With the pace of a snapping turtle, they moved their way through the forest, cutting in and out between the trees. Bo paid attention to the rail cars and pointed at one of the freight cars. They made their dash and all four sprinted as they found the car with the door ajar. Bo helped Miriam and Lydia on, and last Sara. He climbed on as Lydia reached out her hand to pull him into the box car. Miriam noticed the action, and it seemed like the former Mrs. Barnum wasn't pulling her hardest, and from her eyes it appeared as if she attempted to drop Bo. Bo Barnum came close to falling to his death if it wasn't for Sara and Miriam yanking the man into the empty freight car.

"Sorry Bo. Prison must be making me weaker. I thought I could get you in."

During the ride in the box car no one spoke since the steel wheels provided the lone noise thundering down the tracks. That noise became deafening. Sara and Miriam, forever bonding, sat beside one another, gazing at Bo and Lydia.

As expected, the stay at the house turned into chaos. Lydia never even visited her husband's and children's home, because another woman shared her husband's residence and a bedroom with Bo. Bo and the children tried their best to make her comfortable, while Miriam kept quiet, baked the cornbread, and stayed in the shadows. When company came unexpectedly, Miriam retreated to the kitchen or upstairs to her room. She always seemed afraid of someone finding her.

Cecil, his woman, Angeline, and Tomas soon arrived. Angeline brought tamales, jambalaya and crawfish gumbo for the party which already started. Bo, Sara, Tomas, Grandpa Cecil and Angeline scarfed their food down. Lydia and Miriam ate small bites, shoving their food aside, refusing to acknowledge one another.

After dinner all seven of them went across the lot towards the juke, and Bo, Miriam and Sara tuned their guitars and played Lydia some songs. They invited the former Mrs. Barnum to join them since Bo knew how much she loved her music. They played a few songs and Lydia sat there smiling as she enjoyed the show. Bo placed his guitar next to a chair to join his former bride, while Sara and Miriam performed a duet. Lydia checked the Dixie Beer clock hanging above the bar. She jumped, dashed out the door and got in the Barnum's jalopy. Bo ran after her, but he got a late start as he witnessed his former wife bouncing her way through the yard. She proceeded towards the train tracks. Sara and Tomas chased their father out the door. Miriam continued playing, finishing the tribute Sara wrote for her mother. She dropped her guitar once the song finished and stood in amazement, staring at the door where everyone but her, Cecil Barnum and Angeline exited. She stood in shock, mouth wide open, hands on her hips as the man who confessed his love for her chased after another woman.

Angeline, Cecil's woman, a dark-skinned former prostitute, and voodoo queen, walked towards her and put her arm around her hoping to console the young woman.

"I'm never gonna see him again, am I?"

Angeline put her hand on Miriam's forehead and caressed it. A prayer warrior, but not in the traditional way, she tried to read the spirits. Miriam's head pressed against Angeline's bosom, and Miriam prayed for Bo to come to her. Cecil's woman also bowed her head and shut her eyes. Angeline, who came from New Orleans, screamed. She witnessed a vision, even though she never repeated what she envisioned to Miriam, Cecil or the Barnum children. Her scream echoed through the house and shook the portraits hanging on the wall. Bo's copy of *Tobacco Road* fell off the bookshelf and went tumbling to the ground. Miriam noticed the swamp creatures screech with anticipation, and she jerked her head towards the river.

"I got to go see him," Miriam said as she ran for the door.

"No chil' you cannot go." Angeline snapped, her face expressionless. "Stay here and protect yourself." Miriam twisted her head and lollygagged towards her mentor, as Angeline held her close against her chest. "Dere, dere, chil'."

"But I blames myself. I shouldn't have run off like I did."

"Miri, Bo tempted the spirits. Before they met you, the spirits said he would never see her again. He shouldn't have chased her, but I would have done the same thing, if I had a chance to see Cecil again." They both glanced at Bo's father who never adhered to the voodoo witchcraft crap.

136

Cecil took a large hunk of chewing tobacco and stuck the wad in his left cheek. He grabbed his favorite corn cob pipe, stuck it in the bag and scooped a plug of tobacco out. He took a shot of the amber colored whiskey the Barnums were infamous for. Cecil lacked a cigar in his mouth, so Grandpa grabbed his cane and went across the room into Bo's parlor and grabbed a cigar out of the White Owl box. He eyed the two Creole women. "Let's go back to the house," and with the rhythm of the creatures chanting swamp sounds, the three of them walked across the yard towards the Barnum house. Cecil walked towards the rear of the house using his cane, while Miriam and Angeline went inside.

"Come inside dear." Angeline called him.

"I will not. I'm going to the river." Grandpa snapped back at her and spun around, getting out of the wind to light a cigar. He spit the tobacco out on the step and hobbled towards the river.

"Cecil you do not believe in the spirits either," she shouted at him. "Get back in here."

"Mastah Cecil, you don't believe. I believes in dem a little, and it's not safe."

"Listen to Miriam honey, I'm not even sure I could save you. There is something out there." Cecil, light skinned Creole man, wore a tan straw cowboy hat pulled over his eyes, hiding the tears that developed. The pipe dangled from his right lip and he carried his drink and cigar in his left hand. He held his cane in the right.

"Dat's my youngest boy out dere, and da only one that remains a Barnum. Dat other one is Bourgeois and he joined da Klan. I can't even say what happened to the oldest. Can't tell no one." He shook his cane at the two women, as he walked towards the Sabine. "I can't just sit here and wait." The man had a point. Parents never bury their children. Still no proof of the demise of Miriam's lover and Cecil's son existed. Hobbling towards the river, the strong southwestern breezes shifted, and came straight out of the north in violent gusts. The animals communicated boisterously, while the gators sang in harmony. Some bellowed, creating an eerie base line, while the agitated reptiles harmonized with high pitched screams. Bo and his daughter, Sara both liked the resonance of the swamp, and when things got a little spooky, they loved the noises even more. The rest of the family preferred to stay inside. Cecil Barnum retreated and limped his way towards the house.

All three of them sat in silence, scared of might happen. Sara and Tomas remained absent, and near the violent river. The three hoped and prayed nothing befell the children. An hour passed and another one, when Miriam wondered if she made out voices coming from the Sabine. The voices got louder as they approached. She made out Sara's voice, but the man's tone resonated unrecognizably to her. It wasn't Bo Barnum.

Then came a rapping on the door, Grandpa limped across the house to open it. Angeline followed right behind. Miriam slipped into the shadows of the kitchen. She wondered if she remained a fugitive after escaping off the farm. Always mysterious with the law, Miriam hid in different rooms, closets and stood in the shadows. They all heard Sara and Tomas screaming. When Cecil opened the door, they noticed Sara and the Deputy Bourgeois holding the large plastic body bag and struggling carrying it. Miriam disappeared upstairs to her room as she broke into a fury of tears. Sara chased after her and followed her towards her room. She hugged her friend and her father's lover, as tears cascaded throughout the interior of the home. Both women soon became inseparable.

****

Cecil and the rest of the family chunked Bo Barnum in the ground near Cletus tree, a haunting tree overhanging the Sabine River. Following the funeral ceremony Sara, Cecil, Miriam and Tomas doused the land with gasoline. Cecil lit a cigar and tossed the match onto the ground, hoping to burn the place to the ground. Old man Barnum never liked evidence.

Sara, Tomas and Miriam soon moved into Cecil Barnum's place on the Black Bayou, north of Shreveport. The place, like Bo's, was disguised as a bait shop and general store, however the juke-joint, whorehouse, and illegal distillery made the money. The children's belongings had already been moved to Cecil's waiting for them to get settled in Grandpa's larger place. At his joint, there was one larger main building.

Sara and Tomas transferred schools, and Cecil finagled the system to get the children into the all-white Byrd High School where she flourished as a student, and in Sara's free time she taught Miriam how to read and write. They also played zydeco and Blues together, often on the docks surrounding Grandpa's Cecil's place. Miriam taught Sara tricks about the Blues Bo never picked up. She taught her all her songs but one. Miriam planned on taking that one to her grave.

Alone in the bathroom together, after Sara's graduation Sara became interested in attending LSU. Sara, aware of the "one-drop rule," and her wish to study the law developed into one reason she planned to become a civil rights lawyer. However, Sara attended Byrd High, the white high school, but she had serious doubts about LSU.

"Miri, do you think I can pass?" She checked her complexion in the bathroom mirror. She poked her face with her index finger, before she began brushing her thick hair.

"Miss Sara, I can't say." Miriam approached Sara, and Sara saw her staring at her, admiring her skin tone. "My family has people lighter than you, that couldn't get in, and some got darker skin that got in. Dey had straight hair though. I had me a cousin dat graduated from there."

"I guess it would be a crapshoot then, if I went to LSU. I guess there are plenty of good Negro colleges I can go to. Grambling is close by."

"Dat could be better for you. I don't want you to go too far. I's gonna miss you." Miriam walked behind Sara and gave her a hug. "We should have some fun dis summer. I'm ready. I think you are too." She played with Sara's hair, and went outside.

Chapter 16
The Lesson

Sara and Miriam sat on a metal picnic table overlooking Black Bayou. Sara finished high school and was anxious to attend LSU. She paced through the yard, sprinting towards the bayou, where she attempted to catch some bullfrogs, providing a future family dinner. She hoped she'd snag a few snapping turtles also. Grandpa Cecil's ladies cherished cooking turtle soup. Sara wasn't having any luck catching critters as she returned to talk with Miriam.

"What's da matter Sara? You always catch something." Miriam asked her.

"I'm just nervous about going away to college. Not about the school part, but about the boys. I mean what if I go on a date, go to the pictures and then he tries to kiss me? I ain't kissed a boy since your little brother down in Morgan City, and that was a few years ago. I ain't sure I did it right since he didn't want to again."

"If you want to kiss him, kiss him. Dere ain't nuttin' wrong wid it. Sometimes I just want to be kissed by a man, and don't do any of dat other stuff. Your daddy was a good kisser."

"What if he sticks his tongue in my mouth? Your brother did. It kind of surprised me. I didn't do it back. Do I put my tongue in his mouth?"

Miriam and Sara gleamed at one another. Their eyes focused on one another as they spoke. Miriam broke focus from Sara's hazel eyes, and making direct eye contact with her soon became as hard as wrestling alligators. The darker skinned Creole woman glanced at the murky green water of the Black Bayou. The color of the pond scum resembled pea pods. Leadbelly used to live near this lake, and the legendary Cecil Barnum concluded his illegal whiskey business there.

The water stood still, with the wind idle, enhanced the murkiness of the water. A bass jumped, and it made a splash, sending circles of water out towards the cypress trees, while half circles came towards the shore. The jumping fish also broke the awkward silence forming between the two friends. Both sets of eyes followed the water movement, and they returned to their natural focus. This time neither woman glanced away as the eye contact intensified. Miriam shifted her focus away, gaze once again on the moss.

"Are you nervous?" Sara asked Miriam. "You can't look me straight in the eye."

"I'm thinking we need to take us out a boat. Do some fishing or sumfin."

"The water is a disaster right now. I mean look at it." Sara's head switched positions and pointed to the murk. "Grandpa said the lake turned over last night. Dat's why it so green."

Miriam twisted her hair into a ponytail. Her left elbow stuck straight out, and she cranked her hair like she cracked corn in a small corn grinder to make corn liquor. "Take da boat out Sara. I need to tell ya sumfin."

"You can tell me here."

She glanced over her shoulder, turned and faced her friend, put her finger to her lips and grinned. Her neck cracked a bit, loud enough that Sara heard it. "I can't Sara. Little brothers and Grandpas and their lady friends are close by. I need to tell ya something private." She jumped off the table and went to the dock and plopped herself into one of the wooden jon boats Cecil rents out. She fell on the floor of the boat, as Sara descended the wooden steps, untied the knot, and threw the rope at Miriam. Sara climbed in the watercraft and crawled towards the aft side, primed the engine four times, pulled the rope and started the Evinrude. All this time she kept her bottom stuck out.

Miriam sat smiling at her. Sara wore nothing but cut off overalls, with undergarments beneath her pants. Heat and humidity everyday forced the residents to dress casual. The young women dressed the same, but Miriam wore a tee-shirt beneath her overalls. Sara spun around and sat in the boat, bent over, exposing her cleavage. Not unnoticed, Miriam peeked at Sara's chest.

Miriam gleamed and smiled at her buddy, as the red boat bounced across the green water. Miriam developed secret plans for Sara for the summer. The younger friend guided the boat out to her secret spot where Sara wrote her songs. It was the location where they hauled in bountiful amounts of fish and turtles. Abundant wildlife existed on Black Bayou, and Sara and Miriam spotted critters all day. They often composed and performed original songs for one another at this location. Today they lacked musical instruments, and they also lacked fishing tackle.

Miriam tossed the anchor overboard, causing a loud and large abundant splash and she hurried to sit closer to Sara. The anchor descended into the murk as the rope unwound, following the weight to the bottom of the lake. She rocked the boat while she hurried towards the aft. The boat swayed as if the duo sat in a life raft in the middle of the ocean, searching for their freedom from fascist oppressors. Plopping on her ass in the middle seat of the boat, the watercraft quit rocking.

Sara leaned towards Miriam, exposing her cleavage. "Why did you want to come here?"

Miriam's focused followed Sara's cleavage. She smiled as she spoke. "I's got sumfin to tell ya. I really want to show you things."

"What things Miri?" She bent even further.

"Looks like you want to show me sumfin too." Again, she peered straight at Sara, but the eye contact vanished. She focused on Sara's breasts.

Sara peeked at her chest, and back at Miriam and smiled. "What do you want to show me? I asked you first. You wanted to come here." Sara sat straight and flicked her hair behind her.

"You say you would be nervous in college with da boys trying to kiss you and stuff. I just wants to teach you."

"We're both girls." Miriam realized she needed a better sales technique.

"I'll be da guy, Miz Sara. I'll start." She held her right hand up with the palm facing her. She wiggled her pointer finger towards her, prompting Sara to get closer. Sara moved towards her bending down, exposing more cleavage to Miriam. Miriam smiled, showing her crooked yellow teeth.

"So, you want to teach me how to kiss a guy? Is that all? Do I use my tongue? When…"

"Shh." She put the same pointer finger to her lips, brushed it and placed it next to Sara's mouth. Soon, Sara gave Miriam's finger a kiss, a brief kiss, but still the first one between the two. "Don't ask a lot of questions when you kissing. Da boy will walk away."

"Maybe that's what I want."

"Dat's not what I want. I want to teach you how to kiss, so shh." Soon, inches apart they took in each other's breath. Miriam took Sara's face in her right hand and pulled her closer. Miriam opened her mouth a tiny bit. Sara puckered her lips. Their lips met for just a second as Sara pulled away. "Don't pucker so much Sara. We need to try this again. Now open your mouth just a little. When our lips touch just keep dem touching mine." Miriam leaned in and played with Sara's dark hair. She let the hair run through her fingers as Sara moved closer and closer to her. They kissed again. This time Sara didn't retreat.

They stayed out on the lake for hours, while Miriam taught Sara proper ways to kiss a man and receive kisses. She taught her several aspects of loving a person sexually. What if a guy desired to caress or fondle her body? She required learning her response to fantastic caressing, incredible kissing, and where a tongue needed placed, in case a guy asked. She also received lessons in how to caress someone else's body. Miriam taught her, and Sara demanded additional lessons.

They often went out in the boat, stayed in Miriam's or Sara's bed, and they even went for drives. Sara became an eager and willing student, and Miriam taught her without hesitation.

Tears flowed from Miri's eyes as summer ended. She witnessed Sara leave their juke-joint home and she seemed alone in Grandpa Cecil's house. Cecil, his lady friend Angeline, and Tomas Barnum still lived there, but Tomas always bothered Miriam. Maybe she caught the boy trying to catch her naked on several occasions. He hung outside the bathroom when she took a hot bubble bath. He spied in her room, when she changed clothes, to catch a glimpse at her thin young body. Sara's freaky little brother desired to receive a glimpse of Miriam's sexy little naked body and maybe, maybe receive his private lesson. Tomas later confessed to Sara several times he spied on Miriam's tutoring sessions and even swiped a car and followed them to Zwolle to spy. Spending time alone with Tomas would never happen, and Tomas later confessed, "I don't want to go to college a virgin. For God's sakes, I grew up in a whorehouse."

Once the Barnum vehicle faded in the distance, traveling the muddy roads to Shreveport, Miriam followed it with her bindle stick hanging atop her shoulder and she hitched her way to Shreveport. Hitching a ride with the Barnums to Shreveport, a simpler task, but then there were the hugs and tears of saying goodbye. Miriam never said goodbye. Running away was always easier for her.

During the last four years, Miriam developed some incredible survival skills. She cooked, cleaned, played guitar and learned how to hustle. She no longer desired to do the latter, but in times of desperation, she'd hit the streets again. Miriam no longer desired to become a maid. Her last experience worked out for her, but she witnessed death and abandonment. She still remembered the Judge, and his raping and pissing on her. The abuse she'd no longer tolerate as long as Chicago remained an option.

Part 3
Chapter 17
Sweet Home Chicago
August 1944

Maybe Miriam knew, and maybe she didn't. The woman sometimes acted clueless but her timing always seemed perfect, like when she followed the Barnums into the city. Miriam's former lover, now the famous musician, made his way to the South from Chicago. He became part of The Great Migration. This man Miriam used to live with returned to Shreveport, and he hit the big time. Tommie Parker had many followers, imitators, and emulators; some of these men became rock and roll stars in the 1950s. People remember Chuck Berry and Elvis Presley. They made Tommie's moves famous. The media said Berry and Presley invented duckwalks and swiveling hips, but Lightning Bug Parker disagreed. The man performed his moves for years—in fact he stole them from others.

Lightning Bug spotted Miriam standing in the pouring rain outside St. Paul's Bottoms. Miriam arrived and glanced at the large church near the red-light district. The bluesman departed the church, and disguised himself. The man was so popular with the colored folk in the area, he unable to display his face in public. According to the rumors, he attempted to Christianize himself and attended the large Methodist church. Miriam recognized him right away.

The singer wearing a dark fedora hat, with

sunglasses, appearing like a detective in the movies, noticed Miriam glancing his direction. She smiled at him, and with her hobo bag on her shoulder she went toward the crossroads of Fannin and Sprague to get reacquainted with the man who dumped her ass around the corner years ago.

"Pack your stuff pretty woman. You is coming with me."

"This is my stuff," Miriam hollered back at him, as she walked toward the shiny Cadillac he drove.

Lightning Bug hollered again at her as she raced toward him. Soon she sat in his 1944 Cadillac and the duo departed Louisiana. The vehicle sped past Texarkana and they ventured out of Jim Crow.

"Baby, I is sorry I leaves you down here in da bottoms. I have been looking for you. You is da best of da girls. I really is sorry. I got myself Christianized and everything."

"Why you move on up to Chicago?"

"We all move up dere. Mojo went, even Wolfman, all da good ones. Tired of living with fear we gonna be on a flagpole or dangling from a tree. Dey don't treat us too bad. We got us our own community up there."

"What's I going up as?"

"What I told you before. You gonna be my lady. I try to slow da drinking and reefer down. Trying to give up dat white powder also. You coming wid me?" He smiled at her, and he displayed the perfect smile, and perfect teeth. His teeth shined through the southern sunset. His smile melted her every time.

"We's in Arkansas now. Nots in Shreveport, so I guess I is coming wid." She stared at him like she never glanced at another man or woman before. She pondered the idea of real love. She felt it with Bo, and she wondered if Lightning Bug Parker would recreate the feelings Bo Barnum gave her. When Tommie picked her up years ago, she desired getting the hell out of the swamp. Miriam, now a woman, no longer a kid, and she was prepared to stick with decisions she made. Even though he abused her, cheated on her, and treated her like a dog, Miriam still loved the man. Maybe she loved him because he told her he loved her and became the initial man to do so. She gave herself to him and he stole her virginity. Also, she took in his greatness—the talent, and charisma. If Lightning Bug stayed clean, who knew what may happen, and he told her he kicked the narcotic habit. None of it mattered. Once again, her journey took a left instead of a right turn. She ventured out for a different life. She had aged a few years but matured several more in wisdom.

They called it the Great Migration. Ducks and geese, and many species of fowl migrated south for winter. The buffalo migrated because of the climate, and the Native Americans migrated to follow their sources of food and clothing. Between 1910 and 1950 some four million African Americans departed the south and headed elsewhere. They went to the upper Midwest and California. Hunting season also happened during the migratory process. Ducks and geese shot dead for food. The white man came close to exterminating the buffalo. The white man came close to eradicating the Native Americans. African Americans flocked out of the South, abandoning the Jim Crow laws and hoped the path they followed wasn't the same. Equal rights became a pressing issue, but most hoped and prayed they'd share the same water fountain and didn't have to piss in colored-only toilets.

Thousands of people of color fled Louisiana and Mississippi and went to Chicago. Tommie Lighting Bug Parker and Miriam Landry became two of them. Blues musicians also departed the Delta and the swamp and helped create the Chicago sound.

Technology also brought the folks to Chicago and helped create the newer tones. They gathered the mud from the Delta but played the electric guitar and amped their guitars and their harps. A lot of folks still preferred playing on a resonator and singing to the gators in the muddy swamps. Miriam preferred the country style, but Lightning Bug, Wolfman, and Mojo liked the Chicago style. All showmen, they reached additional folks electrified. Plus, plenty of musicians hung out seeking work. Bands formed, drummers beat on drum kits instead of trash cans and they played loud, real loud. With a pretty and talented steady guitarist beside him, Lightning worked on his act. Their life in Chicago started blissful. Things appeared bright for the duo.

The couple settled on the South Side of Chicago. The black families who moved to Chicago either settled on the South Side or on the near West Side. Lightning Bug treated her decent and bought her nice stuff. The gifts, jewelry, new clothes, greater than the presents Bo Barnum or Lucas Turner purchased for her, and greater than the fat judge.

Stopping at one of the black-owned boutiques in their neighborhood, Tommie Parker, bought Miriam a short, tight, skimpy red dress. Miriam added a few pounds since they arrived in the Windy City, and the man liked the tight-fitting, revealing red dresses he bought her. Her small but firm breasts popped out, exposing her cleavage. Through the flimsy material one noticed the shape of her round bottom. The dress didn't come close to her knees.

Miriam ogled over herself in the mirror before showing her man. Her nipples hardened a little, and her breath got heavy. She recognized the additional dampness down there. Tommie Parker peered at her from head to toe, making Miriam twirl around, so he gawked at her entire package. The skimpy dress hugged her curves and gave him the perfect view of her ass. She twirled and faced him. "Damn girl, you looking good. You so purdy in dat dress I bought you. I can't wait to get you home and rip dem clothes off you. Then I guess I must buy you another new dress dat you can model for me. Den I's going to have rip it off you. Baby we be buying you bunches of dresses cause I gonna like to tear dem off you."

The early days in Chicago they evolved into royalty and Tommie treated Miriam like a queen. She served her man with respect and admiration. He became a king in her book.

She spoiled her man in the kitchen too. She made everything from scratch. The biscuits, the gravy—she fried the bacon and eggs to perfection, and sliced the potatoes so fine. For a Texan he didn't mind the Louisiana Creole flavor folks everywhere would enjoy. Tommie Parker came from Northeast Texas, but Miriam discovered there was Louisiana food he wouldn't eat.

The early years in Chicago went as smooth as the ice rinks on a winter day. He took her on the road with him and they shared everything. They serviced one another in several ways as Miriam performed on stage with him, sang some songs, sang harmonies, and even did

151

a few duets. He expanded his repertoire and competed with Mojo as the top dog out of Chicago.

Miriam lived the life she dreamt about, becoming the talented sidekick. As the groupie she serviced his male desires, as the roadie she carried his equipment, tuned the guitars, amped them. Lightning liked one in open G, or Spanish, one in standard tuning, and one in open D tuning. Miriam liked to keep the one she played in Spanish tune. Blessed with tiny fingers, she developed her own method of playing slide. It came from the swamps. She played dirty and she performed mean. She used a sawed-off pipe which she carried with her, but if she misplaced it, she used the switchblade she always kept in her pocket.

Ms. Landry sought marriage, but never pushed it. She took care of her bluesman and figured marriage may happen in due time. She envisioned a life of porch parties, house parties, clubbing and rent parties with different musicians visiting and jamming all night. Miriam made breakfast for the ones too drunk to stumble or drive home.

A few years in, the clubbing and gigs escalated. They became key figures in a growing genre of music called race music. Negro artists made a splash in the American music scene, while rebellious white teenagers started listening. Lightning made several tours to both coasts and returned to the South where he and the record producer hawked his race music to the colored radio stations. Sometimes Miriam traveled with him. Most of the time she didn't.

Lightning went to Memphis on a recruiting trip. Miriam stayed home, cooked, cleaned their apartment in their slum neighborhood. He returned after a week with a guitarist, green to life in Chicago, but that axe man put all the others to shame. Both men returned with fire in their eyes, and ready to play.

Soon party time arrived at the Parker house. Lightning appeared different. The angelic eyes she became used to, were soon replaced with fire-burning devilish red eyes. This man came from Memphis, and Tommie's manager used him to steal the upcoming star away from the Memphis rival manager. They took an extra day returning. Lightning used all his resources.

Two days after returning, a rent party became necessary for different neighbors. Rent parties prevented eviction for a neighbor when they became unable to afford the rent. The band played and collected bills and coins from around the block. Lightning and Miriam fed the guests, as Miri cooked the grub. Beer and whiskey flowed, drugs ran rampant, and the band played all night.

"Miri honey, get dis place cleaned up." Lightning Bug ordered her. "Get dat couch out of da way. We gotta get this place ready. The Jacksons need their rent or get kicked to the curb. Ya hear me Miriam? Get dis couch in dat other room. Me, Mojo and Wolfman needs us a place to play, since it's too damn cold outside. Dis is what I hate about Chicago." A lamp got tossed in the hallway before Miriam acted. She knew about his anxiety attacks.

Miriam enjoyed the rent parties except when the pre-party anxiety hit. Lightning denied relapsing into his coke and smack habits. Even though Miriam believed him, his actions created doubt. Still early in the afternoon, he stumbled, screamed at her, raised his fists, and became demanding. He may have been drunk or craved something or someone besides her. Miriam demanded to find the issue, but when he acted like a lunatic, she decided her safety became a priority, so she kept her

153

distance. She rushed back into the kitchen, working her cooking magic. Tommie raced behind her with elevated fists. Sweat trickles down his face. The stains on his tee-shirt expanded near his armpits.

"I hate me some Gumbo. I ain't from Louisiana. I'm Texan. You Creole bitches don't know how to treat no Texan. Mojo's from Mississippi, he don't want no Gumbo neither." He tumbled through the drawers, tossing utensils onto the floor. He searched for the carving knife, which Miriam held, blade pointed at her lover. Tommie continued his rant, oblivious to a shiny blade aimed at his sweaty face. "Now go makes us some turtle soup. What da fuck you is making some crawfish pie for? You know I can't stand crawfish pie. I want us to have frog legs and turtle soup. Dat's what I like to eat, and dem boys, Mojo and da Wolfman. Dat's dere favorite. Damn bitch. How many times have I told you dat? Stupid little whore."

"My crawfish pie is da best Lightning. Last time Mojo was here he was raving about it. Everyone else was too drunk to eat."

"When were dey talking to ya about it? I tossed ya in da bedroom last time. They didn't want to fuck you. Besides them motherfuckers don't know what dey is talking about. They just stupid foos anyway."

"We talked in da morning, before dey left and..."

"I don't want you talking to him and stop arguing wid me. Mojo is too good of people for you. Now go git some fucking frog legs, and turtle meat for dinner. Go to da fucking store or catch them yourself. Stupid bitch. You know these peoples going to be hungry."

With her head tilted, tears in her eyes, Miriam descended three flights of stairs toward the street. She passed Mr. Jackson as he whittled a stick on the stoop, with his Bowie knife, while the young boys played stickball in the street. She walked to the market; her eyes still focused on the cracks in the sidewalk. Miriam stopped at the store and got herself a pen and paper where she scribbled a letter to her friend in Louisiana. She wrote her seventh letter to Sara the past year and dropped it in the blue mailbox on the corner. This was the seventh she wrote, third sent, and still no reply from Sara.

Miriam returned from the fish market with the proper ingredients for the feast. Miriam chopped and diced the onions, peppers, celery, carrots, and other vegetables. The knife slashed through the vegetables quicker than normal. She hacked, chopped and sliced with so much pressure, she lucked out, and didn't leave a finger in the meal.

Miriam started the gumbo, and prepared the tastiest gumbo in Chicago, but Tommie Parker didn't crave the roux. Roux—a Louisiana French—word and he hated the French.

The frog legs waited until later. Getting the house ready became Miriam's priority. Lightning retreated towards the living room, making sure the room was ready. He plopped in his comfy chair, lit one of his cigars, exhaling the smoke throughout the room. He sat, relaxed from the nicotine, smashing the half-smoked cigar into the ash tray.

After dusting and sweeping, she continued cooking. Most of the dinner already stewing, he returned to her kitchen. "I need your help in da living room. We need to clear a place so we can play tonight. Lots of people gonna show up. Get dis sofa out of here. We're plugging in tonight. Da Jacksons can't complain about us."

Miriam took a deep breath and rolled her eyes at her man. She started sliding their heavy davenport across the wood floors. Lightning Bug wouldn't help her lift it and carry it across the floor. He returned to his plush chair, squishing his ass into the cushions, while smoking a stinky cigar, as he peered at his woman's butt, while she slid the heavy furniture.

"Damn it, Miriam. You must be from Louisiana and used to muddy floors. You're leaving scratches on da floor now." He pointed to the small tracks the legs of the sofa made on the wooden floors. She didn't even notice them as his finger pointed at somewhere near where the marks. Miriam followed the focus of his finger and didn't notice any marks.

"I guess I will help you." Tommie Parker leaned his guitar against the wall, took a puff of his cigar, before placing it in the ashtray. He let it burn, as the smoke encircled the room. He walked to the far corner of the room and hoisted the couch. Miriam tripped a little, dropping the furniture. A solid thud. Tommie spun around and glared at Miri. His eyes shot her dead, like a prisoner trying to escape a Stalag overseas, or a prison farm down south. Miriam needed to speak up, but she realized how her man got, right before a party. Aware if she said something, anything, a bruise on the side of her face may appear, followed by a matching one on the opposite cheek. or worse yet she'd lay stranded in the bedroom, evolving into the main attraction for several of the guests.

****

She   enjoyed   playing   guitar,   when   she

156

accompanied Lightning or the man, they called Mojo Davis. She also hoped Sonny or Walter arrived to play harp. Miriam Landry played a mean harp, when pissed off at Tommie, but no one played the harp like either of those two men.

Miriam got all the cooking done, got the place ready for the guests. She went to the local church and carried home twenty folding chairs to place in the living room. She made four trips to the church which stood around the corner from the Parker residence. At the end of her first trip she piled the chairs against the Jacksons' stoop.

"You bring dem chairs in here and set dem up. Jackson got too much to worry about."

"Just set them there. They don't have to play no rent party for me." Mr. Jackson retorted. Miriam dropped the chairs on the stoop. They slid on the steps, landing on the sidewalk. Lightning Bug Parker hung over the balcony.

"I told you to bring dese mother fucking chairs up here, little bitch."

Miriam rolled her eyes at the man. Mr. Jackson intervened. "Don't you go up dere Miriam. I will take da chairs up. You folks mighty nice for throwing me this party." Mr. Jackson carried the chairs to the third story of the apartment building, while Miriam headed down to the church to grab more folding chairs. Miriam walked around the corner, and returned with five chairs each time, and each time, the chairs fumbled out of her arms when she got to the Jacksons. She repeated this process three more times, dropping the chairs on every venture. She picked up the chairs and struggled climbing the staircase with all five. Lightning Bug Parker met her at their door. He sat in the parlor room testing the corn liquor.

The fire reflected in his eyes when he met her at the door. His nose ran as snot dripped down, and the man paid no attention. Three things on his mind—Miriam's jaw, his fist and how hard they'd meet. It took one punch to knock her down, holding her jawbone, and laying on her ass, spread eagle. Lightning grabbed her by the feet and pulled her into their room. He ripped her clothes off her, while he got his rocks off. She never protested.

Miriam stayed in the room crying, while he continued taste-testing the hooch to make sure it knocked you on your ass. He staggered to the adjacent bedroom hanging on to the wall. He tripped over the wooden floors and fell onto the spare bed. She followed him and caught his face hovering above the coffee table. He whipped out a dollar bill and snorted more powder. Fire remained in his eyes telling her, *"Miriam, whatever you do tonight will not be enough."* The young woman soon played hostess to the Jackson's rent party and served everyone. Miriam didn't jam with the band, she spent all her time making sure the people ate, drank and received gratification. Tommie Parker desired the guests be fed, drunk and entertained. Servicing the guests meant different things to the legend. Having his woman gang raped by drunk musicians wash is idea of entertainment.

Tommie Parker told the truth to Miriam when he picked her up in Shreveport after Sara's departure. His drinking pace reduced to an occasional snort and he eliminated the narcotics. He attended church and became coke free. The last year, the Blues lifestyle rediscovered him, and as a top cat from the hip crowd from the Southside, he forced himself to entertain, and to entertain meant having the best chemicals. Sometimes he forgot about his young girlfriend. The chemicals controlled the man.

Chapter 18
Mojo Davis

On the South and West Side of Chicago, the man called Mojo dominated the scene. Lightning demanded top billing, but with Mojo Davis's talent and professionalism, he'd never relinquish control, especially to narcotic-driven Tommie Parker. He came from the Delta and brought the Mississippi mud with him. Some folks claimed he invented electricity. Ben Franklin's kite shocked the founding father, along with the entire world, but the colonizer didn't bother to plug a guitar into an amplifier and play some Blues music with it. Ben, oblivious on utilizing electromagnetism, never plugged a guitar in. At least Edison invented a record player, but Mojo Davis found the greatest way to use the power and energy.

He displayed a flair for playing guitar, singing, and performing, plus he turned a songwriter's song into his own. It became common practice. The Blues musicians remained in Mississippi, the jazz musicians from New Orleans, and even some of the greatest folk singers traveling the country as troubadours "borrowed" music. Mojo Davis did not bring the Delta with him. He reinvented the South in Chicago.

One Tuesday afternoon, he dropped by, searching for Lightning, but Mr. Parker again went out carousing, drinking, trying to score some cocaine, or whatever powder he snorted or injected. Miriam never knew where he ventured off too. At this point Miriam cared less. She opened the door for the broad-shouldered man and let him inside. Mojo Davis, a womanizer with the best of them, but he also treated women with respect. He acknowledged who the fine lass belonged too, and he respected Tommie Parker's lady. Lightning trusted him. Plus, he liked mates to drop by to make sure his gal wasn't screwing someone, while he fucked some underaged whore around the corner.

Miriam fooled around with one of Lightning's worn guitars, playing and singing something she improvised. "Mr. Davis, let me play sumfin for ya. It ain't nutting very good, just sumfin I been fooling around wid. I been writing when Lightning goes out doing whatever he does."

"Play it for me, I want to hear it. You're a good player, I heard you many times."

"Now this might be for Lightning or someone in my past, dat's anyone guess right now. I let you decide." The soulful Blues song moved the bluesmen to tears.

Mojo wrote a lot of his material, but he also worked with some incredible songwriters. Most of his famous works someone else composed for him. His subsequent recording penned by another songwriter, and her name, Miriam Landry. Miriam abandoned the shuffle on this one, but she used her short skinny fingers for some classic fingerpicking and worked a single chord drone. She got the rhythm going, tapping her feet to the noise she made. She let her smile shine bright, and once she got everything in gear, and guitar came to the exact part she sung.

> *Why can't you just go away*
> *Why can't you go away*
> *And be a runaway*
> *Leave me here alone to play.*

I'll Run you out of town
You got me feeling down
You're just an ol coonhound
I'm gonna run you out of town.

Can't you just runaway
Come back some other day,
And when you are here to stay
I'm just gonna runaway.

Going to that Creole Land
Running as fast as I can
I'll get me another man
Down in Creole Land.

"Damn, dat song is killer. Can I steal that one from you Miriam? Maybe sing it at the club and put it on my next album. I give you full credit. Might have to change the last verse or add something to the first."

"I don't have none of it written down. Not sure I can play it twice. Just something, I been messing with."

"Here grab my electric, let's plug in."

Miriam grabbed his Gibson. She came close to dropping it once he let her hold it. "This thing is heavy, Mojo." She held it a little different, sat down so it rested on her knee. Mr. Davis plugged the guitar into a small amp, while Miriam started finger picking to loosen up.

"Great. You ain't playing with no pick. Now try to play the song and sing it. I'm gonna follow you with da Martin. Now start the shuffle." He smiled as she sang the words. His feet tapped with the rhythm and his Martin guitar and the Gibson intertwined like lovers as they became one. Miriam remembered all the words, and Mojo controlled the song, while Miriam followed.

"I got it down." He smiled at her as they rehearsed throughout the afternoon.

"I need to get going before you man come home, find out we working together. You gonna get full credit. Some folks think I stole that Ray Wilson song, but I didn't. I just liked the phrases he used on it."

Some reason Miriam glanced away from Mojo, and wiped tears away from her eyes, knelt her head down and moped out of the parlor room at the mention of Ray Wilson's name. She cried as if she witnessed a long-lost lover take his final breath. The girl held her head in her hands, hiding the downpour of tears which commenced. She helped Mr. Davis out and gave him a hug goodbye.

Tommie returned soon after the great bluesman vacated. Miriam always wondered if he attempted to trap her cheating, capture a friend of his trying to mess around with his woman, or if he trusted her. She realized it wasn't the latter. "Did Mojo stop by? He s'pose to has some good news for me."

"Yeah he was over. We played a few songs on his gear. We sound good. Maybe we…"

"No one called, did they?" He paced the floor like an expectant father. He went back and forth, to and fro, leaving scuff marks on the oval braided rug. "You say you been playing some songs. You can't hear dat motherfucking phone ring, if you is amped up. Don't ya know I 'specting an important call?"

As always, Miriam took a few steps backwards when Tommie raised his voice at her. She started, "You never told…"

"Damn bitch, I told you many times dis important

163

man I met down South in da prison be trying to reach me. Wants to do some shows and records us some music. I told you over and over. Now when I is gone, I wants silence in here. I don't care who comes over. Fuck Mojo, he ain't allowed here no more anyway." He stomped away and departed for the night. Miriam stayed at home and penned another song.

Miriam received a phone call from Mr. Lomax the following day. Tommie, as usual disappeared somewhere, rehearsing, drinking, or falling off the cocaine wagon. More than likely, he got high, scored some corn liquor, and hit a whorehouse, trading reefer and performing an impromptu concert in exchange for some old-fashioned fucking.

Miriam scribbled his name and number on a matchbook. Her writing, always messy and resembled Chinese. When she took her time and slowed her writing, one made out the chicken scratches. When the girl hurried, poultry remained unable to read it.

Her man returned about one hour later. "Baby light me a cigarette and get over here." She obeyed, and she struck the red tip stick across the flint. She noticed the message on the pack of matches.

"Honey, I wrote you a message. Dis guy called, wants to talk to you. His name is here."

"What da fuck is dis shit? You can't read nor write girl. What da fuck good are you? Can you remember da motherfucker's name? Can ya?"

Miriam retreated and peered at Lightning. Her hands shook as she spoke. "I thinks his name was Louis, A-A-Adam, or Alan Louis?" Miriam's statement resembled a question instead of a solid confident answer. "I can't member Lightning. I is so sorry." She started crying.

"Dammit bitch. These calls are important. Dat's why I got us dis phone." He lifted the heavy black box and shook it in her face. "Dese things can be important. Lomax wants to record and film me. Damn can't you do anything right?" He pounded the wall as he walked out of the room. A small hole emerged from the wall as he removed his fist from it.

Miriam plopped on the hardwood floor. She needed to apologize to her man, but he stormed out too fast. She made a mistake, and realized that fact, and she's aware and capable of greater things. She pleaded to her man, but he already departed, strolling along the streets with the electric guitar strapped on his shoulder, and on his belt, the pig-nose amplifier, hung attached to the leather. He entertained the ghetto block of Chicago's worst hood as he played and sang the Blues to everyone that preferred to listen. His woman gave him the blues, and Miriam's troubles evolved into his ideal muse. He didn't realize the unknown master started to use him to fuel her fire.

Later in the afternoon Lightning returned, and Miriam prepared dinner. Steaks broiled under a pepper sauce marinade, and pinto beans simmered over the gas grill. The cornbread she already baked, painted golden yellow, as the butter melted on top. Miriam heard the phone ring, in the other room, the room where Tommie sat. She took in the baritone voice of her man. "Get dat Miriam. I'm busy."

Totally aware, he sat on his ass, trying to figure out how to make it with the two teenagers across the hallway, without Miriam finding out. The steaks still sat in the broiler as Miriam sped across the floor to answer the phone for her lazy man. "Hello?"

"Is the man known as Lightning Bug there?"

"Who is calling?"

"Alan Lomax. I called earlier but he never returned my phone call."

"I'm sorry sir. He couldn't read my writing." She sat the phone on the table. "Lightning, phone." She screamed across the room, but no answer. She called again, and still no reply from her man. "Sir, can I get your number again?"

He gave her the number, and in her chicken scratch she scribbled his number on anything available. She found a piece of paper, and in readable penmanship transcribed his information. She strolled across the apartment towards Lightning, and she searched room after room for him. This process took about fifteen minutes since her man enjoyed hiding within his own home. Miriam passed him the message, as he ripped the piece of paper out of her hand. The young woman smiled, since she pleased him with the note. Miriam peeked at him and he kissed her, however they both noticed an aroma. As a Texan, Lightning Bug Parker liked his steaks rare to medium well. Distracted by the phone call and locating her man. Miriam ignored the meat broiling in the oven. The steaks, not rare, but well done, no redness in them, and a Texan likes his meat a certain way. He didn't get them rare or medium. Miriam witnessed it in the way he screamed, at her and the punishment she received in bed. It wasn't love making but close to rape.

The following morning when he awoke, her man was pissed at the world. The night before Miriam cried herself to sleep. That next morning, she cried herself awake. She acknowledged the scenario—damned if you do, damned if you don't.

When he came home in the evening, she cooked the dinner to perfection. She fried the pork chops perfectly, smothered in her homemade gravy, peppered the way Tommie liked it, and the way Miriam always made it. The mashed potatoes already mixed by hand, and the corn shucked, boiled, and complete. The aroma in the apartment drowned the smelly cigars out. "Looks and smells good baby, but Wolfman fed me some his fixings. I s'pose to do some shows wid him."

Miriam grabbed one plate, grabbed herself a pork chop, an ear of corn, and threw several servings of mashed potatoes on her plate, and doused them in gravy. There she ate alone. She cleaned the kitchen and went to bed alone and once again cried herself to sleep. He came home and pounded her, instead of making love to her. The girl never won, period.

Tired of getting raped, beaten, and degraded by Lightning Bug and his entourage, Miriam was no longer a partner, and not even a pet. To say he treated her like a dog insulted canine lovers everywhere. Miriam wrote her twelfth letter to Sara in 1948. The letter she sent:

Sara:

I need your help. I going to need rescued. Dis Lightning Bug and his friends keep on raping me and beating me. He treats me like a dog. No, I wish he treated me like our dog. He takes dat little bitch out for walks at least. Even pets her. He pounds me to get his rocks off. He treats me like his cheap whore. Maybe that's all I am to him. Come gets me now.

Love,

Miriam.

Miriam:

The day after I graduate from Grambling, I'll be headed up. I'm taking a semester off also. I'll come get you and we are gonna have some fun. It's about time, right?"

Love,
Sara.

Chapter 19
Finally

When Miriam returned to Chicago from a summer adventure with Sara, life remained the same. House parties, drugs, electric blues, prostitutes visiting their slumlord apartment. Life wasn't much better, and still Miriam remained in the North. Life in Chicago must be better than in the South thanks to the discrimination her friend, Sara Barnum, attempted to outlaw. Laws get passed and discrimination made illegal, but prejudice won't stop. Corporations find loopholes in the system. Prejudice ends when people's hearts change, and the hate can take generations to cease, since hate-mongering gets passed along the family tree like the good china.

Riverview Park in Chicago hosted The Bobs roller coaster. Miriam and Lightning never went, however, their relationship, like The Bobs roller coaster at Riverview Park terrified her. Long dragging ascends, and speedy treacherous descends. For some reason Miriam remained faithful.

Miriam got brave. She evolved into a kitten running into a hound dog. The dog barked at her, but the kitten refused to go instead she hissed at the meaner and bigger dog, tired of his bossing around. She became so sick and tired of the hound all drunk and fatigued from his narcotic use in the slums of the Windy City.

"Lightning, you need to stop dis. You so much nicer when you ain't high. Wishing you can finally stop, so we can get us a normal relationship."

The back of his hand went across her face. He

returned the action coming the other way with the palm of his strong hand, his guitar picking hand.

"Always concerned about yourself now ain't ya bitch. Man, I got these shows, and I needs to make contacts. My damn manager ain't do shit for me. So, before you worry about us, think whats I has to go through. God, Miriam you such a little selfish bitch ain't ya?"

He followed his insensitive comments with another backhand-slap combination. Miriam didn't retreat and for the initial time in their turbulent relationship she went on the offensive. He sat on in his chair high, and she realized it. The pupils in his eyes small, like pin holes, as the sweat poured out of his body, like he did four rounds with Sugar Ray Robinson. Outside, the wind howled like a lonesome wolf, and snow piled. The steam heat wasn't working. She took a few steps forward after reaching into her pocket where she carried her knife. It always sat adjacent to the old gris-gris bag she carried for over ten years. She realized Lightning packed a pistol with him, but she cared less. Several times in Miriam's life she dealt with a death wish. Assisted suicide, and state sponsored murder as he fried in the electric chair. She took the knife out of her pocket, took small steps, strolling across the room. Life moved in slow motion.

Mr. Parker reached into his pants and whipped out the small revolver. "One more step forward, and those would be the last steps you take."

Miriam took him up on the dare and proceeded forward. She stood three feet from him and sniffed the lead of the bullet inside the gun. Miriam stopped on a dime, as she glanced at the end of the revolver, and glared at her man. She swallowed and inhaled and exhaled.

"You is fucked up, Tommie Parker. You ain't gonna kill me, and I ain't gonna cut you up. This is my protection. You're about to lose the best ting dat ever happen to you. If you touch me again in any way, try to fuck me, slap me, I gonna use dat, and if you shoots me with dat gun, I don't care, cause I'd rather be dead than spend my life with you. Now get da fuck out of here. Go live with one of your whores." She let out a deep breath which blew out the pilot light of the gas stove from across the room.

Whatever shit he snorted or injected wore off, because the bluesman, the legend, went to an adjacent room and curled into a ball. He appeared like a kitten as he lay weeping on the floor. Miriam followed the trail of tears, as the salt-water made a small pond on the floor. "I is sorry Miriam darling. I is sorry. You give me another chance?"

For some unknown reason she pondered the idea. The little person on her shoulder told her, *You gave that man way too many chances, too many times*. The voice kept talking to her. She snuck a peek around as if the voice came from a corner in the room. *You have been through so much; yet came out stronger than you think. You already caught the bus, now it's time to drive it.*

"Pack your bags, go gets yourself cleaned up. Stay clean for a year, I just might take you back. Go, I'm calling Mojo to get ya out of here."

Shaking, he eyed her in disbelief, as he remained curled in a ball. He still carried the potential to uncoil and strike, like a cobra snake, yet he did not acknowledge the serious tone in her speech. Even when Mojo Davis came to get him and took him to the hospital, she listened to his pathetic cries. "Miri, I is sorry, I is sorry."

Miriam sat, sighed and witnessed their exit, wondering if she gave him an album worth of material. She wrote Sara her sixth letter during the month, and Sara still ignored the correspondence. It was not necessary for her to respond, since the kiss she gave her years ago lasted a lifetime. Sara missed her friend and wondered about her every day.

Chapter 20
Leaving Chicago

Sara Barnum entered the slums again. This time she paid for a one-way train ticket. Miriam would return home with her, or she'd spend eternity in Chicago, a life she bitched about. Sara once again owned no vehicle since The Klan or the law kept confiscating the cars she purchased in Baton Rouge. A rising star in the 1950's Civil Rights Movement, Sara Barnum defended a dark-skinned Creole from the charge raping of a white society woman, she organized the bus boycott in Baton Rouge, and she returned from Monteagle, Tennessee, trained in nonviolence, so she worked sit-ins, registered Negroes to vote and helped with assorted protests.

Her nonviolence training with Cisco Greene was cut short when she stepped on her trainer's face, cussed out her roommate, and walked out the door. She hopped freights returning to Baton Rouge, and a few weeks later caught the train to Chicago to retrieve her friend.

Miriam stood on the balcony of her slummed-out apartment, hanging clothes on the community clothes line. She wasn't doing the greatest job, and she cared less. She hoped Sara got the letter she sent months ago. Her friend hadn't responded since Miriam mailed the parcel.

"Where can I buy me a car up here?" The voice came from street level and sounded familiar.

Miriam went to the edge of the balcony and peered to the ground. "Get your mixed ass up here, Sara Barnum. What da fuck took you so long? I been needing to get out of here. I thought you gonna rescue me. I don't know where to get a car at. Dat man too fucked up to drive anyway."

"I told you once, I ain't going up dere. Now get your skinny ass down here and let's go shopping. I'm gonna get you for the last time." This time Miriam didn't glance around to note what chores she'd abandon. She didn't pay attention to the dirty dishes, piled up laundry, and the other chores she hadn't finished. Miriam cared less if Lightning Bug Parker escaped rehab and might return home any minute from detoxing or screwing some underage neighbor girl and leaving her pregnant, or on a chemical-induced high after relapsing again. Miriam bolted through the door and soon escaped their urban paradise.

"You gotta know better than me where to get a car. You live here. We gonna buy me a car and get you some new duds. Then I'm taking you home for good, and you are staying with me."

"We gonna take da train downtown." Miriam pointed to the elevated track running through the Windy City.

"Can we hop it?" Sara asked her with a smile as wide as the great lake to the east of the city.

"I stole Tommie's tokens. Now let's get outta here."

Sara counted out C-notes for the replacement Buick wagon, and soon they cruised in the car searching for clothes for both. Sara purchased herself some overalls, and she bought Miriam three pairs and a straw hat. Miriam spotted a tight little red dress and a red hat Miriam said matched. Sara received the fashion gene from her father, She found an oversized pair of overalls fit like perfection on the body and added a straw hat. Soon they departed the North and headed towards a life of segregation.

"We're not going playing, are we? Miriam asked Sara once they scooted down the highway, and the skyscrapers appeared in the rearview mirror.

"What do you mean by playing?" Sara lifted her horn-rimmed sunglasses at Miriam and winked.

"Playing gigs and shit. Last time we got you a boyfriend and ran off dem Klan guys. I don't need no more drama. Dat guy wore me out."

"No honey, I'm kidnapping you for good. Taking you home where you belong."

I don't know. We're much freer up here. We can do things our people can't do back home." Miriam lifted the pair of sunglasses Sara bought her , and winked back at her.

"You guys aren't no freer than back south," Sara told her. "I mean you can drink out of da same water fountain, but you're trapped in a ghetto. We're still slaves Miriam. Do you pay attention to the work people do? They work in the factories, on assembly lines, sweeping floors, for less pay than white folks. You guys do okay, from what you tell me, but you still live in roach and rat-infested mess, and there are drugs all over the place. Hell, the south is better than this." Sara's lawyer accent seemed to disappear every time she got around Miriam. "At least we can farm and live off da land. Looks like up here we still gotta follow da rules. Down home we know what's to expect." Sara Barnum never trusted Yankees.

"I am with you. I ain't gonna be with dat man no more, Miss Sara. I am done. Let's just head home. I miss Louisiana anyway. You're right. Life's much simpler."

Miriam Landry and Sara Barnum lived a

complicated relationship. She had been the former lover of Sara's father, until she ran off with the singer, plus Miriam liked girls, but she never considered herself as bisexual or a lesbian. Miriam already slept with two members of the Barnum family—Sara's father and Sara. Miriam became attracted to the person who loved her and took care of her. Before Sara went to college, Miriam told her their sexual exploits were nothing but a lesson, an experimental relationship, and they remained no more than friends. Sara knew different.

The initial time Sara rescued her, nothing happened between the two of them, but this time fireworks ignited, the fuse lit and burnt, and the two waited for the explosion. Miriam eyed the curves of her friend's voluptuous body a little more closely, as Sara Barnum drove through the winding roads of Southern Illinois, near where the Ohio River surges into the Mississippi. Sara's eyes focused on something besides the road, she studied the curves of her friend, since the car crossed the center line a time or two. The vehicle also bopped off the far side as Sara spun on some gravel adjacent to the highway. Fortunately, no accident happened, and Sara kept the car moving forward as it sped to Tennessee.

Miriam gave Sara a show to distract her former student. Miriam wore the cute, slinky, red dress Sara bought her in Chicago on the road for the purpose of tempting the driver. She always got an incredible reaction from Tommie when she dressed in tight red clothing.

Sara kept one eye on the road, and the other on her friend. The dress must have been uncomfortably tight, since Miriam struggled to remove it. In Northwestern Tennessee she snuck out of the top of the dress. Once she exposed her breasts, she accelerated the passenger seat torture. Miriam caressed her breasts, pinched her nipples, and slid her hand between her legs. She teased herself giving Sara a glimpse of her future, while she stared between Miriam's legs, grinning. Sara somehow managed to get the car to go past Memphis. They crossed the state line and decided they craved food. In Southaven, Mississippi they stopped and ordered breakfast from a Negro only café.

"Besides your Daddy, I thinks you is the only person dat ever loved me. What's I'm trying to say is once we do this, there ain't gonna be no one else. Not for you, and not for me. I don't want to be no sex toy for ya. I gots to be all yours."

It was past time to say it. Miriam took care of her younger friend, ever since Bo passed. They evolved into best friends, they fooled around, and performed satisfying sex as Miriam took Sara beneath her wing. It wasn't the little training session she got on the Black Bayou, or on the Sabine, or wherever they snuck away. Love is always greater than sex, and they both acknowledged it. Love came from the times they spent together on the dock, playing guitars, or the walks they took together talking about life.

"I don't think I'm that way. I like men, I think."

"We don't choose which way we are. Do you love me?"

"Of course."

"Well, I truly loves you in dat way, but before we can love each other I needs you to promise me dis will be forever."

"I promise you," Sara replied, as a hash brown shot across the table and missed hitting Miriam in the eye.

Both women realized an incredible relationship blossomed between the two of them. Sara remained clueless about Miriam's past.

After breakfast, Sara paid the bill, walked Miriam to the car and opened the door for her. Miriam once again struggled in the red sundress, but she got comfortable and started her seduction routine again. The two young women gazed at one another; eyes focused on each other.

In a flash, Miriam changed her focus above Sara's shoulder. She shook her head, pointing to a potential attacker. She reached below the seat to pull out her slide. Since their slides doubled as switchblades, they sometimes become protection from rapists. In 1954, and in Mississippi, Creole women used the knives for safety. Miriam handed Sara the knife and Sara snapped the switch, and the blade locked. Sara spun around and stabbed the man in the chest. The knife slid in like she sliced a turkey dinner late in November. It came out in a flash but stained with a nice bright crimson color. The large man dropped to the ground, clutching his chest. Sara ran around to the driver's side, got in, and backed out of the diner parking lot like a daughter of a bootlegger. "He tried to rape me, didn't he?"

"He had to?" Miriam replied.

"Why else would he be at a colored diner I mean a fat Klan-type guy. It was self-defense, right?"

"Gots to be, but we ain't going to no cops."

"Hell, to the no," and Sara drove faster than her daddy taught her.

The two girls got out of Mississippi like a bat out of hell, retreated through Memphis and crossed the bridge into Arkansas. They didn't stick around to notice if Sara Barnum became wanted for murder, even though it appeared like self-defense. The odds stacked against her, the man she killed, a Caucasian man, and Sara Barnum a mixture of everything, would lose this one. It didn't matter what gruesome crime he may have attempted.

Crossing through Arkansas wasn't always the smartest option when one turns into a fugitive. However, traveling through Arkansas seemed a hell of a lot safer than crossing the Magnolia State, since the murder took place there. Visions of dangling from a tree flashed in both women's minds as Sara sped through Arkansas, with Grandpa Cecil's place as their destination.

Miriam found her calling because near West Helena, home of the King Biscuit Flour Hour radio program, she penned a song called "I Killed a Man." She didn't require much inspiration, since she witnessed it. The anonymously released song became a regional hit. Sara and Miriam never received royalties. No one claimed to author the song.

I killed a man in Southaven
I killed a man in Southaven
I killed a man in Southaven

Tried to rape me, had no time to run
Tried to rape me, had no time to run,
He tried to rape me, but I had no gun

He could have killed me; he had no time to run
He could have killed me, had no time to run,
He could have killed me, but I had no gun.

The knife went in, straight through the heart
The blade went in, straight through the heart

179

Ain't got time for a running start.

I killed a man down in Southaven,
I killed a man down in Southaven,
I killed a man down in Southaven.

On the run, but I got a place to hide
On the run, but I got a place to hide
Can't confess, police will think I lied.

On the run, got a place to hide
On the run for the rest of my life
Can't confess, jury will think I lied

Home in the swamps, I'm forever free
Home in the swamps, I'm forever free
Down in the swamps, I'll always be free.

I killed a man down in Southaven
I killed a man down in Southaven
I killed a man down in Southaven.

Cecil Barnum hadn't a lick of musical talent. He tried every instrument from the accordion to the guitar, but the man never figured one out. The world became a better place because of his whiskey, he perfected cooking the shine his mother Sara, the woman, the younger Sara named after, invented. He made the family fortune in the whiskey business. Bo Barnum's older brothers also lacked the musical ability, but also, they lacked interest. Only Bo Barnum played, and he taught his daughter. His son, Tomas also lacked the musical gene. Tomas, had been relegated to drums and washboard, since he displayed decent rhythm.

After Bo's passing, the rest of the family moved into Cecil's place north of Shreveport. The recording equipment Bo owned went with Sara, Miriam, and Tommy and now languished at Cecil's. They pressed and distributed their own records, and often peddled the recordings, while dumping whiskey off at a juke. The Barnums tried this new business, and a way to make some legitimate money

The two girls recorded a few songs together. They recorded "I Killed a Man." The following tune remained untitled, but the ditty echoed haunting familiar to the lyrics of the song about murder Miriam wrote right after she broke free from the Huntsville prison. The song told the tale about a former lover. A man who misunderstood once a woman gave herself to a man, she'll always remain his property. Big Lucas Turner found out the hard way.

They soon retired to Sara's old room for the evening. The two consummated their relationship, bathed together, slept together and went fishing together. As a couple they planned on remaining as one forever. However, both girls knew nothing about love.

After spending a few days together at Cecil's, Miriam moved in with Sara in Sara's small Baton Rouge apartment. Sara lived in a miniscule place, a one-bedroom apartment, with a small kitchenette, a dining area, and a living area plus a bathroom. The unit, a part of a red brick complex on the corner of black and white had rusted pipes, while Sara placed mouse traps in the corners, but Sara and Miriam called the roach trap home.

Sara tried hard to maintain the relationship, but when folks try too hard to make something work, the pooch gets screwed.

She blamed it on her poor role models. A mother who abandoned her family and conspired in her father's murder. Her father's younger lover, who had an affair with her. She had one affair to this point, which was with the commie folk singer, civil rights trainer, and beatnik. Sara didn't love him, and marriage had never been an option. Spending consecutive days with this man was even out of the question. This time with Miriam she hoped they would last a lifetime. Their loving relationship made it through the weekend.

"Miri what da fuck did you do with the pots and pans?" Sara came into the bedroom as she attempted to make Miri some eggs with biscuits and gravy. She longed to surprise her, show her some love and bring her friend breakfast in bed. Instead Miriam received similar abuse. She accepted the verbal treatment she always received. Miri laid in the bed crying. Sara, forced into doing the impossible for her, knocked on their bedroom door and stuttered the words "I'm sorry." Miriam accepted the apology, they bathed together, and made breakfast. Miriam and gave Sara a gift, containing the small burlap bag Miriam carried forever. Miriam attached the bag to an aqua blue ankle bracelet and tied it around Sara's leg.

"What's this for?" Sara asked her as she adjusted the beads.

"It's to protect you, give you some good mojo. It's my commitment to you." She ran her hands and kissed Sara's leg from the ankle past the knee. Sara stepped away.

Sara's job required her leaving Baton Rouge to attend business. Miriam contemplated her next move. She stayed home by herself waiting for Sara to return.

Sara soon departed for Topeka to be involved

with the landmark case, Brown vs. The Board of Education, a dream of hers. Working on a case of this magnitude might be the greatest thing that could ever happened to her, a crowning achievement. She never made it.

She made it as far as their Zwolle property, and took care of some essential family business. Someone or something told Sara to drive by the old place on the Sabine.

Bo Barnum's killer, and the father of Miriam's aborted child were now deceased. Cecil Barnum had succumbed to the cancer chewing his body to shreds like termites taking to a little bayou cabin.

Miriam stayed in Sara's apartment by herself until Miss Barnum returned, and stayed put, and didn't do too much. She still remembered how Sara reacted when Miriam didn't rearrange anything. Imagine her reaction if the furniture switched places.

Sara returned earlier than expected. "Wacha doing home so soon?"

"I didn't go to Topeka." Water drained from Sara's eyes like a leaky faucet. "Grandpa Cecil died. I was called down there. I came to get you for the funeral." Miriam hustled next to Sara and squeezed her body into her friend's. The twenty-eight-year old attorney always liked it when Miriam pressed her body into hers. "We gotta head up north to the Caddo place."

The two traveled together to attend Cecil's funeral. They encountered Tomas Barnum, a full-grown young man, with a pretty and young Creole wife, named Ruby Barnum. Ruby, a thicker, younger version of Miriam, also played lights out on the guitar.

Tomas also surprised his sister with a special

guest, and Miriam had no desire to visit this bitch. After all the families only get together at funerals and weddings. Sara did not even crave to communicate with her mother—rumors surrounded her about killing her ex-husband. Miriam went to Cecil's funeral, but stayed in Sara's room for his celebration of life at least until Lydia departed.

Guitars and harmonicas drowned out the screeches of the bayou. The whiskey flowed as most of the guests became drunk off their ass. Sara and Miriam remained sober as her lover, since neither woman drank alcohol, but at Creole funerals most folks didn't find an excuse to play music, and drink too much liquor. Cremated earlier in the day, Cecil's wished for his two grandchildren dump his ashes at a certain spot on Black Bayou at midnight. Sara knew the location, a spot on the lake which witnessed most of the Barnum debauchery.

At midnight, Sara and her brother went out on the boat to dump Cecil Barnum's ashes in the family site, while their partners, Miriam and Ruby Barnum, a younger version of Miriam, cut heads, or dueled on the guitar.

"You start, bitch." Mrs. Barnum told Sara's lover.

"No, you're starting bitch. Dat da only way you can win, cause I'm much better. If you ain't starting, I win. I'm waiting, whore."

"Okay, bitch. Stretch out on da dock dere, and I's gonna play shit you could never."

Ruby hated Miriam from the days in Zwolle when her mother was a former whore at the Barnum's. She couldn't stand Bo, Cecil, Sara, or even Miriam. Her mother became a close friend of Lydia, and accepted Tomas into the family. Her father was a talented Blues

184

musician, but his life ended before his time. The death, still stood as an unsolved murder in West Texas. She stretched her fingers and started playing. The strings and neck of the guitar soon ignited as she played.

Miriam followed her, still laying on the deck, she matched her note for note, same speed if not faster. They went for two additional rounds. A gunslinger from East Texas judged the contest, and the man seemed familiar. He judged Miriam the winner, even though the results were a toss-up. Once again, she fled with a Bluesman.

Chapter 21
Christianized

Miriam Landry witnessed enough death in the last fifteen years of her life. It started when she walked towards a hoodoo practicing midwife who handled a coat hanger, like a cowboy tossed a lasso. She didn't take any chances and realized Sara Barnum couldn't be counted on to fall in love with anyone. Before she departed, she went into the room she shared with Sara, found the bracelet on the floor. She nabbed it and stuffed it in her overall's pocket.

This Texas bluesman acted different than the rest. Maybe he learned about the jinx. The man, aware of deep dark secrets about her and the Barnums. He recognized the curse Miriam lived before she knew about it. The curse played out only if he took a roll in the hay with her. He took on the mission of ending Miriam's condemnation, and created an idea how to conclude whatever followed her around. The man kept quiet, while they rolled over the highway. A few miles past Lufkin he broke the silence. "You friends with da Barnum's then?"

Some folks say Miriam ain't nothing more than a naïve country girl, surviving on the streets and jukes of Louisiana with nothing but a guitar and her sexy assets. Once meeting her, acquaintances described a certain coyness about her, as her beautiful and big brown eyes never gave anything away. She glanced at the man and gawked straight into his eyes. "Of course, I was da maid, and we all just went to Grandpa's funeral. I knew Cecil's kid Bo, and Bo's kids, Sara and Tomas. Y'all just saw me at his funeral."

"Well, I never trusted the Barnums anyway. Specially dat Bo Barnum. Da only thing I can tell you about him, is he don't like to play no games. I'm a man dat likes to play games, and that motherfucker ain't about games. I should have respect for him, but I don't. In my line of work, we need to get some deals done. I need to get me some bribes, get some gifts, like tobaccy or some good booze, like rum or whiskey. Cecil always gave me some good whiskey and tobaccy."

"I loved Cecil like he was my pa and grand-daddy, but I loved Bo. I think he was my best lover, and the man I loved the most. I still loves him and miss him."

"I ain't had no use for Bo Barnum, got sad when I heard he died. He never wants to play with me. Wouldn't give me nuttin'. Damn straight shooters ain't no fun. Bout da only thing different between Bo and Cecil, besides they were both non-believers in da spirits. Dat was another reason I didn't like Bo."

"You had nothing do with him getting kill…?" She didn't even finish her question.

"Oh no. He tempted da spirits. Dat why he dead. I ain't never kill my flesh and blood. Now Miriam Landry, do you remember when you had dat abortion? There was some guy on da street corner, and you dropped your pouch of tobaccy. I never thanked you for it, but I been watching out for you ever since. You just never knew it."

Miriam gleamed at him with the white of her eyes lighting the man's Studebaker. "You making dat shit up, aren't you?"

"Hell no, I keeping you out cause I knows they trying to kill da Barnums. Barnum's are my flesh and blood. Why da fuck you think you won da contest? That li'l bitch can play lights out."

Nothing phased her at this point. Was this trip a figment of her imagination, or possible that little bitch, Ruby, be the devil. "So, I wasn't better than her?" Miriam scowled at the man and wondered if he noticed her with the darkness of the night. She even pouted with her lower lip extending.

"It was close, but I gotta get you out of there. I'm feeling something bad might happen, plus you need to change your life. Dat's why you coming with me." The man exhaled like he developed the perfect lie. Miriam grunted and twisted her head and peered out the passenger window as the car headed further west into Texas. She still didn't recognize this man from Adam, or Papa, or anyone, and she didn't recognize where in tarnation they headed towards. She checked for roadside signs and didn't spot any. The car sped across East Texas and they hit a town with a motel. The shack took coloreds, as the sign said, and the man got a room and checked them in. The man set his suitcase on a dresser and sat on the bed. He loosened his Mississippi string tie and tossed it on the suitcase and kicked off his loafers and they landed on the floor.

Miriam sat beside him and started removing her clothes. She set her hand on his lap and moved it closer to him. Miriam only brought the clothes on her back; she wasn't planning this trip. She skedaddled on a whim. Her clothes hung scattered across the country, Some in Baton Rouge, some at Cecil's, and the rest in Chicago. Miriam Landry never packed.

"What da fuck you doing? I don't want to fuck you. I be just like da rest of them fools dat used you. I know all about you too. You need to learn for yourself.

Plus, I know all about dat lady you was with." He glanced at Miriam and he noticed her exhaling. Relieved, she returned the mysterious man's smile. He stood and walked to his suitcase and removed the string tie from the top of the suitcase, opened it, placed it inside the blue suitcase, and removed two books and came towards her and faced her, as he tossed his straw cowboy hat on the brown suitcase. "I am a married man now, Miss Miriam Landry. I is married to The Lord. Me and you cannot be together, cause it is a sin against da flesh. Lemme open dis book up and show you. You can read it for yourself. It's right here." The man thumbed through his worn good book. He skimmed through The Bible, towards the end where the New Testament verses sat. A smile came on his face, brightening the room, which was only illuminated by a flickering bathroom light.

He squinted as he jumped up and down pointing to the Bible. He read out loud. *"Galatians 5:19-21 ¹⁹Now the works of the flesh are manifest, which are these; Adultery, fornication, uncleanness, lasciviousness, ²⁰Idolatry, witchcraft, hatred, variance, emulations, wrath, strife, seditions, heresies, ²¹Envyings, murders, drunkenness, revelings, and such like: of the which I tell you before, as I have also told you in time past, that they which do such things shall not inherit the kingdom of God.*

"I'm a sinner then? I just trying to survive. They say the only way out is to be a whore or play music. I does both."

The man paced around the room, putting footprints upon the dirt floors of the seedy hotel room. "Someone told you wrong, Miriam Landry. There are other ways out of da swamp. There are other ways out of the poverty of Louisiana. It ain't migrating to Chicago, just to be part of da devil's playground either. Your answers are all in here." Again, he pointed to his book. Miriam gawked at this mysterious stranger, still nameless to her, wide eyed, as the whites of her eyes seemed to brighten the room.

"I wants to read some now, but I can't read dat good, plus it's dark in here." The man walked towards her and laid on the bed. Miriam scooched her little butt aside, so he stretched out. One Bible rested on the table beside him as he opened it to read in the dark. The straw hat covered his face. Soon she listened to the abnormal breathing of a man sleeping. Familiar grunts of an old man sleeping from Shreveport years earlier.

She grabbed the second Bible and walked over to the far bed and placed the good book on the table adjacent to the bed. The rustic lamp didn't work, however when she sat her copy of the scriptures on the furniture, the lamp flickered. Goosebumps rolled up her body, like a marching band in a parade, and vanished as rapid as they arrived. She grabbed her Bible again and curled into a ball on her bed. She opened the book again. The light flashed on and off. It stayed on as she read for a bit. She closed the book tight and replaced it back on the table.

She flopped around on her bed all night. If anyone watched her, they'd imagine she transformed herself into a little rubber ball, the way she curled up, and tossing and turning and bouncing on the bed. That entire day exhausted her, her mind and body craved sleep, but she bounced on the flimsy mattress. Something in this room made the hair on her arms stand and salute.

From nowhere, a guiding light from outside shone through the ripped curtains. Her eyes focused on the light, as if Jesus himself called her home. The lamp soon flickered off and on, and soon darkness enveloped the motel room. A sudden flash of light came into the room, and the notion hit her. She seemed to recognize the fool as the man in the Terrebonne Parish juke joint. She didn't say nothing to him, and figured she sat in this motel room for a reason and refused jinxing the moment. Soon, she fell asleep in the same fetal position she flipped and flopped in.

She awoke as the man brought breakfast in. He carried a sack with extra clothes stuffed inside for Miriam. "I gotcha breakfast here, Miss Landry." He tipped his hat to her. "Also went to dat old thrift store downtown and got ya some new duds."

Miriam eyed the man and smiled, but still apprehensive about this relationship, and wondered the man's real identity. People hide their devil's work behind God's mask, and this drifter may do the same, or maybe he became her guardian angel, who arrives in the movies? She ate the biscuits and gravy, as a starved puppy attacks his bowl. She wiped the gravy off her face, licked some spilled gravy from her fingers as the man handed her a couple pairs of overalls.

"They didn't have no lady's overalls at the thrift store, so I gotcha some boys. Hope they fit ya. Go in da bathroom and try dem on. I didn't gets you anything else. I didn't want to get your underthings. I is gonna take you out to get some before we start studying dis book." Miriam eyed the man with her chin on her hand, and her focus moved to the Bible he held. A smile appeared on her face, but it disappeared. Miriam ripped off her clothes as she walked to the bathroom to change and peeked around as her clothes fell on the floor, before the bathroom door. She spun her head and glanced at him, checking to notice if the man spied on her. He did, and the man possessed a smile as big as the state they stayed in.

She came out of the bathtub with the aroma of lavender, her essence tempting and her physical body, clean on the outside. Her inside still craved cleansing, but spiritual cleaning takes time, even a lifetime. Still unaware of what town they spent the night in, the man took her for a drive. They found a creek in town called Wells Creek. She soon found out they bunked in Palestine Texas. Miriam wondered in solace. *"Could God's will a brought me to this town with the Biblical name? Was it a coincidence that this is where he was from? Did this have anything to do with Lucas Turner? Was this man even real?"*

In the past Miriam encountered people that may not be human. Angels, fallen Angels, or just the devil, she never realized.

She sat in the passenger seat of the Studebaker as the man opened the car door for her. He reached out his hand and helped her up. There he took her to Wells Creek, where Miriam searched for sticks and rocks to throw in. The little creek cut through a forest of Dogwood and Magnolia trees. The trees stood at attention to witness the goings on. If trees owned vision, they witnessed the teenagers coming down to explore carnal desires, as the young football players took the cheerleaders out for the customary deflowering. The trees also took notice of the preachers, pastors, and other men of the cloth, or those playing preacher, taking the sinners hand and laying them down on the bank of Wells Creek. Townsfolk of Palestine and the surrounding areas called this a Wells Creek baptism, just as the young football players called the deflowering of the high school cheerleaders a Wells Creek Baptism. Daytime or nighttime, the only difference.

The man asked Miriam some questions about her life and her future life with Jesus. He quoted scripture. He talked to her again. "Miriam, I have seen you since you were a little gal, hanging out with Lightning Bug Parker. I heard he done did some mean things to ya." He spit out some snuff, nowhere near Miriam. A small stain developed in the dirt. He lit his corncob pipe. Miriam's eyes focused on the pipe, and the crusty thing seemed familiar. The aroma of the pipe tobacco tickled her nose, making it twitch. The fragrance radiated a familiar and eerie scent to it. "I hears you was sent to work on da streets, and no girl should have to do dat. Dat is where I lost track of ya, but that might be part of the plan. Now Miriam Landry, what would you want to do with your life, if ya had a chance to start over, cause Jesus can give you a new life."

Miriam sat on the banks, tossing some dogwood branches into Wells Creek, where they floated downstream into the Neches, and into the Sabine, and last into the Gulf of Mexico. "Three things sir. I wants to be like dat branch, and just float away from here." She tossed a decent-sized log and witnessed the wood float away. "If I can't do that, I still want to sing da Swamp Blues. Da kind my daddy played, but better." The man still glared at her shaking his head. "What's the matter?"

"It's all about yourself isn't it? You wants to run away, you wants to play music, what about da others. Ya think you is the only girl dat been raped and, da only girl dat walked the streets of Shreveport. Listen Miriam, ya ain't the first, and you ain't gonna be da last. Hell woman, I is just gonna walk away if you can't figure this one out." The man started walking towards the Studebaker. He opened the door, which creaked like a door in a haunted house. Miriam's goosebumps reappeared with the resonance of that screech.

"Wait!" Miriam shouted. "I can help those girls on da streets. Help get them off da streets." The tone of her voice changed into a polite scream. She hollered to make sure the stranger acknowledged her. She noticed him, and a smile appeared on his face. It appeared in slow motion. He stayed out of the car but proceeded at a turtle's pace towards her. In fact, a painted turtle walked with him as it also made its descent to Wells Creek.

"I can see you helping those girls. You been there and survived. I'm sure you known some that haven't. There gonna be a girl just like you, Daddy's friend rapes her, she aborts the baby and runs away, and ain't no one gonna give her a job, except some pimp or madam, or even some junk dealer, wanting you to hold his smack. He tells someone it okay to sample, and she does and gets herself hooked. Now she hooked and hooking. She ain't gonna be so lucky. Now Miriam Landry do you want to commit your life to Jesus Christ? To help these girls, you gotta find da Lord? Now I am here to help you find him." The man kicked off his loafers, as one went flying and missed the turtle, who lost the race towards Wells Creek. His argyle socks also tossed near his shoes. The man rolled his pant legs and started walking in the little river. "Now Miss Landry, I wants you to repeat after me." *John 3:16* *[16]For God so loved the world, that he gave his only begotten Son, that whosoever believeth in him should not perish, but have everlasting life.*

"What does dat mean sir?" She asked the stranger. "Why does I have to repeat it?"

The man paced around in Wells Creek. He circled around and crossed the narrow stream. He stopped in his tracks, spun around and walked towards the west bank. "Well, all dat means if you believe in Jesus Christ and He is our Lord and Savior, your life gonna be in heaven. Now before we rescue and reform them streetwalkers you care about, you needs to commits your life to Jesus Christ. Now to do dat, He's got to be in your heart. Is Jesus in your heart?"

"I'm not sure, sir?" He ain't never been in my heart before? How do I know it?"

The nameless preacher shook his head. In his heart the man realized Miriam required a country baptism, so he'd return her to Shreveport, so she'd be qualified working downtown. In silence, he closed his eyes and said to someone above, "This should be easier, Help me Lord." He glanced towards the water and smiled and took a gander at the girl. "You know it if you have to ask, Now do you Miriam?"

"Yes sir." Her response wouldn't have been one hundred percent convincing to most people, but for the mysterious minister she convinced him. Miriam repeated John 3.16, as she entered Wells Creek with him. He held her hand and he read Matthew 28:19-20 *[19]Go ye therefore, and teach all nations, baptizing them in the name of the Father, and of the Son, and of the Holy Ghost: [20]Teaching them to observe all things whatsoever I have commanded you: and, lo, I am with you always, even unto the end of the world.* Amen."

Miriam repeated the verse. The man demanded her sitting down in Wells Creek. This portion, shallow, while Miriam plopped her butt into the water with her legs crossed. The man stood beside her and grabbed the back her black hair. "Now hold your nose closed likes you going for a swim." With her right hand she squeezed her nostrils with her thumb and pointer finger. The man pulled her head, it retreated as if time stood still. Her head splashed backwards into the water.

"What da fuck you doing?" Miriam came out splashing her arms in the water. It wasn't the ideal response for a woman who committed her life to Jesus and reborn. "Why you dunk me in da water?"

The preacher rolled his eyes at Miriam. "Now you watch your mouth. The dunking in Wells Creek is for cleansing your soul. We must do this. Now since you swore at a disciple of The Lord, I thinks we need to do this again. It's about faith, before you can trust the Lord, you need faith in him, and you have to trust me." He repeated the two Bible verses and she read them to him. He immersed her into Wells Creek again. This time Miriam Landry kept quiet and trusted the man. He pulled her head out of the water. She shook her head in a futile attempt to dry off. "I don't feel no different, just wet." She walked out of the creek and water cascaded down her body as she went to the car. "Sir, you says Cecil and Bo Barnum you kin? I don't believes you. Prove it."

"Me and Gramma Sara. She made da whiskey for me. She knows I like to haves me some snorts." Well dat's how Cecil was born, buts he's mortal since he don't believe. Bo be mortal too, 'cause dat son of a bitch don't believe neither. You gotta believe. Now dat daughter, if she believes in da spirits, she might live forever, but she can't know about none of this." The man and his car disappeared. Miriam shook her head, confused she

196

strolled towards the business district of town.

A Hudson sedan waited for her as she hit the corner of Birch and Moody. "I been waiting for you to take you back to Shreveport," The well-endowed Caucasian woman told her. "Now hop in and trust me this is the plan for you. If you need to do your calling, you need to have faith and your plan will work. Now get in this car. Your stuff is all here. I got it out of the hotel."

Miriam gawked at her confused. "Where did dat man go? He just disappeared. Was he real?"

"Do you think he was real?"

"He seem very real to me?"

"Then he was real." Miriam studied her face. The woman, in her mid-forties, appeared pretty, but she also buried her face in a foundation, covering a hard life from her younger days. She dressed better than most women. She stranger wore a flowered dress which dropped below her ankles. Miriam wondered why she didn't dress casually.

Her car sped out of Texas, and the lady never said her name. The blonde woman, a former prostitute in Shreveport, worked in one of the classier houses in town, until it got raided. The woman got busted, did six months in the Caddo Parish Jail in 1952. Once released she vowed, she wasn't returning to jail, and never selling her body again, promising to help anyone in the same situation. She ran a halfway house near Fannin Street and Miriam Landry came recommended as one of her mentors. Discipling the hookers walking Fannin wouldn't be easy. She walked these same streets some fifteen years earlier.

After the woman retrieved Miriam, they arrived in Shreveport in three hours. Miriam returned to the place she got dumped off by Lightning Bug, the place where the obese Judge pissed on her, where she once lived in a two-story shanty and shared a room with another young hooker. She loved and hated this town, but it became time to make a difference in some girl's life. The redemption she required, waited.

The halfway house sat on the Corner of Caddo and Cane in St. Paul's Bottoms, the area Miriam got banished from years earlier. "First thing we need to do is take you shopping. We will go to the thrift store down around the corner. I have a surprise for you. Felicia is taking over now." They walked into the house before they went clothes shopping.

"Miriam Landry? Is that really you?" The thicker dark-skinned woman asked her as she went into the two-story house. "Come here and squeeze your body into mine." All grown and appearing incredible, Miriam remembered her as a hard worker, but also a girl who wouldn't tolerate the crap of several of the older clientele, and the immaturity of the college age boys. Felicia liked her regular johns, the clients she did her specialty with.

Felicia remembered Miriam loved her lemonade and a nice big glass sat on a coffee table waiting for her. Miriam downed a big gulp, scrunched her face, set the glass on the coaster and smiled at her old friend. "This shit's as bitter as my life's been." She continued. "Remember back in thirty-eight when I found you?"

"You save my life Miriam Landry; I will never forget. Dat is why I'm saving yours right now."

Miriam sat on the davenport and got comfy. She kicked her shoes across the floor as she wiggled her toes, waiting for Felicia to return. When Felicia returned, Miriam started.

"Dat rich attorney, named Sylvester, he da same man that visited The Mitchells. You was with him."

They toasted each with their lemonade and snuggled. Felicia continued. "Yeah, he wanted the Red River special, but I don't go nowhere outside da Bottoms. Too many of our girls don't return. Dat man promise twice, or three times da money, but dat money still ain't shit to get dem to go. Now I don't do dat shit at all."

"I don't blame ya, I always thought there was something about dat guy. Dat time he came to visit da judge, I thought they was lovers or something."

Felicia took another swallow of her bitter drink, made a face, gleamed at her partner and smiled. "I heard dat too about dem." She caressed Miriam on the thigh and peered deep in her eyes. "He whipped dat roll out and I eyed it like I wanted it. I knew he wasn't after a good screw or even what I always got extra for, but he wanted the power trip. You know what I mean by dat?"

"I always hated dat shit. I didn't mind da job, if they just wanted to talk, be held or something like dat, and then we could screw up like we was there girl, but once they looked at us like they were better, then those men got dangerous." She cuddled with Felicia, but the older thicker woman stood and walked around the room.

She stood before Miriam as Miriam admired Felicia. They both smiled a little at one another, remembering the times they enjoyed their private moments. "I grew up in da Bottoms. I ain't never gonna leave it. I born and raised here and ain't never gonna leave it. I especially ain't leaving for a man with a wad a cash, and a bigger stash stuffed in his bank account."

"You showed me a lot baby, showed me how to roll some fool dat don't wanna pay, you show me how to protect myself."

I knew dat foo Sylvester didn't wanna fuck, he's even told me he wanted Da Red River special."

"Glads I got there when I did. You know some girls never come back. Da judge and Sylvester didn't kill all them. Some got out da business right then and dere. They say it was a spiritual cleansing. Just like a Baptism as da girls got dunked into da river."

"Yeah but there were others that never came back. There were news reports of bodies being found down the river. We never knew why dese fools would save a girl or kill a girl, and I didn't wants to know."

Miriam pushed her petite body off the couch and walked to her friend and hugged her. "I don't blame ya. I do da same thing."

Felicia stared deep at Miriam and walked away from her. "Then he says, 'You are coming with me. We are going down to the river. I want your special, Miss Felicia.'"

"I says, I don't go to no river. We do it in that shack over dere, or you don't get nuttin from me. I looked at dat wad of do-re-mi stuck in da money clip, took a deep breath and thought about it for a second. Dat man that had his cane or da judges and looked like some guy on Halloween all dressed up like a foo from da olden days. You know the men dat thinks us Negress has a place, and dat is to service a master."

Miriam sat again as Felicia joined her. "I know baby. I hate dat."

"I told him I ain't going nowhere but over to that shanty, I ain't walking or riding in your carriage down to da river. Some girls never returned from there. I don't give a fuck who you are mister aristocrat. I see you getting into some music before, and dat's okay, but you come down here chasing these women, and some end up missing. Dat not gonna happen to me, and dat ain't happening to no others of dese girls. You know it Miriam. Dat man looked at staring at my mouth and lips. I could see him getting excited cause I was staring rights at him. I knew he wanted some release, so we wents back to da shack. He says to me, I come with you as long as we can walk in da Bottoms."

"So, you sucked him dry?"

"Of course. Dat man had money, and I was still in control. One wrong move, and I know how to chomp. He knows dat." The two women exchanged snickers. Miriam's much louder, as Felicia continued. "Well I finished him and spat dat shit out. He saw me spitting into the mop bucket and he comes alive, mad as a gator and started wrestling me, slips me sumfin dat I tried to spit out also. He dragged me to his fairy tale carriage and must have slipped me sumfin. I spat that shit out too, but I must have gotten a little in me, cause I felts real tired, but I stills tries to fights dat man."

"Dat must be where I's come in then. I sees ya fighting, but not very good, but I's still far away, but I's starts running toward you and makes you two out. I recognizes you and then him, and I move faster."

"Yeah we ride down in his little carriage dat was straight out of a fairy tale, and he tries to drag me and throw me in da river."

"Dat's when I shouts at ya, and dat fool skedaddles out of dere, and I took care of ya. I stays wid you for a week and den I mosey on down da road."

Felicia never turned another trick again. Instead she worked to protect the girls. In her eyes, the girls, powerless against the societal folks renting them, required empowerment. "Miriam," Felicia said. "It's da same ol' song and dance. We just work to satisfy dese men. The girls need to take control of their lives, so we not worked to death, get hooked on dat shit anymore. Even if we all got seamstress jobs like I'm trying to set up we still just working for the white man. He gonna pay us what he wants to, but it's a start."

"Felicia, I gotcha. They piss on us and tell us it raining, then don't pay us shit, and if we bitch about us, dey gonna fire us." Felicia started an advocacy group, and she welcomed her mentor. She owed Miriam her life and fifteen years later Miriam got a fresh start.

"Wait Miriam, the devil is my great grandpa. They just called him papa, never even had a name, and you just told me. You told me I am kin to some Haitian spirit. I don't believe you anyway, but I want to be Haitian." The girls hugged.

"Is that all you asking about? My life changing for the good, and all you care about is you self."

Chapter 22
The Folklorist

Miriam spent most of her time in Shreveport. She took a trip to Chicago to check on Lightning. The Palestine preacher told her she was required to make amends and forgive the people who did her wrong. Another pilgrimage to Chicago needed to be taken. Step one: her commitment, when the mysterious minister dunked her in Palestine. Step two: asking Lightning for forgiveness, the man who dropped her off at a Shreveport shanty, and said, "you don't fuck good enough to be my wife. You need to learn it here."

"Felicia, I need to head to Chicago. Some man say I need to ask for forgiveness to get redemption. Not sure what dat all means. I mean why should I say I is sorry to dat junkie dat abused me with his mouth and fists, but I needs to get out of here for a little bit."

"I know Miriam. That's what they told me, so you get yourself a bus ticket and be back here in a couple of weeks or less. Then we will get started."

"But why is I sorry?" He da one dat do shit."

"His response will tell you everything. Usually, a man will admit his failure, after one opens up to him. We're all guilty." Felicia hugged her, got her the bus pass and dragged her to the station.

Several times she desired to slice the man to pieces like the chickens she used to catch for him in Texas. In both their attempts at a relationship she also longed to blow his brains out, but she'd fry at Goree or Dwight, with no chance to meet her potential.

At this stage in her life forgiving the man became a necessity, but she thought she already had when she departed with Sara the last time. She wasn't even sure why she returned to the Windy City, but something made her return. It wasn't the electric atmosphere of Maxwell Street, but something, or someone beckoned her.

She got off the Greyhound and ventured to the southwest section. She found the old neighborhood, the area she missed and glad she abandoned in equal measures. Two men studied her, as she headed east on Maxwell. The two gentlemen walked adjacent but did not acknowledge one another. Miriam got closer to them, and noticed one man, an older drifter, but dressed like a Mississippi bluesman. He paid no further attention to her. The gentleman walking beside him, a Caucasian, stood taller and smiled. He didn't fit the demographics of the neighborhood,

A gray fedora topped the white man's head, and a goatee covered half of his face. The man dressed and acted like a hipster. He didn't seem like the young college students, who started hanging out at the folk festivals rising on the East coast. He seemed too old. His hair, not well groomed, blew in the wind, and the breeze messed with his narrow tie. He spotted Miriam Landry and for some unknown reason he recognized her, even though they never crossed paths before. The man who seemed familiar as a bluesman vanished.

The remaining gentleman approached her, and Miriam, always suspicious of strangers, stepped into the doorway of one of the markets which frequented Maxwell Street. His eyes still focused on her, as he made his way closer and closer to her. She didn't run and appear guilty of anything, when she wasn't. She wasn't aware of any charges still pending against her.

The man stopped at the market where Miriam ducked. She stood behind a philodendron with long vines, spread across the red brick. The vines stretched like a daddy long-legged spider. She already missed the weeds and foliage from Louisiana. The man brushed his hair with his left hand and returned the fedora to his scalp. He took a photo out of his pocket and eyeballed the image. He peered at Miriam's face, as a small smile came on his face. "Miriam Landry?"

"How you know me?"

"I've been on your trail since Friars Point, looking for you. Now, I am not the law, nor am I a hellhound. Some folks down South say you're a key person to the music of some well-known and not so famous musicians."

"What folks? Most folks I know from there is dead."

"I can't tell you that, but can we grab a cup of coffee, and can I show you more photos? If you are who I think you are, I want to get some stuff recorded, also."

They wandered Maxwell Street from the grocery store to a diner. The man held the door for Miriam, as they sat and ordered coffee, and some breakfast. She got some grits and eggs, while he ordered a stack of flapjacks. He opened his attaché case and whipped out folders, placing them on the table between the two of them. He opened a manila colored folder.

She gazed at the photos inside. Her eyes scanned each picture as if she studied a map while taking a car trip.

In the opening picture appeared a tall dark-skinned man. He wore sunglasses inside, sported a fedora and did the splits. "Lightning."

"I take it you know this man; I have had a demanding time locating him. Mojo and Wolfman have not seen him. They said he has checked himself in a hospital, again and again. Mojo also said he lost the only good thing he had ever had, when you left him. Wolf told me Lightning muttered something to him, that not even the great Willie Dixon could write a song about the way he felt. Mojo wrote the tune we're hearing on the radio. His song is about you and Lightning. Most folks thinks it's about his wife."

Miriam lowered her guard for a second. She relaxed and hummed the ditty that made her a trivia answer in years to come. A smile appeared on her face.

"I used to live with him, but I ran away from dat man. I was looking for him. I needs to forgive him for treating me like shi... I's sorry sir, I meant to say for treating me bad."

"That's okay, I say nasty words too." He smiled at her. Miriam returned the grin. He took out another photograph. I only got this one of him. It showed a man and his guitar—a handsome light-skinned bluesman from another era. He appeared as a light-skinned Creole man, that lived up and down Arkansas, Mississippi, and Louisiana. Some say he played in New York City, others said he went all the way to California. The man never made it to Chicago, but he wrote a song about the Windy City. The iconic photo had been taken between 1936 and 1938. The man died in 1938.

He showed her a photo of a man called Lucas Turner, another tall, dark and handsome Negro. The photograph taken in Tyler, Texas as he strutted around the girl. Miriam Landry played her guitar in the background watching him circle her.

"Obviously you know this guy." He pointed to Lucas Turner in the photo, and to Miriam playing slide guitar in the picture.

"Lucas Turner. I knew him, and dat's me in da photo. He dead, too. I knows what happened, too." She hung her head, noticing the butter melt in her grits. It meant a confession the man cared little about.

He cut his pancakes in small pieces and drenched them with additional syrup. He took a swig of coffee and wiped his face with his shirt sleeve. "Self-defense?" Miriam nodded her head. "Some folks said he made a deal, a deal with the devil, some drifter, a lighter-skinned man from Louisiana. Folks says that drifter is the guardian." He poked the flapjacks with his fork and took a big bite and chewed them up and took another shot of coffee. "You know anything about that?" A gust of wind rushed through. In Chicago, the Windy City, it's not unusual, but both parties jerked their heads towards the window, witnessing nothing. Not even a piece of trash bounced down the sidewalk.

"I don't know nothin' about that, and I don't know what's to believe, even though I lived it." Miriam sprinkled additional pepper on her grits, stirred them and scooped a spoonful. She glanced out the window again and noticed the drifter walking. He smiled at Miriam and got lost on the city. "You knows sometimes I don't thinks we're in control of our own lives." She took a bite of her eggs.

The man produced an artist's rendering of some fiddle player. Of course, a scar slashed across his face. "Cover dat up. I knows dat man real well, and I knows he's dead. If dat man just stuck with playing fiddle he could have been famous."

"What do you mean?" The folklorist poured extra syrup on his pancakes. The cakes drowned, and the folklorist rescued them with his mighty bites.

"He played with my daddy down in Morgan City way back in 35 den dat man must have drifted all over." Miriam grabbed the breakfast menu and covered her face with it as she continued talking. "He was good, but a sick man. I think he was looking for me all along. He found me once, but I ran away from him."

"So, the rumors about him were true? A possible hit man for the government?"

"I don't know nothin' 'bout dat. All I know is he raped me when I was a kid and got me pregnant. Dat's why I run away from home after I had me an abortion. I also knew he used to run with a friend of mine way back when."

He stuttered. "I'm sorry, Miss L-landry?

The folklorist rested his face in his hands as he gazed deep in Miriam's eyes. Tears dripped down her cheeks, cascading onto the table. He found the correct person from talking to her.

They continued eating breakfast, while he showed her additional pictures. Miriam's eyes still watered when he showed her the next photo. The guy appeared mixed race, someone who could pass as black or white.

The woman focused on the Creole man. She shoved her breakfast aside and put her head in her hands. She lifted her hands but kept her face buried in them. "Bo." Nothing else said, and she sighed. "Dat fiddle player used to run with Bo too. I'm pretty sure he killed Bo."

"You are the woman I have been looking for.

Maybe it has been for fifteen years." He placed the fork on the table, took a swig of coffee, and smiled at her.

"Fifteen years. You sure you aren't no cop?"

"I'm no cop, but I've recorded folks that have been in Louisiana, Texas, Alabama and Mississippi prisons. I've talked to the ladies at Goree, men at Angola, and Parchman, and everything I have been told is confidential. I want to record you. Some woman I talked to at Gorree said you were the best singer. Some kid down in Roseville said you got it on. Right now, all I'm interested in is that Creole folk singer. Folks across Louisiana said he inspired them. Do you know how I can get a hold of him or his family?"

"I can take you to his kin folk. I just needs to get a hold of Lightning Bug. After we gets hold of him, I can take you to meet him. I just don't know what's gonna happen when I hook up with Lightning again. I just needs to talks to him and see if he okay. I just need me a minute of his time." Miriam glanced behind her shoulder, and out at the sidewalk as they remained adjacent to the window at the Maxwell Street diner. She didn't notice anyone she recognized—the city changed a little since Sara grabbed her and tried to make Miriam her property a few years earlier.

"I'm pretty sure I know how to find him. It's a hunch anyway. Thought I saw a little porch party starting up at this hour." The man finished his food before Miriam and started puffing a large cigar. He blew the smoke away from her, so she finished eating without smoke in her face. He's around here somewhere, and I need to find him too." The man inhaled another puff as Miriam downed her last bite of food and scooped the little crumbs on the spoon to take her last bite.

"Let's go find him, then we can goes back to Louisiana. I knows where we can meet Bo's kin. Bo ain't alive no more. He passed a long time ago." Miriam tilted her head, she couldn't face the man, instead she peeked again at her bowl of grits. She didn't care to say what happened, but she also realized this man didn't care.

"Alan Lomax." He shook her hand. "This is what I do for a living. I look for lost songs, lost recordings, and look up the people that wrote and performed them. Let's go get Lightning Bug." Mr. Lomax tossed a five on the table to cover their bill plus tip, and they walked out the door. Mr. Lomax, a large and healthy man, blocked the wind for Miriam as he walked ahead of her, heading east towards downtown and the Great Lake. The winds blowing off the lake knocked a horse flat. Miriam stayed behind the man.

They took a turn on the corner. The house party started already. Miriam played hostess to these parties as Lightning played his guitar on the porch before the neighborhood kids, and there he stood. Lightning Bug Parker performing his patented—or stolen—moves in front of a group of young kids. Most of the teens that flocked around him were young girls, but he also showed some of the boys how to play guitar. He showed the kids how to play the correct way, and with their teeth. He carried a portable amplifier on his belt as he strutted up and down the steps. Lightning stopped dead in his tracks when he noticed Miriam.

Mr. Lomax addressed him. "This woman wants to talk to you, then I do too." His eyes pleaded for Miriam's forgiveness. Tommie's eyes locked with hers, and not in an attempt to seduce her. The saying goes, "if looks could kill…" Miriam stood firm again.

"What do you want Miriam, and where da fuck have you been?"

Required by the Palestine preacher to complete the ordeal, she spoke with caution. "I just want..."

"What da fuck do you want?"

"If you quit interrupting me, I will tell you."

"You ain't told me shit."

She took a deep breath, and her eyes stayed focused on him. Under her breath she counted to ten. "I'm forgiving you for dropping me off on Fannin Street way back when. I said my piece, now I'm getting da fuck out of here." She peeked at Mr. Lomax. "I will meet you back at dat diner. Just because I forgive dat man don't mean I want to spend any more time with him."

"Miriam, wait. There sumfin I really need to tell you. Lomax, I wants to tell her in private." They went inside the house passed the guests and into the parlor, as her acquaintance waited outside. "I'm sorry, and I know I said it too many times, but I got messed up on da junk. Strong shit makes you do crazy things. I was doing it all along. Well dat shit probably gave me the cancer I is fighting. Not sure how long I got. I needs your forgiveness too. Dat's all I want."

Miriam gave the man a hug, additional words no longer required. She forgave the man, spun and raced towards the diner.

Miriam realized trusting this man became essential, and the name seemed familiar, but still they had just met, a stranger to her. But she had run off with strangers before. She remembered the Lomax name from taking phone calls for Lightning Bug, when she lived with the man in Chicago, but sometimes putting two and two together was not her greatest asset. Also, she longed to remain anonymous and live the rest of her life helping the helpless, giving young girls a chance in life, when they abandoned all hope. She completed her mission and started to walk towards the "L." Mr. Lomax caught her walking the wrong direction.

"Ms. Landry, there isn't a need to run from me. I will take you where you need to go. Possibly, it is the same place I'm going, and I'll give you a lift. I promise everything is on the up and up. I'll buy your meals and get you your own room. I don't mind crossing the tracks in the South. Like I told you earlier I've been in Angola, Goree and Parchman. I talked to some of the meanest guys and ladies around and I'm not afraid on the outside. Maybe on the inside I'm shaking like an LA skyscraper in an earthquake, but I don't let them mean and ornery folks see it in my eyes. Now come on in. I got my recording equipment in the trunk, I'll show it to you, because I want to record you. I want to find Bo Barnum's songs, and I want to hear his daughter sing too."

She gawked at him, still in disbelief. He hooked her arm in his elbow, as if they danced a country square dance at the Haymarket in Shreveport. He stopped and faced her. She gazed at the tall man straight into his eyes. "I'm serious, Miss Landry. This is what I do for a living. I got the best damn job in the world."

"Ok let's go. Not sure if I got me enough money for the bus anyways." They walked down Maxwell Street and got into Mr. Lomax's vehicle. He opened the door for her and drove her to a studio. Mojo and Wolfman sat smoking cigars in plush chairs. "You need to sign some papers too for a couple of those songs Mojo recorded."

"He say he got me covered on dem."

"Well, I trust Mojo, but some of these others are

crooks, they might have signed your rights away. Some kids overseas are playing records now."

Lomax and Miriam rushed up to the receptionist desk. The first woman they met, a redhead, ignored Miriam, but Lomax got her attention. "I need international rights." He told her. The woman, named Emily, sat in her chair painting her fingernails, ignoring both the tall white man, and the colored woman. She tossed a piece of spearmint gum in her mouth. The aroma matched the pennyroyal Miriam inhaled so many years ago. She stuck her tongue through the piece of gum. "International rights down the hall." Her voice muffled from the gum.

They hurried down the corridor. Miriam needed to get out of the city, but other business needed attention. There sitting at the desk sat a woman, a brunette. She wore spectacles, horn rimmed. Her hair sat up in a bun. She also reeked of spearmint gum and chomped it when Lomax addressed her.

"Mr. Lomax, always a pleasure." The woman, named Madeline, spoke while chomping, her voice muffled by the gum.

"I'm hearing "Won't You Go Away" has been picked up by some blokes overseas. I want to make sure all the I's are dotted, and T's are crossed on the contract. Don't want this girl's rights to the song taken away."

Madeline replied. "Here, Mr. Lomax read it over." Lomax skimmed the contract. Miriam tugged on his shirt.

"I is sure everything is in order. Let's get rolling. Do I have to sign anything?"

"Nope." Madeline replied. "Everything is in order." Lomax kept reading it. The contract looked good.

He gave it back to the woman, and she placed it in the file cabinet behind her desk. Madeline rushed to the office carrying the folder and returned as fast as she left. They both thanked the woman, scurrying down the hall and out of the office. Mojo and Wolf hugged the two. "You going to Newport, for the festival?" Mojo asked Lomax.

"I'll be there recording. I got to get Miriam home first."

"Well she should be playing." Mojo replied.

"I is retired, Mojo. I ain't playing no more, just teaching some girls to play guitar down home. Might play and write some stuff for me, if I get a moment for myself."

"I do wanna play with you again. You better than most of these fools." Mojo stared The Wolfman down, as Miriam and Lomax walked out the door and into his car, and soon they abandoned Chicago.

Miriam never wanted to return to Chicago, but that was the step needed for her redemption. She enjoyed her life in the Windy City, but home was Louisiana, and Sara Barnum convinced her she belonged in the Pelican State. "I ain't going back." She never peeked out the rear window as the Chicago skyline disappeared.

Chapter 23
The Road Home

The folklorist kept true to his word. He paid for everything. When they got to Memphis, he got her in a Negro-only motel, while he stayed at the Peabody. Getting Miriam a room at the Peabody would have been his preference, but the man traveled several thousand miles in the South during segregation. His job gave him survival skills, even if he didn't like it.

He got her breakfast to eat in the car, and later in the evening they pulled into Shreveport at the halfway house near the hookers and drug addicts. The man, well received by the ladies of the night, but a quick rendezvous, or venturing into the Shreveport nightlife, didn't fit his agenda. Miriam stood as his one and only focus and recording her songs.

She'd sent a letter to her friend; however, Sara Barnum refused to answer her. She wondered if Sara received the letter, or if her friend ditched her, like everyone else in her life. Miriam Landry evolved from a person other people drug along, so they felt charitable and raised her up, for the sole purpose to knock her flat. It became a life she was custom too, a life she lived, but in her mid-thirties, Miriam arrived.

She built her reputation as an amazing musician, but better yet she became an amazing human. Maybe she always was, but her life evolved once the girl craved an existence larger than being a sidekick. She still cut heads with the best, when challenged, and she still wrote incredible songs, but Miriam didn't demand the lifestyle.

She ached to teach, she desired to help the women struggling and suffering from life on the streets. Miriam sought to help the girls pondering the easy money of prostitution being the only way out. The former musician helped the addicts, even though she never got into drugs.

Miriam ran into Sara again, right after they got back to Shreveport. "This man been looking for you Miss Sara. He wants to record some of Bobo's stuff, some of yours too." She gawked at Miss Barnum, eyes devouring Sara's face and body, as she stood in Tomas Barnum's home. Afraid to move or come closer or to show Sara some real affection. Sara craved a hug. Miriam kept her distance.

"I can record some stuff. Damn, what month is it? I've been living in the swamp too long. I'm supposed to play at Newport in a few days, at that Folk Festival they have. Miri, you need to come along. I need another player. It would be great if you came along."

"Sara, I retired. I don't play no more, just teach them girls how to play, and we sing hymns and stuff." She required a better rejection, besides Sara knew she wanted to play again. A rotten liar, Miriam tried again, this excuse worse than the first. "We don't have no way out there."

Lomax interjected. "I'm headed out there in the morning. Again, this is what I do, I can take you gals out there." A sigh came from Miriam, acknowledging defeat.

Tomas entered the room, he leered at Miriam, winked at his former crush. "What's going on?"

"Miri and I are playing at the Folk Festival in Rhode Island. I signed a contract, let's go, you can watch Berto." Sara, always quick with a retort—one of her many strengths.

Miriam glanced up at Mr. Lomax for approval, but she recognized defeat. He nodded approval for what happened next.

The next morning the five of them departed Monroe and drove straight through to Rhode Island. Lomax, Tomas and Sara split time driving. They arrived two days before schedule, Lomax got them all nice rooms. Miriam shacked up with Sara and the baby, while the two men received individual rooms, all overlooking Newport Harbor.

"We ain't doing nothing, Sara. You know I'm married to the lord. I can't be with no one."

"Miri, I know. You told me about five times. Dat means secretly you do, but I'm respecting your wishes. Acting like dat is a big turn-off anyway. Plus, we got Berto. Let's just rehearse a few of Sammy's songs. We'll do fine. Dat's why we're here." She put her guitar down, turned her head from Miriam. Miriam sighed and they fell asleep on the bed. The baby slept in between them.

They attempted to enjoy the ritzy city, but the city didn't match their lifestyle. Days and nights spent rehearsing; recreating sounds created on the Black Bayou. Both women longed to return to their ways. Sara on the lam, Miriam helping the helpless.

They played for forty minutes, the show perfect, the rehearsals paid off, but no one paid to see the two, who weren't the highlight of the show. The crowning achievement came when established artists performed a mini tribute. The bluegrass duo of Flatt and Scruggs played a Sara and Lydia Barnum-penned tune, called "The Ballad of Bo Barnum." Lightning Bug Parker played a Miriam Landry-penned tune, "The Bo Barnum Blues." Lomax handed the family a few recordings he pressed. One, a live recording, and others he made of Sara back in Louisiana. Also, he recorded Miriam singing, one penned with a famous collaborator.

They drove back the same way they came—straight through, alternating drivers.

They got back to Tomas's residence, and Miriam escorted Sara to the door. She stepped close, opened her mouth to give Miriam a kiss. "I gots to go Sara. I missed enough time already."

"Come see me. I need you back in my life, even as a best friend. I ain't got no one. I'm on the lam here. I live in a little river shack with Berto, and who knows how long that's gonna last."

"Sara, you don't gets it, do ya? I's needed. These women, little street whores likes I used to be, needs me. I'm keeping them from hooking. I do more in one day, than I used to do in my life. Let me gives you my number." She chicken-scratched on a piece of paper, her info, handed it to Sara. They exchanged pinkies, and hugged. Miriam turned and walked away. Lomax drove her back to Shreveport.

Sara craved Miriam in her life. She didn't realize it, but Miriam had evolved, no longer dependent on Sara. Miriam figured out life on her own, as the gifted woman settled in Shreveport at the house she shared with Felicia in the Bottoms. Their home became a shelter for women, who no longer desired to sell themselves. The house became a home for the women molested by a family member, a shelter for those women, both black and white, trafficked by pimps into an already-established sex industry in Northern Louisiana.

Partnered with her former lover, the former

prostitute, and drug dealer and Miriam's mentor-in-vice Felicia Baptiste. Felicia evolved into a glamorous woman. She received her Master's from Grambling University, sixty miles down the road.

"Glad you could make it back Miri."

"I got me a calling dat says I needs to help dese women dat was like us. Dat ain't no way out of the swamps, or from the poverty." You gotcha an education, I got me talent, and we got it through challenging work and hard living. I ain't gonna recommend the hard living as a way out, but I recommend dat dese girls work hard at what they want. At least now dere ain't no discrimination on education. Plus, I'm getting me bunches of money to finance all of this. I found my calling."

"I got the government help we need. Got me a big grant. Now I know the government wants to keep us down, but I told them there's a way we can clean up Shreveport. We can get these girls some jobs and teach them things. I can teach them education, give them some working skills."

"I's can teach dem da guitar, and how to write songs. Tough market to get into, but this guy told me dat playing music is much better for your exteem, whatever da fuck dat is."

"The main thing we are doing is giving the girls a chance to empower themselves. We need to train them they don't need a man to provide for them, but it is not about woman power. It is about survival. Women need to be taught survival without being a whore, without catering to another person."

"Well when we were hooking, we was working. We was surviving."

"Yeah but we were dependent men using and abusing us. Dat Judge I heard he pissed all over ya. You don't want him pissing on no one else do ya?"

"Of course not." Miriam smiled at her mentor like she understood. Her eyes widened. "So, we need to teach the girls skills that can give them real jobs. Teach them to sew, cook, several types of people's skills. I know I cook and play guitar. Not sure if dat helps."

"Miriam, when you started playing guitar, were you any good?"

She contemplated Felicia's comment, and smiled. "I was terrible, but I worked hard. We teaches dese girls how to work hard at something, den they gets better at it, den have dem get out in da world with a job."

"Now I've been talking with different stores, and they need seamstresses. We can teach the girls how to be seamstresses, plus how to talk professionally with people."

"I don't know how to sew that good."

"You couldn't play guitar either. Probably couldn't field strip a chicken without someone showing you how. Someone told me you killed gators before. Now that is something I wouldn't do unless I knew how."

Still smiling at Felicia, Miriam replied, "My daddy taught me how to do most of it. Mama taught me the rest except for guitar. Lightning helped me a lot on da guitar." She took a deep breath, exhaled and gawked at Felicia. She smiled her irresistible smile. All them mean people in your life can teach you things, can't they? I think there is something in The Bible about it."

"You got it, Miri."

"When we get started?"

"We already started. We're working, I'm training

you to help train them. In turn we're going to teach new members to mentor the girls. In religion it's called discipleship. Now I gotcha a Bible verse on that too. Go grab a Bible from over there." Miriam walked across to the center of the room where there sat a stack of Bibles and grabbed herself one. "Now turn to da back, but not in Revelations. It's in the Second Timothy, chapter 2.2 *Timothy 2:2 And the things that thou hast heard of me among many witnesses, the same commit thou to faithful men, who shall be able to teach others also.* Now read it back to me."

Miriam repeated the verse to her several times, her smile got bigger each time she recited it. "I knows what I's doing now. We just keep bringing girls in and out of here, teach dem skills, teach dem Da Lord, but more important dey gonna learn Da Lord for themselves, so after a while, we don't need to teach no more."

"Sister you got it." She came and gave Miriam a nice big hug, and it reminded both of earlier times bathing and sleeping together in the shanty. "Now show me dat guitar, and I will teach you how to sew. You can teach guitar to the girls, so the girls feel good about themselves. I heard learning guitar is an effective way. Teaches discipline in other things too. You need to study to play guitar, you need to study to get an education. Miriam Landry, I think we will be good partners."

"We already were partners." Miriam eyed her former mentor in prostitution different than when she noticed her way back when. Felicia's eyes focused on her former shanty-mate.

"No, we can't do that again. That is what they want us to do. The local government and the white man will look for any excuse to see us fail. Wacha think the city leaders will say if this place is run by two lesbians. The place being run by two black women is bad enough. Two colored lesbians would be a death sentence." Felicia sighed, exhaled as Miriam noticed her sigh and took in her breath. "I like the offer though." She smiled and returned to her office. She shook her hips, showing off her bigger bottom. Miriam followed her, afraid to make a move. She failed in her relationships and figured a business partner didn't mean a life partner, but it meant a lifetime friend.

Felicia strolled to the kitchen and got them each a glass of lemonade. "Say did you hear what happened to the judge and his male lover, that guy named Sylvester? Well with your testimony, they both went to Angola for da Red River murders."

"I thought they were involved." Miriam took a big swallow of lemonade. She scrunched her face a little, since the lemonade seemed sour. I's glad they put dem away for life."

"Yeah dey put them away for life. Dey both dead now. Some homo black man that the judge sentenced took to both of them. Dat man was innocent and knew he was, I mean everyone knew. Well he stabbed them both. When he received his sentence, all he says was, if you do the time, might as well do da crime." Felicia went to get some sugar to sweeten the drinks. Miriam smiled and shook her head.

Miriam and Felicia ran the rehabilitation center with an iron fist. They kept their relationship platonic and professional. Miriam Landry never forgot her past—it always haunted her, no matter how hard she tried to extinguish it. Nightmares of the Judge brought night sweats. Flashbacks of Tommie Lightning Bug Parker's fists still haunted her. Forgiving someone can be easy. Forgetting emotional and physical abuse is damn near impossible. The two women worked hard running their center. Both women gave their life to Christ and Christianized themselves, incorporating a Faith-based format into their rehab program.

Chapter 24
Sabine Lake

A few months into their work the phone rang, and Felicia answered it. "Miriam, I got a call for you. This man says he is your brother from Morgan City."

"How da fuck he know where I'm at? No one knows where I work at but you, and some of these other women. Can you see what he wants?"

Miriam noticed Felicia talking on the phone. She dropped it, and the receiver dangled from the chord as if Miriam's mentor took a bullet. Miriam rushed towards her business partner, wondering what happened. Felicia reached towards Miriam, gave her a hug, but she didn't say much. "Your father. He died last night. They want you to come home. I will get you a bus ticket."

Miriam broke the hug and backed away from her partner, but peered at her, while Felicia returned the deep eye contact. Tears fell from Felicia's eyes; Miriam's face showed no emotion. No frown, no tears, and no smile. "You ok?" Felicia asked her.

"Just my daddy. If he gave a shit about me, I'd be doing something else right now." She gathered a suitcase worth of belongings, and in her prettiest dress departed the halfway house, Felicia dropping her off at the bus station. Dressed nice, with a nice hat and a flowered sundress, she took the seat furthest to the rear of the bus. Nighttime hit the city, as the coach departed the Greyhound station in Shreveport and headed south towards New Orleans. Miriam never made it there.

Somewhere past Natchitoches, where Miriam Landry first met the Barnums, she was startled by boisterous noise, like a thunderclap during a severe thunderstorm. However, the night stood calm, and the full moon shone straight above. A vision of a man standing in the middle of the highway appeared to her. She wondered if that image she witnessed was Bo Barnum, as an ear-piercing yell echoed throughout the bus. The fat Caucasian bus driver threw her off the motor-carrier for her raucous behavior.

Standing beside the highway, she took in another face. Covered in grease, grime, moss, and mud, she stank like the roadkill next to her. "Miriam, I knew it was you. I just knew it." She hurried towards her friend forgetting she stunk to high heaven and gave Miriam Landry a hug lasting a lifetime. Sara looked a complete mess, with mud and moss caked over her arms, face and legs, and she stank worse. "Tomas and Uncle Jeb are somewhere out there." She shook her head like a junkie seeking a fix. Scared and paranoid, she shook like the pecan trees from Northern Louisiana. "I need to go to Haiti. You are coming with me."

"Sara my daddy died. I'm going to Morgan City. I was on dat Greyhound, but I heard and saw something. I think it was your daddy, and then I screamed, and this fat man threw me off dat damn bus." Miriam expected another hug but getting closer to the stink she hoped Sara wouldn't hold her. She wondered if Sara might try to kiss her, but when Miriam got close, she tilted her head away. Sara's reek emanated like she had eaten a dead skunk. Miriam, dressed in her Sunday best, and Sara acting like an escaped convict, a fugitive from the law, dressed in muddy covered overalls. Her straw hat ripped and torn, but still covered her head, and it also appeared caked in mud and moss. In the moonlight Miriam noticed her arms and face streaked with the wet dirt. Sara still carried two guitars.

"I need to get to New Orleans and meet someone, so I can get to Haiti. You're coming with me Miri."

"I can't come wid you. I got my life to lead Sara."

"Miri, I need you with me. I love you Miri, trust me. We're destined to be together, and you are my best friend,"

"You doesn't need me, but I got to go to see my daddy off to hell. Come with me to Morgan City. Then I sees you off."

"I got to go to Narleans anyway. Got business with the guy that's helping me to Haiti. I'm gonna borrow a boat on the Sabine. You come with me at least?" Sara smiled, and Miriam noticed the mud on her teeth.

"You needs to get yourself cleaned up."

"I'll tell you on the way to the river. We can borrow a boat from someone."

They cut across the bayou towards the Sabine. It took another two days for the women to make it to the river. Miriam wished she'd stayed on the bus, but at this point she realized she needed to remain with her friend.

Maybe Sara grasped the truth to everything, or at least she'd found a key to something. Of course, Miriam stood aware of secrets about the Barnums, which Sara may or may not realize.

They kept trudging through the swamps towards the old homestead. The old Barnum land would soon be flooded by the damming of the Sabine for hydroelectricity. The Barnums already knew the area was damned.

"Remember Cletus Tree. We fooled around in it. I need to climb it one more time." Sara struggled to get inside. Her chest had developed a little further since teen years, plus she'd added extra pounds in her butt, but Sara Barnum still looked great. She climbed into the hollowed out, old and dead cypress tree. "Miri, I can't get my fat butt in here. Get your scrawny ass over here. I think there's some crap down at the bottom."

Miriam climbed the tree to crawl in. She still wore the same pretty Sunday dress, but this day, now Tuesday, and the dress also plastered in two-day old mud. Miriam crawled through the opening in the tree. She descended the ladder which still hung inside the tree. From the center of the hollowed-out tree, Miriam called out, "There's a strongbox at the bottom. I need to get it out. Climb up, and I'll drag it up here."

Miriam struggled, pulling the small chest towards the top. The ladder had been built in the tree long before the civil war, but it still held together. Maybe someone replaced the crossbars.

She struggled to the top of the rungs and slid the chest out the opening. Sara grabbed it and tried to navigate to the bottom of the tree with it but dropped it towards the bank. She splashed into the Sabine, a game they played as kids.

Miriam slithered through the hole like a snake and took one last leap into the river. They shook themselves dry as their clothes clung to their bodies, gathering their gear and their treasure. They struggled walking the riverbank, searching for a boat to borrow.

Hoboing south on the Sabine River in a stolen jon boat may not be the ideal way for Miriam to attend her father's funeral, but somehow, the perfect way to say goodbye to her friend, Sara Barnum. Sara, the disbarred attorney, now forced into living in Haiti, her homeland.

Her contact with her legal documents waited in New Orleans for her. Still wanted for murder, she was destined for exile. It took them another day to get to Sabine Lake at the mouth of the Sabine River. There they landed the boat and collapsed below the bridge.

"Dat's my story Sara. Da whole truth and nothin' but da truth."

Part 4
Chapter 25
Tallulah Til

"Miri, didn't you say you left that fat lawyer in April of 1938? Papi picked you up in the early fall. I think it was September." She glanced away from me for a minute, as her head shook with the breeze of the tall trees standing high above the waters of the lake dividing Texas and Louisiana. "Miriam Landry you haven't told me everything, have you? You know you can trust me." My lips puckered up and gave her a fake kiss from across the table. After twenty years, I'd never figure out our relationship and probably never will.

"Sara, I is glad you is sitting down. This is gonna knock you on your ass."

"Ou se pi bon zanmi mwen "

"Oh, I'm gonna tell ya everything, and I'm glad you got dat notebook. Got yaself a pen or pencil?"

I sat with an open notebook on a large rock, with pen in hand, and her hand on her chin. My gaze focused on Miriam, waiting for her to reveal the lost song. My family always wondered if she kept a secret, the way she hid in the shadows. Yes, there was something about her, and now Miriam would reveal her secret to me, Sara Barnum. I was about to get that elusive lost song of Miriam Landry.

April 1938

229

Miriam crossed the tracks in Shreveport and went from the ritzy upper-class white section of town, where she lived with the obese piss-ant Judge Mitchell towards the section of town where the petite girl seemed at home. Prostitution used to be legal in the Bottoms, and in 1917 laws passed to make it illegal, but the different bills didn't stop the trafficking. It created additional bribery, and different ways the elite made unaccountable money.

Miriam Landry no longer desired to work the streets, and no way she was going to be anyone's whore. She lacked in confidence and required that someone believe in her. The woman, stuck with the Blues inside her, became angry after leaving the Judge. Although her musical talent developed, she lacked confidence or flair.

If the Indians walked to Oklahoma from Georgia and the Carolinas, Miriam Landry started her own Trail of Tears and hiked towards Mississippi. She pocketed money from The Mitchells, plus what she saved, and managed a few dollars she got from hooking the last few days. She'd hit a pawn shop and get herself a used Stella once she crossed the river.

Miriam knew she required extra money. Worn out from freelancing on the street, she needed a bed to sleep in, and give them boys something they craved. The younger boisterous boys desiring their noodle wet. Miriam became picky about the boys, however her heart set on a Stella guitar.

She preferred to only give oral sex. The boys didn't care, they lusted to get off, and older married men whose wives refused to go down on them also came calling. They carried extra money.

Some piles of garbage separated Fannin Street from a row of shanty-appearing shacks she used to call home. As she stumbled and lost her balance, she reached with her left hand to break her fall and grabbed a shattered empty bottle of Jax beer. The girl balanced herself without slicing her hand. The government camps designed for the Okies and Arkies during the dust bowl seemed better constructed than these pieces of plywood and cardboard. After stumbling across the garbage, she meandered along the street. Miriam knocked on the door on the third to last house on the block. Knocking too hard made the shanties fall like dominoes. The flimsy houses contained no toilets. She glanced at the outhouses and took a deep breath before she knocked.

A short heavy-set woman opened the door. The prostitutes living in the shanty wondered what gender Madam Lavell was. She always received the most money, the sum of an average prostitute in Shreveport. The girls living in the shacks made half as much.

"What you doing here?" she asked Miriam.

"I'm looking for some work. I don't like working the streets. Is Felicia still here?"

"Fuck dat bitch Felicia. She ran off with half my money, so fuck her, and fuck you. Do you remember the looks you was giving these hoes when da Judge hired ya? You was strutting all over da place like some uncooked hen. You just a ungrateful l'il bitch. We all know what dat fat judge is about. We all knows what you put up with, cause most of these girls were there too. I even 'member telling you not to ever set foot down here again, and I hears you is walking round the Bottoms here. Get the fuck out of here, or I'm calling the police on ya. You know I gots me p'tection.

"I ain't gots nowhere to go. I ain't goin' back to dat judge."

"Go home to your mama, little bitch. I know you want to." Madam Lavelle smiled at her, exposing the gums where her three missing teeth once were. "Now stay da fuck out of da Bottoms." She slammed the door in Miriam's face.

Miriam spun around and retreated, climbed over the stacked garbage and tramped to the business district. Beer houses, juke-joints, and groceries stores sat abandoned as the streets ranged empty without their weekday parked vehicles.

Miriam decided leaving Shreveport behind would be her best option. Sitting underneath the Jax Beer sign at Freeman and Harris Café, she plotted her excursion towards Mississippi. The café's sign said *open*, but she had no desire to spend the cash she earned on anything, not even a bowl of grits.

Sitting outside on the step with legs spread, Miriam lowered her head towards her knees and started speaking unintelligibly. Those who passed figured she spoke in tongues, but no one knew for sure. Miriam had been raised Creole, with several religious influences, but she never went anywhere without her gris-gris bag.

Somehow, somewhere. and sometime a 1935 Cadillac parked besides Loves Café. The woman driver went inside, grabbed a seat and got herself a nice big breakfast, eating it without a care. The larger woman sliced her grub and sipped her coffee as she read the Shreveport paper. Oblivious to this woman, Miriam sat with her head buried in her hands, praying. She paid no mind to the car and started her walk towards Mississippi.

The headlining performers learned the Blues from pain escaping body and soul. The music served as a release from the suffering and torture of a miserable and abused life, passionate and beautiful. The greater the pain, the more incredible the music.

Miriam possessed the demons, and she acquired the talent. She required confidence, and an opportunity. Miriam continued her own Trail of Tears.

Ms. Landry was aware her talent exceeded most of the female Blues singers she listened to. Her music wasn't raunchy, even though when she relaxed and had some fun, she whipped a ditty, making an old bluesman blush. Her songs weren't about sex, but she sang about men who abused a fifteen-year old girl.

Mississippi lay one hundred seventy miles east of Shreveport. It lay across the river from Tallulah. Miriam, young, pretty with nice legs and a cute bottom, could catch a ride easy. She made it out of town on the opening day of her journey. The Bossier City water tower stood tall five miles behind her when a bright shiny Cadillac whizzed by. Inside was a woman driver who carried a few guitars and several suitcases in the rear seat with. Miriam toted her bindle stick with the red and plaid bandana. Her gris-gris bag snuggled in her overalls pocket.

The car sped past her at about fifty miles per hour, she figured. In the distance, she noticed the vehicle stopped and parked beside the road. She didn't remember how the driver looked, since the car sped by too fast.

Miriam wished she possessed a gun for protection instead of her switchblade. She had her looks and gris-gris bag, but her pleasing appearance could get her into trouble. She continued to walk towards the car, hoping the driver turned out to be a courteous soul, who would be willing to give her a ride to the neighboring state.

Miriam had run into celebrities before. After all, Tommie Lightning Bug Parker was with her when she was fifteen. They visited several juke joints, beer barrel houses, and fish fries where they met famous and not-so-famous bluesmen. Also, local politicians stopped by the whorehouse and she served the governor, mayor and one congressman. She recognized them from their pictures in newsreels and newspapers she couldn't read.

The driver refused to put the car reverse, while Miriam made her slow stroll towards the Caddy. She observed that the person in the car was a woman and took in three guitars in the rear. Miriam exhaled as she quickened her step. She hurried to the passenger door of the car. The woman sat waiting and smiling at her.

"Where da fuck you going?" the woman asked her.

"I don't know. Maybe Miss'ssippi. I wants to play some Blues, but I ain't got no guitar no more. I had me an ol' cigar box, so I kick ass on da slide."

"Hop in. You is coming with me." The woman smiled at Miriam. Her grin beckoned Miriam towards her, as she strolled closer. The driver's smile would make any stranger comfortable. It made Miriam anxious, but putting Miriam at ease took more than a suggestion of happiness. She opened the car door and sat in the passenger seat, setting the bindle stick in the back seat next to the Stella guitar.

The woman continued gawking at Miriam, hoping she recognized her. "I seed you down on Fannin before. You was hooking where I did me a show last night. Dat's where I seed you before."

The previous night Miriam Landry worked a barrel house where the famous woman Blues singer Tallulah Til performed to a drunk Black audience and put on quite a show. Miriam Landry sat in amazement as the woman shredded the guitar, making men and women eat out of the palm of her hand. Miriam refused all her suitors. She realized what she desired in life and realized there were other ways out of the swamp. She already tried two of the three methods her mama told her, and she played the guitar better than most people she ran into. Performance issues haunted her.

Miriam flashed a rare half smile smiled at Til, "Ms. Til, can you teach me to play like you.?"

Til smiled at her. The car still sat stationary east of Bossier City. "Let me hear what you can do." Til gave her the cheap guitar, the one ordered from a Montgomery Ward catalog. It evolved into the six-string which would give its life for the owner if she was attacked by a jealous fan or even the Klan.

"It's set for open G." Til whipped a knife out of her purse, and the blade snapped out towards her face. Miriam's eyes followed the it as the shiny blade reflected the high Louisiana sun, and she jerked a few inches in the seat. "Don't worry none, sweet girl. This is my slide. I want to hear you play the slide guitar. You says you can, now I wants to see if you can."

Miriam strummed the guitar, tuned in open G, in perfect rhythm. Short fingered Miriam preferred playing with this tuning, but she still loved her finger picking.

The rhythm of the South, more than banjos, guitars, fiddles, and washboards, was that of the river flowing downstream. Miriam heard the rhythm of canoes paddles slashing the water, and the cadence of the freight train rolling towards the gulf. She nabbed the blade of the glowing knife and tore it across the strings, placing the knife, blade down, on the fifth fret, slid it to the seventh and down to the twelfth fret, producing a G chord of a different octave. She slid the knife back and forth, performed a turn-around with her finger picking and repeated.

Ms. Landry never performed better than her initial performance for Til. She smiled at Til, as the Blues Mama took her hands off the wheel and applauded her. Miriam returned the guitar to the rear seat, wiped her hands against one another, rotated her head and smiled at the driver.

"Congratulations. You play just fine. I'm gonna take you under my wing."

Starting the car, Til and Miriam drove east towards Mississippi. Til got the car going straight, and removing both arms from the steering wheel, she stretched out her hands. Her left arm hung out the driver's window and her right arm went around Miriam.

"Ya sees I'm taking you under my wing. Now com'ere." Miriam scooted her little ass alongside Til's thicker butt. The blues woman embraced her. She held her closer as she pulled little Miriam into her large bosom. She peeked down and smiled at her. "I's gonna teach you everything you need to know about da Blues. What you say your name was?"

Miriam still snuggled her head into the large breasts of Til. She peered up at her. "Miriam, but I got friends that call me Miri."

"Mara. I like me Mara. Can I call you Mara? 'Cuz that's gonna be your new name."

"Teach me to play like you and you can call me anything you wants." Miriam smiled at Til. "So, Mara like Tamara?" Miss Landry let out a little laugh.

"No sweet sugar. Like today. Like right now." While driving east along the road, Til ogled Miri. She leaned towards Miriam and kissed her on the lips. Miriam reciprocated. The Caddy drifted off the road while Til controlled the car. It rested near a forest of Pecan trees west of Monroe. The two women kissed for a few hours while their hands explored.

The origin of the word Mara is death, but Miriam had no clue. Buddhists believe Mara means the devil, although Miriam stood ignorant of this meaning.

Miriam's accent grew thick when dealing with another South Louisiana Creole. When she lived in the northern part of the state, her speech was more understandable to non-Southern speakers. When she met someone from "Da Boot," she damn near lost it. Til came from New Orleans.

Til's competition included Memphis Minnie, Bessie Smith and Ethel Waters, plus women like Mattie Delaney. Til displayed her talents, but she was deficient in the charisma Bessie exuded. She lacked Minnie's flair and she palely imitated Ma Rainey's smut. Except for Minnie who played with another guitarist, the rest employed orchestras, showgirls and the whole bit. Til played the country Delta Blues, like Minnie, and the woman played better than most. Some of Til's listeners thought there was no one better. Til yearned for a larger fan base. She sought something or someone special.

Chapter 26
Lovers

The Barnum family loved Til's music. Radio stations from Memphis to Macon to Mobile played her music. Bo and Sara Barnum, both huge fans of Til, listened to her on the radio and purchased her records. In fact, he pondered the idea of becoming her chauffer, before he met Miriam. Bo, had been a professional driver at one time, and Til liked her whiskey. The combination may have been perfect. Sara quit playing her zydeco for a period thanks to Til's greasy playing. Til's influence was responsible for the grit in Sara's voice.

Til also kept with a large stable of lovers. An open bisexual, she adored her younger prodigies. Rumors circulated around the Chitlin Circuit that she screwed the younger Ray Wilson and took him beneath her wing and tutored him.

Ray Wilson was the latest phenomenon in the Delta, hoboing across the country, doing backdoor loving, making husbands jealous, and increasing the murder rate in Arkansas, Louisiana and Mississippi, one ex-wife at a time. Before she gave him the lessons, the light-skinned Creole man was nothing but a two-bit hack, following Son House and Charlie Patton around hoping for a gig. He made his second trip across the Sabine River to make another record.

Nobody realized how influential of a record this would become. No one ever figured some British blokes twenty-five years later might cover his songs. There wasn't a soul who predicted the modern-day folk singer would cherish his music. Nobody predicted this man would become a legend.

Miriam stayed snuggled in Til's boobs, without a care in the world, while they crossed Louisiana in a warm spring evening in Til's Caddy. They scooted along US highway 80 east of Shreveport, headed towards Monroe, Tallulah and the state line. Billboard signs and mile markers flashed by like one of those animations you draw yourself on blank pages.

"Right there, look Mara, right there." Miriam broke loose from Til's bosom and sat upright in the passenger seat. Til's right arm went across Miriam and pointed out the window. "Dat motherfucking Henry Melvin bitch, or something like dat, set up them crooks, Bonnie and Clyde. Dat's where's dey were killed. Took about one hundred- seventy-five bullets. Do you know who Bonnie and Clyde were?"

"Dat fat Judge Mitchell dat I was living with was talking about how bad they was." She paused as her eyes got brighter. Soon she smiled a small smile—witnessing Miriam Landry's smile is nothing short of a miracle from God. "They must have been heroes."

Til glanced towards her new-found friend Miriam and smiled back at her. She ran her fingers through her hair as she held the steering wheel with her left hand. "Mara, they weren't no heroes. They robbed little stores and gas stations. If they was robbing banks, it would have been different. Stealing from those that steal from black folk and poor folk is one thing, but you begin stealing from working folk, dat's another show. You follow?" Til punched Miriam on the shoulder and smiled at her.

"Yeah, I think so. Them folks dey was stealing from just hard-working folks. Dey should have been stealing from the rich folks like that Robin Hood guy." She continued to smile at Til. She swished her hair as it blew in the breeze.

"Back in thirty-three, me and my chauffeur was driving east of Dallas, down by Tyler, and this car comes a'rolling up at high speed. Guns were firing, and they ran us off the road. We was lucky to be alive. Not sure if it was them or not, but folks were saying they passed that way."

"They wouldn't scare me none. I'd go after dem with this knife. They wouldn't know what hit them." Miriam smiled at Til again, pointing Til's blade at the singer. She snapped it shut.

"You know Mara, I used to support folks that robbed from the rich, but once I started making me some money, I looked at folks different. I used to think dat poor bank robber, robbing banks and gas stations, just to feed his lady and kids, well now that I got me some money, I wants to hang on to it. You hear me? You might wants to buy a new purdy dress for yourself, or a purdy dress for some purdy girl you met dat used to walk the streets of Shreveport, selling herself for five bucks so she can get a meal. Maybe some purdy dress dat young girl could wear, that would take me to the Promised Land. I'm gonna look her all over and look down and imagine dat Promised Land. Like I is doing right now." Til placed her index finger of her right hand on Miriam's lips. Miriam kissed her finger and sucked it for a minute. Without breaking contact Til's hand caressed her face, neck and between Miriam's breasts towards her Promised Land. Miriam smiled at her older mentor and placed her hand on Til's holding it in Paradise.

Til parked the vehicle before they reached

Monroe. She couldn't wait until they got to her home. Til found a spot secluded off the highway, so they got comfortable together. She ravaged Miriam, and Miriam returned the favor. Miriam enjoyed the ride from Monroe to Til's hometown.

The woman kept Miriam happy as they chatted. "Do you believe in The Lord, Mara? I know I believe. Money changes you. Even the Bible says the love of money is the root of all evil."

Miriam sighed and moaned, responded. "I'm not sure anymore. When we was little, I believed, but since I been on my own, I'm not sure if I do. Was The Lord p'tecting me, when dat fat judge was peeing on my little tits, and in my face. Taking his goo was bad enough. Why wasn't The Lord p'tecting me? Dat's why I'm not sure if I believe in him or not."

"You have a lot to learn, pretty girl. The Lord works in mysterious ways. Oh, baby, he's there. He was just teaching you some lessons. Sometimes you have to know what you don't want to know what you want." Til used another finger as Miriam let out a beautiful scream of pleasure."

"I knows what I wants now, and it ain't no rich judge."

"What do you want?"

"I want to be your lover, and you can teach me guitar better and how to perform, plus all dat other stuff too."

Til removed her extra-long fingers from Miriam's love pocket, brought them to her own face and kissed them. She smiled at Miriam as they entered Tallulah Til's hometown in Northeastern Louisiana.

Her home, located in a nicer area of the black

section of town wasn't electrified yet, but at least the plumbing worked. The porch wrapped around her house, making a perfect place to play some zydeco or Blues music. The porch, elevated from the ground a few feet, contained a wooden rocking chair, where Til smoked her corncob pipe, cigarettes, and cigars. Her home contained six rooms with two bedrooms, living room, bathroom, large kitchen, and a small dining area.

"Let's take a bath first Mara, then a nap and I will teach you everything."

She swatted Miriam on her butt and Til yanked her own clothes off her body. Her oversized breasts lost some perkiness and dropped a tad. She shook them, so Miriam got a glimpse. Til hugged Miriam from behind, squeezing her body against her back, then squeezing Miriam's tight bottom. With a quick motion Miriam pulled off her flimsy summer dress.

The tub filled with bubbles and warm water. Both naked women climbed into the white porcelain basin. Miriam sat astride Til while they got clean. The older lady washed her young protégé, not missing an inch of her young torso.

Their bath lasted a while as Til took advantage of the willing Miriam. The girl relaxed as Til catered to her desires. She led Miriam to the bed where the famous woman singer gave the young girl a deep back rub and let Miriam nap in peace.

When Miriam awoke they moved to the kitchen where the crawfish boiled, the gumbo bubbled, and the cornbread baked in the oven, and the stove released a tantalizing aroma of Louisiana cooking. The South always breathed sweeter when someone cooked something, whether inside or outside.

Til filled a mason jar of shine for herself, while the non-drinker Miriam drank a jar of lemonade. Til tuned both guitars, initiating her plan.

"OK Mara, you is my girl now, and I going to teach you everything you need to know about being a blues woman. I know that's what's you wants to do, but first things first. Lets me feed you some gumbo." Til grabbed herself a big spoon, a bowl and a big piece of cornbread. The cornbread came out of the oven a nice brownish yellow, while the gumbo came out a deep shade of brown, and the crawfish floated around with the okra and sausage in the stew.

Miriam inhaled, taking in the essence of Til's culinary skills, as her sweet smile took hold. The girl didn't smile much, but she could make a man or woman fall in love with her when she exposed her crooked teeth. Her big brown eyes got wide, as her lips raised and separated and she exposed her crooked, yellow teeth. Her smile wouldn't appearing in fashion magazines, but genuine smiles conveyed sincerity, with her teeth exposed to the world. Everyone realized she stood in bliss. Her grin melted hearts.

Til sliced off one big hunk of cornbread. She took a bite and licked her chops with a slow movement of her tongue. Miriam's eyes focused on her mouth. Til stretched her arm and gave Miriam a bite of the bread. Miriam returned the tongue waggling. They continued sharing the cornbread until the yellow bread was all gone. Til took the spoon out of the gumbo, and some of the broth spilled off the spoon and into the rice filled bowl. She placed it directly into Miriam's waiting mouth. Miriam opened wide, allowing herself to be fed. They exchanged bites and slurps and Til even dunked the

243

cornbread into the gumbo as she fed Miriam.

Food can be seduction, and another love making session followed Then it was time for the music lessons.

The mentor walked towards the kitchen wearing her untied robe and returned with a butter knife. "You got no pipe, no bottle, you can use one of these things to go up and down da strings. Makes da guitar cry and scream. Dat's da sound you want."

She threw the knife towards Miriam, and it flipped about four times. Miriam, still naked, caught it by the handle. Til walked towards her and sat beside her on the bed, eying the girl again. Til's lips scrunched a little and so did her eyes. "If you is out on da road, and don't got no butter knife, you can use this, if you carrying one. I think you should carry one of these at all times." She pressed the button on the switchblade and the blade flashed near Miriam's cheek. Miriam eyed the blade as it rested about an inch from her. "You carrying a blade, aren't you?"

"Yeah, I got your blade from earlier, plus I always carry me another. I just use it to slide down the strings. I don't think I could cut anybody."

"That's da best news I've a heard in a long time, Mara, cause I get to teach you everything now. You gonna be my student, and my little bitch. We gonna do right. Just stick with me girl. Ya hear me?" She stood and walked across the room. Her smile reminded Miriam of a scientist in a monster movie, and her laugh resembled one too. Miriam glanced at Til, confused and wearing a blank expression that told it all. She began to wonder why Til called her Mara.

"So, Mara, you have already pass da first lesson. Dat is to keep me satisfied. You do them things well to me baby. You also so sweet and taste so sweet. I want you all da time. I got to make sure you can cook, so you is making dinner tonight. If I doesn't like your cooking, you could be out da door. I can teach one to eat my pussy, but making good chicken, and gumbo outranks your pussy licking, baby."

She strolled towards Miriam and kissed her cheek, licked her face with her long tongue. She resembled a dog when the master came home, the way she slurped Miriam's face. "I don't give a crap about cleaning, just pick up after yourself and me. I ain't dat messy so it shouldn't be no problem." Til dropped something on the floor behind Miriam, so the girl leaned over to retrieve it. Miriam exposed her bottom, and Til grabbed a handful. Soon Til carried Miriam into the bedroom. Once again Miriam passed Lesson One.

They stretched out on Til's large bed as Miriam set her head on Til's stomach. "I cooked for Lightning Bug. Grabbed chickens out of da hen house and stripped dem clean and cooked dem in da fryer, da oven, and on da firepit. I been doing dat all my life. My crawfish pie is da best, and I make me damn good gumbo and turtle soup. Breakfast is biscuits and gravy, and my gravy is da tastiest."

Til stroked Miriam's hair. "Sweetheart, I know your gravy is da best thing in da world. I loves ya sweet gravy baby, but we gonna have some work for ya. So, sugar, do you wanna stick wid me?"

"More than anything. I wants to play guitar and sing songs with you and on my own. I wants to be your lover. I don't want no man fucking me. You make me feel things inside dat I never felt wid no man. Dey just stick it in and explode. You treat me so good down dere."

"Okay, girl, just tells me you loves me, and will be my girl forever, and I'm gonna give you more magic. Also means dat if you fuck any man or woman after me, dey gonna have some bad luck. Dat ways you can't cheat on me."

"What's if we ain't together no more? Then I can't fuck no one?"

"You can't fuck no one as long as I live, and them voodoo queens says I can live forever. Now do you still love me? This is your last chance."

"I love ya, Til. Now I want to take more lessons."

Chapter 27
The Deal

Til never told Miriam who taught her the Blues. Folks near the Tallahatchie River, in the Mississippi Delta, acknowledge no one learns the Blues, you're born with them. Til, not a natural musician, worked hard perfecting her craft. She practiced, met other musicians and challenged herself to improve. Folks like Early Greene played anything and everything he desired. Bo Barnum worked his butt off learning to play. No one considered him talented, but he played with passion. Sara Barnum, unlike her father, was a natural musician, since she learned guitar and harp at an early age and made music all her life. Lightning Bug Parker, Miriam's former lover, another natural talent who also practiced, practiced and practiced, but he worked hard on his performance, and hid his deficiencies with some fancy moves. Miriam's skill took off after the abortion. Maybe the spirit inside her helped.

Til's family came from New Orleans, and prior to the living in the Crescent City her family immigrated from Haiti. The singer was known for her magic, or at least she became well versed in it.

"Mara, come here and sit down." She patted the edge of the bed as she smiled at Miriam. With her other hand she pointed at the spot beside her, where she wanted her young lover to sit. Her index fingers, longer than most, aided her in seducing the guitar. Longer fingers enabled an axe player to barre the chords much easier. Miriam stuck to playing the slide with her dainty hands.

Miriam also wondered in the three days she spent with Til, why the hell hadn't she noticed the gross digits. "I don't want you telling nobody about this."

"I promise ya, Til. I ain't telling nobody."

"I cross da river in Mississippi and went up where highways sixty-one and eighty-two intersect. I know me a couple men up there near Indianola. Ones of dem is that singer Ray Wilson and dis other man, well, I just call him Papa. Papa is Papa Legba. Dat man's a nice man, as long as you does what he asks you too."

"I think I saw dat man down in Ter…"

"Hush girl. I is still talking. Anyways I met Papa where the highways cross. I don't see him at first, so I goes by da only tree nearby. Can't believe in this damn delta dere aren't any trees around but this one. It's real hot out, and I wants to sit in da shade. I sits down under dat tree and starts a'picking my guitar, playing the Blues dey play over here, singing one of Charlie's songs, and dis man show up out of nowhere. Whoosh. Straight out of nowhere, like he drop from da sky." Til pointed towards the ceiling, dropping her arms with a vengeance.

"Well, he says his name is Papa and he wears hisself a nice suit, with dat silly string tie, and is always smoking hisself a corn-cob pipe. He's also wearing a big straw hat, to protects dat scaly scalp from da hot Mississippi sun."

"So, this man teaches you guitar?"

"I says hush girl, shuts you trap, I's still talking." Miriam rolled her eyes a little, but the narcissist woman didn't notice. Til continued, "Anyways dat man takes my National guitar, looks it over really good, from neck to the body, just like I looks you over real good from your purdy face to that nice little bottom of yours." She

248

stopped for a second. "Now stand up and turn around." Miriam twirled like a ballet dancer, as Til gave her bottom a swat. Miriam smiled and sat closer to Til. Til continued, "Now where was I? Dat bottom of yours got me distracted. Oh yeah, dat man grabs my guitar, starts a'strumming it. I always keep dat one in G, but he played with da tuners, tuned it down to open D, and gave dat motherfucking thing back to me. Dat was it."

"Was it like magic dat he appeared?"

Of course, Mara, dat's why you can't tell a soul, and I mean no one." She winked at Miriam. "Papa took him a big puff on dat pipe of his, blew himself a smoke ring. I swear I thought I saw smoke coming out his ears. Then he says, Miss Til, I been expecting you. Glad we finally meet. He takes off that ugly hat and bows down, sticking one hand over his belly. Den he ax me, 'What you need me for?'"

"I told him, 'I wants to have da best of everything. I is tired of scraping da bottom for my young girls, and I needs to be better dan dat bitch, Memphis Minnie. I is da best Blues singer. I also needs me a real talented girl to take over for me in case I gets killed or something.'"

"'Where are you staying?' He ax me.

"I says, 'I is flopping out in a barn down yonder.' I point east towards Indianola. 'Why ya wanna know?' He bows again and tips dat hat. 'I need to know what you like, so I get the right girl for ya.'

"He smiles dat sly grin of his and we walk to da barn and fuck. Damn devil, he ain't even fuck good."

She laughed out loud. Her laughter bellowed throughout the room, and Miriam fell on the floor listening to her story. Til helped Miriam stand and pulled her onto her lap. "Da Devil told me I liked young pretty women dat play guitar."

"What happened to him?" Miriam asked her mentor.

"After we was done, he just went out da door and he's vanished like a little black boy wanted for stealing bread for his family."

"Now you sure you want to go through wid this?" She studied Miriam, seeing her prodigy fit her idea of perfection. Papa's work, always out of this world. The desperate become perfect partners or employees. They rose from the dead countless times, only to be kicked to the curb. You push them around and around, and they keep fighting forward. On occasion, you flatten your partner, to witness how they rise. Plus, they never leave. Once departed, one starts on the bottom.

She gazed deep into Miriam's eyes, and she scanned Miriam's body. She undressed her with her vision. "Mm-mm-mmm," Til kept repeating as the smile came on her face. She placed her giant fingers between Miriam's legs and rubbed as Miriam opened for her. "Now I know we've been doing this since we met, but dat was all in fun, this is real." She massaged Miriam's privates.

"Of course, Til. I ain't got shit for a life anyway. Some motherfucker just going to rape me. My daddy's fiddle player raped me, dat judge raped me, Lightning Bug didn't rape me, but beat me. The only nice guys in my life were those kids that paid for me. Unless you set me free, it's going to be more of the same."

"Once we finish there can't be no one else but me. You screw someone else man or woman, your life will be jinxed, and I'm eternal now. Understand? Ain't many ways you can get rid of me now. I like you Mara, and

250

you're free to go if you choose. Just can't say nuttin."

Miriam beamed at Tallulah Til. "I prayed out there on Fannin, and suddenly you showed up. You might be da answer to my prayers." Miriam arose, walked closer to Til and wrapped her arms around the wider woman. "Will I be eternal?"

"No Mara, you still be mortal, but there be a spell on ya. Someone can kill ya just like dat." She snapped her fingers close to Miriam's ear.

Miriam didn't flinch. "I think the devil already got a spell on me. I needs me to do good in life. Prove all dem mudderfuckers wrong."

"Les go in da bedroom again Mara. You gotta do things to me. Then I gonna teach you guitar, da Delta way. Teach you all da licks. You know a bunch already."

She flicked her tongue out at her young girlfriend and winked. Miriam swirled hers in return, as Til grabbed Miriam's hand and led her to their bedroom. Til showed her licks and Miriam once again reciprocated.

Once they finished, Til showed Miriam the way the masters play guitar in Mississippi. Rumors said she taught Ray Wilson how to play and no one compared to him. Ray evolved into the leader of the Chitlin Circuit, as he hoboed across the country hitching rides, hopping freights and entertaining the countryside with his dancing, singing and guitar playing.

Miriam didn't seem any different. She didn't notice the spell on her, in fact she got blessed with something unfamiliar to her. Confidence in her abilities, shown in her face and the way she moved her fingers across the strings. In some worlds a shot of confidence is called a magic spell. She found confidence and someone to support her abilities. Still she wondered if the gypsy, back alley abortionist put a spell on her, or if her aborted baby carried one. She often wondered, but she traveled with someone named Tallulah Til, and the witch trusted her.

Til took her as far north as Chicago, and they played Memphis. Miriam treasured riding in Til's Caddy. Traveling in her Caddy became much safer than hitching or train hopping. She loved it as the wind blew her hair all around, as they cruised the country with the top down. The two lovebirds caressed one another as often as possible, and often gave the truck drivers a quick little thrill as they passed the ladies. Besides Chicago, Til took Miriam all the way to Atlanta. Miriam performed with Til but never soloed. She played the slide and harmonized with her mentor. With the Blues inside them, they shared them with the world. Miriam craved more.

"Can I play some of my songs baby? I wants to do dat one about da whorehouse in Narleans. You know I play and sing it really good." She made her eyes so big and shiny, it was inconceivable mortal human could resist her charm.

Til, put the kabosh on her notion, and Miriam began to wonder she resembled something rhyming with witch. "This is my show. Folks ain't paying no two bits to come see you. Who da fuck you think you are?"

"Just one song?" Miriam pleaded with her, rubbing Til's upper thigh as they crossed the Tennessee River near Muscle Shoals, Alabama on the way to Atlanta.

An eerie silence filled the car as they crossed the river. Crossing the bridge, noises emerged from the water as the river sang its song. They glanced at one another speechless, as if magic came from below the bridge.

252

Miriam's eyelashes fluttered several times as she continued to stare at Til. Miriam concluded she's irresistible.

"I says no, and I means no, bitch. Now gets your hand up dere where it belongs and do your main job. Next show you ain't playing at all. Know your role, dat's da first thing you gotta learn." Miriam realized what she meant and kept her trap shut. Alabama's history was as bad as Mississippi for their treatment of Negroes. If abandoned beside the road, she wouldn't even qualify for a statistic. She'd go unnoticed, another missing Negro girl, and no one cared if anyone kept track of the dead or missing.

Besides Til and Miriam scorching Dixie again, becoming mainstays in Coahoma County, in Mississippi, the other Blues players included Son House, Muddy Waters, Ray Wilson and Mojo Davis. The latter was a younger man Miriam met later in her stay in Chicago. Mud and Mojo led the great northward migration, and along with Son House and Charley Patton, influenced hundreds of players throughout the region. The torch passed to the stranger in town, and a kid rumored to receive Til's special training. Til bragged about it, but others in the Delta disputed their relationship.

Chapter 28
Raymond Melvin Wilson

As a young musician, Ray Wilson lacked talent. He hung out with Son House, Charley Patton, Willie Brown and other famous bluesmen in the Delta. Never the prodigy some of the other men claimed to be. His playing ran to the mediocre and his songwriting skills needed improvement. There was no way the crew could have predicted the future that lay ahead of him. There wasn't any way this man possessed the ability to change the face of music thirty years later. In fact, a few of these legends and future legends treated him like a stray dog. The men often threw him a bone, or tossed him a stick, hoping he would run off, but the youngster kept returning. They couldn't shoo him away easy. The clique sought extra creativity.

Ray met Til at a show near Friars Point, across the river from West Helena. She changed his life forever, and Til assumed Ray would remain grateful towards her through eternity.

Mr. Wilson appreciated three things. Women, whiskey and music. The rankings of his priority were questionable, since they changed every night. It depended on the woman, or the whiskey. Til also loved whiskey, women and her guitar, but she took a liking to the devilish handsome Raymond Melvin Wilson. Til confided to Miriam that Ray had been her sole male human lover. Her encounter with Papa at the crossroads didn't count, since the man wasn't human.

Three years earlier Til took Ray under her wing and taught the twenty-four-year-old young man everything he knew about singing, guitar playing, and loving and leaving women. The budding star changed lovers like socks. There were no issues with abandoning lovers, as a young bride waited at home in Louisiana for him.

Months into their relationship he traveled to Texas to record an album in a San Antonio hotel. Til acted like he abandoned her, stranded by a lone tree, where the highways crossed. She got on her knees and vomited as the flames burnt inside her gut, and the firestorm burnt inside her spiritual heart. She had been rejected by her lone mortal male lover to date.

****

Crossing into the Magnolia State from Alabama, Til told her little protégé something she shouldn't. Steering with her left hand, she placed her right hand in Miriam's lap. She massaged Miriam's thighs a little as a large diesel truck made a daring pass on the narrow highway. He had little room to pass as the driver hooted at the ladies and honked his horn. "Ray-Ray was my favorite loves of all da folks that touched this." She yanked Miriam's hand and placed it between her legs. "No one does me like he's ever done." She kept pressing Miriam's hand towards that special spot. "I means no one." Til glared at Miriam without her normal wicked, flirtatious smile, her sexy demeanor, or her demanding and demeaning actions.

Miriam glared at her mentor, wondering what the heck she'd been doing for the last few months. She pleased her lover, made her some grub, and she evolved into the magnificent little girlfriend Til required. She did Til right, but the loving words quit coming from the witch's mouth. The loving kisses Til gave Miriam, got replaced by forceful acts of desire for pleasure. As always Miriam obeyed, but pleasing your master as survival, and not for the sheer sake of enjoyment began taking its toll.

Til's old student was rumored to be playing on the West bank of the Mississippi, so she drove the scenic route home from Chicago, cutting through St. Louis. An old lover of both his and hers, knew of Ray's whereabouts, so Til and Miriam dropped by and spent the night. The three women spent some memorable time together. She also hinted to Til of Ray Wilson's itinerary.

Highway sixty-seven became Til's bitch as they headed through Missouri and sped across Northern Arkansas. Til heard rumors that Ray was playing at a small-time juke in Paragould, north of Jonesboro.

Somewhere near Jonesboro, Arkansas she spotted a man, playing guitar on the highway, trying to hitch a ride. She recognized his style, the way he shook. The light skinned Creole man hopped in the front seat blowing the harp, while the guitars, Miriam and the rest of the baggage piled in the rear. Til, grinned ear to ear, since her two proteges rode with her and the one in the next seat over, provided Til with something Miriam didn't possess.

It all went down in the middle of the town
Of Jonesboro, Arkansas.
There was the man, guitar in hand,
But blowing a harmonica.
Til was driving, I was riding,
In Jonesboro, Arkansas
I climbed in the back of her new Cadillac,
In Jonesboro, Arkansas.
In hopped the man, with guitar in hand,
But blowing a harmonica.

256

Summers in the Mississippi Delta weren't for the weak and weary. Endless heat, sunshine and humidity made for long days of sweat, anger and despair. Only the beauty of the people surpassed the beauty of the land. The farmers inherited their work ethic, plowing fields, sharecropping, and working eighteen hours a day.

A man pounded two rusty nails in the side of his house and hooked a single string of baling wire between them. He lodged a bottle neck under one end of the wire for a bridge. He built the toy on the side of the house, so his child wouldn't be running all over creation with it. Soon his kid played a one-stringed guitar, a diddley bow. The child plucked the string, slid a butter knife down the string, and made music. Pure beauty resounded in the way the kid learned his craft as he graduated to a cigar box guitar and played on the porch. Patton, Wilson, Waters, Johnson and Landry all learned this way.

Many former slaves moved to the Delta region for the fertile soil laid down by the Mississippi River floods. It spurned the talents of Charlie Patton, Son House and others. The area filled with large plantations, and each plantation became a little community with a grocery store, apothecary, and sometimes a juke joint, and whore houses for entertainment. Some of these little villages cooked their own whiskey on site. Others brought in bootleggers, like Bo Barnum.

By 1936 these singers either died, plotted a migration North, or went into semi-retirement by living the life of a Baptist preacher. This opened the door for the man from Houma, Louisiana to take control.

The musicians sprung from the area worked the fields all day for fourteen to fifteen hours, changed clothes, played until four in the morning, when the men went home and changed, and go tend the crops again.

Raymond Melvin Wilson soon became the biggest name in the Delta. The man became a gifted musician, whose original songs aided him in recording in San Antonio and Dallas. The man, a drifter, played anywhere and at any time. Not a natural musician, rumors around the South, in the Delta area of Mississippi said a devilish deal happened. Wilson, quiet in the Delta for about a year, left the likes of Patton, House and others. Rumors floated around he found a mortal teacher, a human who showed and taught him the techniques required, and ripped the soul out of his gut, enhancing the music. Locals said he met this woman, a heavier set woman, who sang incredibly. Nobody knew for sure if the bosomy dark-skinned girl, rumored to partner with the devil, made a deal. She either taught him, or seduced him, or both, passing on the skills. His everlasting soul given to a thick but chesty singer, but she taught him well. Til missed the man, and still desired him, and made plans.

The Caddy sped along Highway One in Eastern Arkansas leaving Jonesboro and heading towards West Helena. Til eyed the young, male singer. The Creole man's physique seemed average, maybe a little thinner than a field worker, and he was shorter than average. His light skin would never allow him to pass for Caucasian. Light skin meant privilege in Mississippi and Louisiana, at least more than the ancestry of slaves imported from Ghana and the other west African nations. The local bluesmen never developed privilege, even though their forefathers may have been kings and queens in their villages. He always seemed to dress nice in a suit and tie.

Creole and black musicians in the South never

knew when they'd get discovered, so they needed to look their grandest all the time. Til not only loved her women, she also loved one man. Ray Wilson, the man with small hands, but like Til, blessed with extra-long fingers. Til smiled, recognizing the meaning, and not about barring the strings. She smiled again, remembering their time together, and with Miriam Landry on board, the three became merrier.

The man hopped in the Caddy carrying a Stella and a Kalamazoo guitar. Miriam eyed his instruments like she desired them. Her eyes circled the curves, the body, the neck and the strings. She admired the craftsmanship of the guitars, like she admired Ray Wilson's physique. She also eyed him like she craved him, and she assumed they'd share the love. Her bus ticket already punched, she needed to hang on and enjoy the ride. Miriam didn't expect what was coming. No one did.

"Ray-Ray, I got you a little treat." Til said as they drove south across the Arkansas highway. Mr. Wilson scanned Miriam's body and smiled at Miriam, then smiled at Til.

"I likes what I sees, Miss Til." He kissed Til's hand, and gave Miriam's hand a quick peck, as he flashed his smile at both women. Not much conversation happened on the trip. In the month of August the harsh winds in Eastern Arkansas blew furious and loud, and with the top down on the Caddy, no one engaged in any conversation, but Ray Wilson spent most of his time glancing behind him at his new acquaintance. Miriam sat and smiled closed-mouth at the singer.

We were on the run, down Highway One,

Leaving Jonesboro, Arkansas.
Til had a plan with that Creole man,
Blowing that harmonica.
Until he looked in the back of her new Cadillac
And liked what he saw.
That brown skinned girl became his world,
South of Jonesboro, Arkansas.

Right before West Helena something popped in the rear. Til blew a tire on her car and she pulled off the road. "Mara, you need to change that now."

Miriam Landry with all her skills, from field stripping chickens, killing gators, making boots and belts from the reptiles, her music skills better than most, had never worked on an automobile. "I don't know how to change one."

"Til, I think we should just walk. Hoboing better for da Blues than riding around in a Caddy anyway. Plus, no better way to get acquainted with your friend."

Til obliged, and after Miriam pushed the car to a safe spot adjacent to a West Helena juke, they took off walking down the highway.

West Helena, Arkansas, lay across the mighty Mississippi from Clarksdale and the delta region. Clarksdale, the county seat of Coahoma County, sits near the Northern end of the Mississippi Delta. Cotton fields spread across the area outside the town limits, and inside the city boundaries. Shanties spread across the villages in which the sharecroppers lived, making a meager living off the landowners. A lot of the Negro sharecroppers worked the land and made enough to pay the rent.

On weekends the residents liked to drink the homemade whiskey, eat the fried catfish or chitlins, and listen to the local players troubadours traveling through. Men, women, boys and girls congregated, even though the stories of the juke joints didn't scare the young ones away. Shootings happened every night, and the sheriff's office didn't do a thing about it. If a killing occurred in a juke, that was one less Nigra to worry about, and they'd bleach Mississippi one person at a time.

"Over dere. Dat looks like a barn." Miriam pointed to the lone building standing above the horizon. She carried the man's guitar as they crossed the cotton fields towards the wooden structure. There are no beds in barns, but haylofts sit atop the storage facility. Haylofts make for comfortable sleeping, and a discreet place for sex, if the horses don't mind.

The first two nights the three of them enjoyed the pleasure a third wheel provides, especially when two thirds of the partners like each other, and don't mind sharing. Ray enjoyed his time, but he started to take a liking to the younger, thinner gal a little too much, and they often spent the intimate parts of the sex together. Til laid next to them snoring.

Walking into town for a quick breakfast of biscuits and gravy, eggs and grits, Miriam took the part of Ray's roadie as she carried his guitar. With her free hand, she held his as they strolled behind Til.

"You are something special," he told her as they walked past a silo. "I been married before, but she died delivering our baby. Got married a second time, but she done kicked me out. I like my rambling and such." He produced a grin stretching across the vast river to Mississippi. Miriam squeezed harder on his hand.

"Dat's ok. I's used to people rambling around on me. Go out playing dese jukes, it's gotta be hard to keeps to one woman."

She wet her lips with her tongue and smiled at him as the three of them walked south towards the ferry, which crossed the river into Mississippi. A couple of cars sped by. One flew the Stars and Bars flag. Slurs and insults followed, but nothing came of it. Soon, another Caddy came calling. This one stopped, and a well-groomed, tall, older Negro man got out. He wore his straw hat pulled down so it covered his eyes. He took a puff off his corncob pipe and waited for them. Ray recognized the second man still sitting in the passenger seat. The two old chums played the jukes together for a few years.

All three of them settled in the rear seat of the Caddy. With the gear stashed in the trunk, the well-groomed man in the passenger seat shook Ray's hand, while the driver focused straight ahead. "We got us jukes hooked up all da way to Indianola for next weekend. Think we mosey on down dere."

"You folks know Til? She's gonna wanna play, and dis special gal is Mara."

"Miriam." She interrupted him and hid behind Til, ashamed of her intruding.

"Sorry, her name Miriam, and she play purdy good. We gonna throw them on the show too. Plus, I'm hooked up already the next three days. We can meet you down there. We gonna hitch, just drop us off at the Ferry, so we can cross dat river."

They all gawked at Ray like he's crazy. Mouths and eyes wide open, like a freight was a'coming, but he was also the king. Not a demanding man, but his patrons knelt at his feet. Ray's friend dropped the group off near the main intersection in downtown Helena, Arkansas, next to the river. West Helena became famous for a radio show transmitted throughout the South. The two men recently left there.

After crossing the river, and hitching with a farmer, they found a different barn to snooze in. Inside sat plenty of stacked hay for the three to get comfortable together. Once again Miriam became the center of attention as two people desired her. One loved her, and the other used her. Miriam became aware of which one would evolve into the real lover, and which person toyed with her. However, given her past, sometimes distinguishing between the two becomes difficult.

After breakfast they hitched down Highway 61, as Ray opined to Miriam. "It's bad luck for me driving to gigs. I need to hop freights, or hitch. Brings out da real Blues in me. Folks driving fancy cars ain't got no blues— they got a car. We be down in Indianola before we know it. I just want to get to know you better." He flashed his smiled, started to play something funky on the guitar and danced in a circle around her, smiling all the way. Miriam blushed as Til led the way, oblivious to the goings on behind her.

Miriam glanced at him. She tried focusing her eyes on the swirling movements of his hips and torso, but it became difficult maintaining solid eye contact with him. She gasped when she took a breath. Her heart fluttered and skipped a beat. Her body temperature increased as if it was a Mississippi summer day. She considered herself knowledgeable about love and what it feels like, but she never experienced that special sensation. She never got mushy about Lightning. After all the man got her out of the swamp and helped her escape from the trauma of an abortion and rape.

Miriam glanced ahead towards Til. "Maybe we should catch up with her. Don't wanna make her mad. I's heard some stories."

"Les walk faster then." Ray increased the tempo on his guitar, and quit doing the circles around her, but he strode beside her, playing an up-tempo ditty, as Miriam carried Til's guitar towards her mentor.

Til heard the music playing behind her, and she spun around to see her former lover serenading her gal. Til eyed her young lover mooning over the legend like she loved the man, and Ray drooled over the young Miriam Landry. He gazed at her with simple innocence, gleaming at her with enormous brown eyes, and a smile, as wide as the river. They resembled two teenagers in math class, gazing across the classroom at each other, while Mr. Beauregard explained Geometry.

The man had seduced this child like a master how without even caressing her. Miriam at last became flirted back. Ray Wilson showed his love for her.

A pickup truck came cruising by heading south. An old white man dropped them off near Indianola in the early evening. Once again, the three shared a barn, and once again, the attention focused on Miriam from both. One of the two stimulated and pleased the young woman, while the older woman used her extended fingers for intense and pleasurable torture that surpassed the sexual torture she grew accustomed too. The music gig for the evening went off without a hitch, and the three returned to the barn for additional fun.

The following day they returned to the juke to play another show. They met Stoney there also. Together the foursome tore the signs off the walls with their music. The nails shot from the shingles on the rooftop. The joint, emitted a raucous racket, but no real damage was done. It didn't matter since the state police or the county deputies never did a thing. They always hoped for trouble. In 1938 Mississippi, the local law encouraged the killing of Negros. It didn't matter if a white man raped and lynched a black girl. It didn't matter if a white man shot an African American. The white folk stood their ground, defending their property. It didn't matter if the Negro passed by. Most of all the Mississippi politicians and law enforcement encouraged boisterous fighting in the jukes.

Chapter 29
The Deed

Could this have been Til's plan all along? She found the perfect bait to trap the trophy fish—the superstar who shunned her. Til loved fishing, and she never cherished cranking in the big ones right away. Let him run with the line, and yank him in. If the fish gets loose, too bad. She enjoyed the action. She loved hooking and landing the sweetest, spiciest and meatiest ones. Nothing beats a Louisiana fish fry.

After the show Til led them to the barn. Bound and determined to stage the proper send off, she planned a smorgasbord. Til swung the picnic basket of goodies she took from the juke joint, including boiled spiced crawfish, fried catfish and fried shrimp. For drinks, she had a jar of shine for herself and a jug of lemonade for her little vixen. She even packed some peach cobbler for Miriam and Ray although she desired something else for dessert. She craved her own all-you-can-eat buffet.

Miriam Landry demanded freedom and Ray Wilson gave her the greatest chance at independence. He yearned to roam alone, or he'd let her join him. Or maybe he'd ramble on and hobo to a different part of the country while she remained a homebody. In time he'd abandon her, play his little games with another woman in another town, county, state or region.

She desired indulging in the pleasures and music of Mr. Wilson. Miriam envied the passion he possessed, and she wanted the role of his muse, the inspiration behind his lustful, sinful songs. She pondered the idea that people all around might figure she was the girl in the song lyrics—the back-door romances, the back-alley abortions, the clap, whiskey dick, and body fluids dripping down her legs. She smiled at that idea. Miriam never caught a dose, but she experienced everything else in the last three year.

Most women swooned when they eyed the light-skinned Creole man. They loved his sandy-colored hair, covered by a dark fedora hat, and he always wore a suit and tie when performing. He performed about 300 days a year A sweet-talking man, he romanced Miriam either with a song on the guitar, harmonica or by singing acapella. He enjoyed doing jigs around her, and he even two-stepped with her. The man performed pirouettes, as he danced circles around her.

His music lit a fire in her. She no longer desired the oversized lesbian in her life. The spell Til told her she laid on her, she figured, was nothing but bullshit. Besides she still carried her gris-gris bag. Plus, she wondered if she might gander at the man again, driving Stoney's car, the man who played a song in Terrebonne Parish, the song she picked up in Shreveport, and the tune she listened to on the radio. Leadbelly performed it.

Til prepared her picnic dinner in the hayloft they shared the previous two nights. When the other two arrived, she greeted them at the barn door. She kissed them both. She kissed Miriam first, and she kissed her deeply, grabbing her butt, and licking her ears. She went to work on Ray and rubbed him up. "Wait here, guys. I gots a surprise for you." Til peeled off her clothes, hurling them here and there, and strutted towards the ladder, jiggling her bottom all the way.

Miriam and Ray followed, holding hands and

carrying guitars. They moaned as they watched her climb the rickety ladder, and both smiled as she ascended. They enjoyed the view.

Til climbed into the hayloft, naked as the day she came into this world. "C'mon sugars. Get dem sweet bodies up here. I got food, and we all gonna be dessert for each other." Til beckoned to them, but she should never have gone up first. Ray gleamed at Miriam. He kicked the ladder aside, and when it thudded, a puff of dirt rose the earth floor.

"Timber," Miriam said as they both found a private retreat away from the livestock that shared the bottom of the barn with them. Miriam took off her remaining clothes and wandered through the bottom of the building. The young girl took care of her lover, and he succumbed to her charms not once, but twice. Even with the loud shrill of Tallulah Til in the background, he fulfilled his obligation to Miriam a second time. Ain't that a man!

Miriam rested her head on Mr. Wilson's chest stroking his torso with her unkept fingernails, as he attempted to twirl her long nappy hair. She leaned to kiss him again, and he reciprocated. She smiled as the man caressed her. "Baby you must be something special. I'm usually long gone by now. We gonna do another show with Til tomorrow. I think I's gonna write us a duet. Gonna call it 'The Unmistakable Shrill of Tallulah Til.' You can help me write it baby." She pulled away for a minute, in wonder about the song the two might compose together.

He pulled her closer and whispered in her ear. "Some of you Louisiana women are sweeter than Molasses. Others…." He tilted his head towards the loft and the lady they stranded. She released a barrage of swear words about a fallen ladder in her unmistakable shrill which only Tallulah Til could release. Her booming voice echoed throughout the barn and woke the livestock. The horses started to whinny, and the cows mooed in harmony with the devilish female singer.

"Well they is not as sweet. I travel all over the country hopping freights, hitching rides and dat woman terrifies the bejesus out of me. She's da only bitch that scares da living shit out of me."

Miriam leaned in and whispered to her man. "She scares me too baby, but I thinks I owes her. She got me off da streets in Shreveport. Not sure where I'd be if it wasn't for her. Might be dead, and dat would have been better off."

"Don't say dat baby. You is cute and sweet." He leaned over and brushed his lips with hers. This time it wasn't about sex, but about intimacy. The greatest moments between a couple laying together, naked and vulnerable, caressing and kissing become electrifying.

They had piled their clothes beside his guitar case. He hovered above her still naked, while Miriam smiled. He strutted to grab his dark dress pants and returned to her. Miriam laid there smiling as a part of him swung like a pendulum. Tossing his trousers towards her, he curled beside his girlfriend. "Hey Baby, this is da best I got. Now I can't promise to be faithful. My life is to keep moving. I don't want no hellhounds a 'chasing me. I wants you to come out on da road with me, but baby, I needs my space. I likes to hobo around, but I ain't gonna leave you in no faraway place."

"Well I'm afraid of being attached too, baby, but it's something I wants to try with da right man. I knows we just met, but I think we gots what it takes." Miriam twirled her thick hair around her finger and wet her lips. Her eyes, big and brown, like a doe's that runs through the forest, gave Ray Wilson the image no living person could resist.

The man stuttered and took a deep breath. "B-baby, da way you just look at me, I couldn't say nothing." He caressed her face with his long fingers. "Since no girl ever made me speechless, you must be da one." He moved to where his jacket lay, placed a piece of a pipe that he used for his slide on the ring finger of his left hand, and returned to the pile of hay.

The slide, one of several in his collection became a memorable gift for Miriam. He struggled for the perfect wording, but he could barely get the sentence out of his mouth. He choked on his words, still stuttering while removing the pipe from his long digit.

The livestock still hollered in the background as Ray took Miriam's hand and separated her ring finger from the rest of her dainty hand. "I…uh, I ain't got no rings for ya, well, 'cause we just met, so this slide…it will have to do. Ya know, folks says this slide be magic, but it ain't." He hefted the metal in his hand. "You just gotta know how to use it, and baby, you know how to use your fingers," Ray laughed. "As well as other things. Uh, I mean, this ain't no magic slide at all, and I don't know why folks thinks I made me a deal with dat devil up there. Anyway, Til ain't no devil. She just a bitch."

Miriam busted a gut laughing with saliva spitting from her mouth, as tears of joy fell from her eyes. She attempted to wipe the grin off her face, but it seemed embedded. Now engaged, Ray sat back and admired his lover, giving her a huge smile of satisfaction.

His last wife had grown tired of his shenanigans on the road, after returning to their sharecropper quarters. He had sometimes taken the girl on the road with him, and sometimes she waited for his return in their cabin back in southwest Louisiana, fixing up the best gumbo. The woman claimed to have no respect for the well-spoken, well groomed, and talented performer, and the man possessed no self-control regarding the ladies.

Miriam was certain she couldn't control or even contain the man, but the one thing she did know for certain, she loved that Creole man. She wasn't sure if she had figured out the meaning of the word, but he would receive her greatest effort at it.

Ray stretched out on the bed of hay smiling, and ready for his future bride. She knelt between his legs and pampered the man. They both slept peacefully, stretched, repeated the love-making, and got dressed. "Are we going to leave her up there?" Miriam asked pointing in Til's direction.

"Wish we could, but we gots a show to do, so run along and start dat song we gonna write. You gonna get some more inspiration once I gets dat ladder set up. I is gonna take care of everything. Run along baby." He gave Miriam a long kiss on the lips, and she skedaddled out of the barn to the highway. He assisted Til from the loft in the barn, and a fatal mistake took place. In the distance Miriam listened to the unmistakable shrill of Tallulah Til.

Miriam ducked in the cotton fields. The miserable Mississippi sun already took its toll on the young woman, even though the time read eight o'clock in the morning. With the heat and the humidity the Delta region spawns, Miriam already started to sweat. She wiped the sweat off her brow and waited until her companions came out of the barn. The three were already scheduled for a show, and Miriam and Ray desperately wanted to write a couple of songs, including Til's tribute. Ray planned on calling Miriam out for a duet during his set, while Til watched. "Dis is a 'fuck you' to dat bitch."

His records sold regionally, and Ray reigned over the Delta. Folks came from the Hill Country, from Bentonia, and from across the river in Arkansas and Louisiana. They came all the way from Tennessee, and even East from Alabama to see him play. Mostly folks came from the Delta to listen. He shared the bill with his buddy and the two ladies.

Miriam and Til opened the show and the music was top-notch. Til never sounded better, while Miriam didn't miss a note. No one gave a damn about the perfection of their act. People weren't there to witness their performance, people weren't even there to listen to Tallulah Til, whose name had started to fade from the public eye. Til blamed her young lover as the reason, and never figured people knew her reputation. Incredible music was always easy to find in the South. It was finding musicians with the talent and the heart that took effort.

Miriam joined Ray for a few duets, and to add a little accompaniment on a few songs. Both lovers, played their hearts out on stage, and didn't notice Til leaving the juke. She disappeared when they sang the homage to her, "The Unmistakable Shrill of Tallulah Til." Til slipped away and went to a nearby farm to get some whiskey. She returned to the barn where they were sleeping and found Miriam and Ray rehearsing.

Til observed Miriam fingerpicking the six-string. She noticed a nice hunk of pipe on Miriam's ring finger, and it shone like a diamond ring. Til rushed towards Miriam. "I gotcha something as a present. I guess you won, Mara. I ain't gonna fight this battle no more. I ain't sure which one of you two I'm fighting for. Might be fighting for you or for him. I kind of loves both of you. Anyways, I got this whiskey for the two of you. Make sure he has plenty of whiskey tonight. Oh Mara, I know you don't drink, but if you have some snorts, don't you drink too much. This stuff can kill ya if you drinks a lot." She winked at Miriam and pulled her young lover into her bosom one last time. "We can still be lovers, if dis don't work out for you. Now turn around. I want to give that little butt of yours one more spanking." Miriam spun around, allowing Til to give her ass a nice affectionate swat, and she headed out the door. Miriam took a deep breath, loud enough so Ray heard her exhale.

"You got us some whiskey?"

"Yeah, Til give us a bottle, but I don't drink nothing. I ain't gonna have none."

He smiled at her. "Dat's ok. More for me, but I don't want none. Maybe some for later. Let's go up there in dat loft and write some songs." The man grabbed Miriam's hand as they walked towards the hayloft, dancing a little jig. Miriam shook her bottom to the rhythm of the impromptu song he sang.

> *I ain't need no whiskey, when I'm with you.*
> *I ain't be drinking, when I with you.*
> *Oh, my little Miri, I just get drunk on you.*

He played some of his fancier chords, ones only he played, ripped his turnaround that folks around the Delta copied and continued singing and dancing. Once again, he danced circles around her, and Miriam got dizzy watching him.

I said I don't need no whiskey, cause I wid you,
I ain't doing no drinking, cause I wid you
Just loving you, gets me all drunk on you.

He led her towards the ladder ascending into the loft. The hay stacked high, and the two of them were alone except for the livestock. Ray let Miriam climb ahead of him, and again it wasn't because a true gentleman lets ladies go ahead, but like most people, he liked to watch Miriam climbing a ladder. She gawked at him, and his smile illuminated the dark barn. They didn't need the lantern.

"Wacha looking at?" She smiled also.

"Just watching you. I's coming up in a bit." He waited for Miriam to get to the top. Finally, he grabbed the jug of shine and ascended the ladder.

Miriam started to give Ray some nice kisses on the cheek. She wanted to please her man, but the womanizer was still ready to sing.

"Not yet, sugar. We needs to get this song down first. We needs us to do a duet, so we get "Louisiana Girl" down to a tee, and we sing it together. I don't do duets, but I really think we…" He rubbed her cheek with his long index finger on his guitar picking hand, and he also stroked her chin with his thumb, as if he played the bass line on it. Miriam smiled at him. "When we get it right, I's gonna to take you to Texas to record so you can be on a record. We'll sing into a can with those lights a'flashing and we gonna make a record. Once we make us a record, we gonna live and love forever baby. Just you and me will always be together. So, let's get us this song written. I gonna let you use Stella. Looks like dat bitch Til took da guitar you use."

He handed her his most prized possession, and she cradled it in her arms like the baby she'd never conceive. Ray Wilson loved his alternate tunings as Miriam found out when she strummed their baby.

"What da fuck kinds of tunings you got here? Can I switch to open G?"

"You can change it to anything you want." Dat's drop D, and dat's the way I likes it. By da way Louisiana girl, I got me another guitar and a couple extra slides."

"Oh, I got the slide in my overall's pocket. I's gonna get it." Miriam already undressed and naked, ached to play something else besides the guitar and desired to sing a different duet than the one her man preferred to perform. She bent to get the three-inch pipe out of her overalls pocket, sticking her butt in his face. He gave it a smack as she spun and smiled. She plopped before the man and played her version of his standard intro. She started the shuffle and used the slide on the strings like Til. Lightning Bug, and even her father taught her on the Diddley bow years earlier.

Ray got comfortable, and he smiled, and tapped his large feet in rhythm to Miriam's guitar playing. He enjoyed his gal's performance, while she played the guitar naked. Ray Wilson tapped his feet and clapped his hands as his head rested on a stack of hay. Miri got the rhythm, and her cadence smooth as silk, while she strummed. She contemplated the words to sing, and she found them.

Come on in baby, got the hotcakes cooking,

Get over here baby, got the hotcakes on.
Once you get your fill, you gotta move along."

She continued to play and got her Stella ready for the second verse. She gazed and drooled at the naked Creole man, as she expected him to take control of the vocals. After all, they had rehearsed a duet. He sang.

This Lou'siana girl, She's with me tonight,
Lou'siana girl, gonna be with me tonight,
Lou'siana girl, I gonna be supper tonight."

Miriam hit all the notes and played the guitar in rhythm. She smiled and laughed a bit and peered at the man she desired. Her eyes focused below his stomach as she strummed. She started the third verse.

Come on baby got dem sausages grilling,
Come on baby got da sausages grilling…

"No, No Miri baby. Not sausage. Way too common of a metaphor. We don't want to be like Lucille. Fucking metaphors need to be cleverer. Got to change sausage to something else." She smiled the prettiest smile she gave to another human. She missed a beat on the shuffle. "I had my mind on something." Then she continued through the song again.

Come on in baby, got dem hot links grilling,
Come on in baby. Dem hot links are sizzling.
Dipped in syrup, much sweeter than kissing.

He moseyed towards his gal, grabbed the Stella

and placed it a few feet from Miriam. She eyed the man from head to toe. She already breathed heavy, as she wet her lips and leaned against a hay bale. "You got me all revved up baby. You and me gonna shake this rickety barn down."

He took Miriam's face in his hands and caressed it before he gave her a short kiss, and one a little longer, until the kissing no longer satisfied their lust. Miriam craved something else. Miriam was thankful that she worked under the tutelage of Felicia at the Shreveport whorehouse. She satisfied her man, and he soon attempted to meet her desires. An hour or so later. Miriam sank into a deep slumber, and Ray decided to take a shot or two of the whiskey in his flask. Whiskey dick arrived at the proper time, since his satisfied lady slept next to him. The man swallowed several additional snorts.

Ray's empty flask laid next to him. The man lifted the jug Til give them, sniffed and made a face. The stuff stunk to high heaven. He set it on the ground just as Miriam stirred. She figured she was special since the guy refused the whiskey and chose her as they worked on another verse. Miriam floated in the high loft. She'd never achieved such blissfulness; she'd grown afraid that she'd never live the Blues again. He peeked at her as she woke up. He swallowed every inch of her petite frame with his hungry eyes. "I'm gonna get you your own Stella. Gonna find one wid a thinner neck, so it be perfect for dese pretty hands."

The song provided the ambiance for another round, and round three satisfied them. Miriam fell asleep on the hay bale as Ray descended to the floor of the barn with his whiskey. He took a snort, and another two, and in addition several more shots, and climbed to the place

277

where they made love. The jug still sat on the soiled floor of the barn. Ray kissed Miriam on the forehead and returned the short piece of pipe to her ring finger. "One day I is gonna get you a real ring. I wants you to be my wife." He went down the ladder one more time and took another shot of whiskey. He passed out on the dirt floor.

I was on the run on Highway One,
Headed for Jonesboro, Arkansas.
Til was dead and so was the man
That played that harmonica,
I had to run, but I had no gun.
Hopped the freight to Arkansas.
With nowhere to hide, and no one on my side.
I had his slide and harmonica.
I was on the run on highway One
Heading to Jonesboro, Arkansas.

Chapter 30
The Hellhounds

"Girl, get yo ass outta dere. Dey gonna blame you for it. Getcher scrawny ass out of there."

Miriam awoke to the haunting shrill of Tallulah Til. She hoped she'd never have to hear it again. "I needs to wake him, den. We's gonna get married."

"You ain't gonna get married. I'm one hundred percent serious on this. Dey gonna blame you for it, now run."

Miriam got dressed, but she took her sweet time and enjoyed walking naked around him and sensing his aroma across her nude body. Miriam tossed on her overalls on and kept the slide on her ring finger. She leaned to kiss her man, assuming he lay passed out drunk, since she noticed an empty whiskey jug on the ground. She grabbed one of his Stella guitars and departed from the barn, glancing over her shoulder as she walked out.

She walked with the same cotton fields at her feet where she had walked hand-in-hand with Raymond Melvin Wilson as if they were innocent school children. She approached the intersection of the two country roads where the highways crossed—at the crossroads. There the man stood, not her fiancé, but an old man in a straw hat, smoking a corncob pipe.

The man tipped his hat to Miriam. "We meet again." His complexion appeared dark as coal and his matted hair framed his face. His smile, full of shiny white teeth, would have brightened the darkest of nights. "I been looking for you. I just want to thank you for the tobacco you left me back in Morgan City. I was all out."

The southwestern winds blew strong, as Papa put

some tobacco in his corncob pipe, and lit the match. For a mortal the match stood no chance of lighting, but the old man lit it and took a puff off the pipe, blew the smoke out and took a deep breath. He spun around and in a twinkling held the guitar Miriam carried. He smiled at Miriam and sang a song, which she once performed.

There is a house in New Orleans.
They call the Rising Sun.

"You been p'tecting me?" Miriam asked him.

Out of nowhere, a shiny Caddy came flying through the intersection, as Papa pulled Miriam out of the way. He didn't contact her, but she somehow managed to fly far enough off the road not to get flattened. She recognized the driver, since they spent the last five months together. "Watch this, and you decide." He said nothing else.

The car sped past the crossroads, into the path of some giant hounds. Flames engulfed the car as the vehicle disappeared and the enormous mutts feasted on the corpse. Miriam, with Haitian heritage, was aware of the capabilities of Hellhounds, and now she was aware of the cartoonish looking man. She relinquished her position on the highway. The man protected her, but she realized trusting him may cost her everlasting soul.

In a thick Haitian accent, he said to her, "Move along pretty lady. Best run along. Dem crittahs you mortals call hellhounds ain't gonna do nuttin' to you if you innocent. Dat spell wid dat bitch is ovah, 'cuz dose mutts jus' took care o' her. Ya hear me, run along and get yo self out o' dese crossroads. However, if you want to make anudder deal, we can stay and talk." He dumped the tobacco out of the pipe, repacked it and lit it in the swirling, gusting wind. He took a big puff and blew the smoke into the Mississippi blue sky.

"Sir, I'm not sure if I know ya or not, but I'm done with deals. I best be moseying on out of here. Not sure where I'm headed to."

"Very well," the man puffed his pipe again and exhaled the smoke in the direction of the hellhounds who ate Tallulah Til as breakfast. He headed towards the mutts and the fire. Miriam headed off towards Indianola, Mississippi.

Miriam arrived in Indianola and pondered the events. She assumed Ray died, and she acquired no clue as to who killed him, but realized the last person to see her man alive would be accused of killing him, and she'd be charged. Plus, the events happened in Mississippi. She wondered about telling the police what happened, but she doubted the law would understand.

Checking her surroundings, Miriam spotted a phone booth and made a call about a dead body. "Dere dis body in da barn I work at passed out, wouldn't move. He just off da highway." Miriam hung up the phone, and wandered along the dusty road, leaving shoe prints, wherever she stepped.

She spotted the town police and decided on not telling them what happened, and soon wondered to herself, *Did the all-white police force believe in the guardian? Did they believe hellhounds existed?* She laid down on the park bench located across the street from the Indianola police station. There she covered herself up with a newspaper, shut her eyes and fell asleep.

The voices of people talking startled Miriam awake. She glanced up and a familiar-appearing African

American man stood talking to a white police officer. Miriam eavesdropped on the conversation. "They say he left the joint with a woman, might have been two since they was playing a show with me. One of dem girls was skinny, da other was bigger. Da bigger one was Tallulah Til. Don't recall the skinny girl's name."

She couldn't make out the police officer's voice since he talked with a much softer tone, but the guy who they questioned possessed a booming voice. Miriam recognized him as Stoney. He continued to answer questions Miriam ignored. "I didn't see any of them after last night. I thought I saw Til go to that barn over yonder." He pointed the opposite direction of where they went. "I think the last person dat saw him was that skinny girl. I think there is your answer."

The policeman shook his hand, but Miriam already snuck off towards the highway. There she spotted the railroad tracks, where freight trains came rumbling along. Miriam found the rails and commenced to walk across the cotton fields waiting for the Delta Pacific, or the Arkansas Pacific to take her anywhere but there.

Miriam hadn't even poured him a shot. She was aware of her innocence. The hell hounds stayed put, and didn't follow her, so the proof of her non-guilt was obvious. Did white police officers and white judges in 1938 Mississippi care about what a runaway Creole whore told them about Hell Hounds, and their myths? Advising the police she gave Ray Wilson some whiskey meant her death sentence, since a star musician ranks higher on the food chain than a runaway prostitute.

She walked behind the tree line hoping her moving shadow went unnoticed. She moved faster with her butt to the sun going west towards Louisiana.

Catching the right train meant arriving in Louisiana in less than an hour. Catching the wrong train meant delay and being arrested. Miriam remained hidden as she marched to the edge of the railyard where she boarded the Arkansas Pacific.

She stepped on the ladder and pulled herself into the yellow boxcar. The car appeared empty, but she imagined she noticed the man in the straw hat again. She inhaled the tobacco smoke coming from the opposite end of the car. The aroma, powerful and fruity, but pleasant and reminded her of innocent times in her life, before the fiddle player became part of the band.

Miriam sighed, since she smelled her daddy's brand of tobacco. She noticed his straw hat in the shadows, but never saw his face. He sat in the shadows, or perhaps the man was nothing but a shadow. Miriam didn't have a clue if he existed, and she cared less if someone else sat in the freight car. She longed to depart town. He played a song; the song Miriam and Ray wrote together. It was the last thing he ever wrote.

"No one heard this before, how did you…?" Her mind stopped and she listened as the man sang.

> *He Ain't no devil*
> *He ain't no saint.*
> *Ain't white man's Jesus.*
> *He makes demons faint.*
> *He ain't no prophet*
> *But he got a voice.*
> *Share your smokes.*
> *You got no choice"*

Smiling, she grabbed the slide her man gave her

and put it on her finger. From her bindle stick she grabbed her gris-gris bag and held to her lips as she gave it a soft kiss. She kissed it again like the bag was her loved one. She rode in silence while the mysterious shadow sang his song. Then he also sang another. This song came with a dedication to a former female protege of his. The ditty was dedicated to Til. He brought her to fame, but he eradicated the woman and her unmistakable shrill. Miriam made it as far as Monroe, where the railyard cops tossed her off the train. The mysterious man vanished like mash.

Railyard police, sometimes called bulls, can be helpful, or downright mean. Train hopping happened. Millions of people hopped freight trains across the country. After all, folks hopped freights to run away, and that's their sole means of travel. Some scouting for better jobs. Some flee to escape oppression. Others forced from their homes, escaping Jim Crow, while others escape abusive situations. Former prostitute, Miriam Landry ran from a potential murder rap, but she wasn't sure.

Monroe, Louisiana, a booming oil town, was full of drillers. The roughnecks liked their whiskey and women. Miriam, was aware breakfast and lunch money waited and became hers for the taking. She'd sell herself and get a bus or train ticket to Shreveport, or maybe she'd return home to the swamps. No longer desiring to turn tricks anymore, she soon finished her whore's life, but a girl does what she must do.

She whored herself out for three days. Drillers didn't care what race they drilled. They craved to drill something or someone. Miriam made enough money whoring herself out, and made enough coins, to rustle some grub, gather a change of clothes, and splurge on a bus ticket to Shreveport. She didn't care if these oilers received the wrong end of a make-believe spell or not, she cared less what happened to the large, greasy men. The way they treated her, and sometimes two, maybe three of them sticking stuff at and in her, made her hope and wish a spell would transform her. When she got to Shreveport, her life required reevaluating.

In Monroe, while eating a breakfast of grits and biscuits and gravy, she noticed the photo, and even though her reading skill and comprehension wasn't the greatest, she made out the words. "Music Star, Raymond Melvin Wilson murdered in Mississippi barn." In smaller print towards the rear pages of the paper, another article read, "Woman singer missing."

"I do have the spell on me," Miriam whispered to herself. "Now I have to run." She boarded the bus to Shreveport, where she walked to Southern Avenue and hitched to King's Highway across the Red River.

She hitched her way south, hopping a ride in the bed of a pick-up truck. The truck dropped her off near Coushatta, in the middle of Creole Country, near the Cane River. The sun shined straight above her as noon approached, and it took its toll on the girl. Augusts are unkind if one walks for miles and miles, and you're a fugitive.

Miriam strolled along the highway through the bayou. The trees stood thick and green. Spanish moss hung on the branches of the cypress, while magnolia trees also stood tall along the road. Miriam kept her pace, walking steady down the road until she found a bridge crossing Cane River. She stopped, contemplated jumping, but instead began tossing stones into the water. Bo Barnum's jalopy came rolling by and stopped.

Chapter 31
Conclusion

"Are you serious Miriam? You were with Ray Wilson before us? No way! And you knew Mojo Davis and some of them other cats also? I don't believe it."

"It's da truth, Sara. Every word of it. Dat's why I can't go wid ya to Haiti or anywhere. I got stuff to do back here. I just wanted to see my daddy go off to heaven, or hell, wherever he's going."

"Come on, it will be one last adventure."

"Sara, have you been listening to me? I run a little place for prostitutes back in Shreveport. I run it with Felicia. I just gonna be gone for Daddy's funeral."

"I need you there."

"I don't need you, though. I got me a job taking care of these girls. They needs me. You just need someone for sumfin you have no idea what you need dem for." She made a face, understanding what she meant to say, but it came out wrong. Somehow, I comprehended her message. But I needed her back in my life.

"Now I's got some songs we's can record. We can do dem under this bridge before we moves on. We sang the collaborations with Ray Wilson."

That Louisiana woman,
She done me no good
That Louisiana woman,
Always up to no good.
The only good thing about her
She liked to chop that wood.

This other Louisiana girl
Gonna treat your right
I'm a Louisiana girl,
And I'm gonna treat you tonight
My baby gonna be thinking tonight.

We rehearsed the song a few times, and it hit me. At least, I imagined it smacked me in the face. "Miri, wait a minute. This bitch, Til made a deal with you, if you fucked her you have to be faithful to her?"

"Right. But…"

"Well, you cheated on her with Ray, and now he's dead. Next person you were with was my father. Now he's dead. Lightning Bug lays dying of cancer in a Chicago hospital, and me, I'm going to a fucking third world country in exile. At least four people you've had sex with since you were with Til, and three are dead. One is about to die, and the other one's life is so fucked up, I can't even say."

"The hellhounds didn't follow. There weren't no spell, and I's not guilty."

'You were part of all of this weren't you? You were part of the conspiracy all along."

"Sara, I knows nothing at all. Plus there wasn't no curse either. Just 'cause you don't believe no hellhounds exist doesn't mean they doesn't. Now how we gonna get down to Morgan City?" She tossed some stones into the lake, still clutching her little bag, and the slide Ray gave her.

"We're gonna hitch." I glared at her.

"We got no money with us, you stink, and got no clothes except dem dirty rags you wearing. Who gonna pick us up?"

"We will find a way. I always do." I shook my hair at her, and we strolled towards the highway.

"I gots a plan, but I don't like it. This might let you know about da curse, also. Follow me, Sara."

Miriam for once took charge of the situation, and we hitched to a truck stop on the highway near Lake Charles. I tried leading the way, but Miriam walked in front. "Now stay back, I don't want ya to see this." She vanished for about an hour. "Goes and gets yourself a shower. It's gonna work out."

I ran into the truck stop to clean myself off, but I peeked behind me and noticed Miriam climbed into the semi-truck with an overweight driver. Miriam still never told me what happened, but I knew what they did. I got a brand spanking new straw hat and a couple changes of clothes from her transaction. The whore's life behind her, but it seemed like this intruded into the agenda. She planned on assisting me in my exile, where I would spend the rest of my life, while all Miriam wanted was to see her father go to his grave. She had matured, and no longer catered to others. From now on, she'd live in peace.

Miriam convinced the trucker to give us a ride to Morgan City. His had a scheduled delivery at the Winn Dixie in her hometown, and he gave her spending money. The professional skills she put on the shelf for years required refreshing, but the trucker didn't mind, as he drove the rig with a giant grin on his face. Miriam spent her middle adult life teaching women not to use those skills for prostitution.

The driver dropped us off at the store, and after the trucker and I engaged in a lengthy debate, we headed for Miriam's mother's house. I was to meet a business partner in New Orleans and one of Miriam's cousins drove me there. The meeting was essential for my survival, while Miriam socialized with her family and prepared for the services.

Miriam spent most of her time in her old room, writing music. She walked around the house and sat by the diddley bow her father had built for his toddler. She slid Ray's slide along the strings. Tears came to her eyes, realizing the countless numbers of people who had died. She wondered about the fate of the truck driver.

Epilogue:

We met again on a Haitian beach before the failed coup in '63. The smuggler flew her to the poor end of Hispaniola, and I longed to deliver to her the story and add the finishing pieces. I wondered about her life and what direction it moved towards, so pen and paper in hand we ambled towards the golden beaches.

Her life evolved. Her and Felicia worked incredibly together. Platonic business partners, they never crossed the line. It seemed like Felicia liked a few of the girls they worked with. Miriam became afraid to give her love away. The lives of all the people she gave gratification became destroyed. Believe me I'm aware. I became one of them.

Tommie Parker died of cancer, but also became stricken with several health issues. He passed right after playing at the Newport Folk Festival. Miriam and I played at the same show, while he sang a song Miriam wrote. Judge Paul Mitchell and Sylvester—both arrested and convicted of the murders of black prostitutes on the Red River. Miriam Landry, a witness for the prosecution's testimony, got him sent away. The man, well into his sixties, was remanded to Angola, and was slashed by a gay male prostitute he sentenced for crimes the kid didn't commit.

Miriam's songs floated around the Chicago Blues scene, and she received credit for a few of them. Mojo Davis sang, "Gonna Run Away," and it became a hit in the USA, but when he toured England, a group of English kids liked it. They recorded her song, and it took off as the young Brits invaded the States with their music. This band even got their name from one of Mojo's songs, and they recorded additional Miriam Landry-penned songs. She continues to collect royalties.

The folk singer changed the world. Well, he's a huge fan of Ray Wilson. Beatniks, journalists, folklorists all started searching for his songs, and even though Lomax collected most of them, the general population did not. If the songs he wrote with his lover could be found, the duets especially meant a gold mine. As far as I knew, only two people listened to the lost songs of Miriam Landry, and that was Miriam and myself, and maybe the ghost if you accepted every part of her story. We recorded them beneath the bridge near Lake Charles. I still play them in my Haitian hut, even though I adapted the beat to Caribbean rhythms.

"Come back to Louisiana. Maybe I needs you more than I thought, or maybe you needs me more than I thought."

"I can't go back. I got that murder rap. You remember your first hit song? 'I Killed a Man.'"

She smiled at me as the biplane circled, and the smuggler wondered where to land the plane, so he could return her to Louisiana. "Come Sara, I gots me a lovely place, we can just sits on da porch and plays our guitars. Dat's all I does now, collects checks, drinks my lemonade and writes songs. It's what I imagines heaven to be like."

"That sounds like heaven to me, but I actually got work down here. This president is crazy." I wiggled my finger towards me, signaling Miriam to come closer. I whispered in her ear. "I'm organizing a coup. We are going to get Papa Doc. The people will be in charge."

The plane splashed in the blue water as we sat

close to one another. Destiny brought us together, but it also kept us separated. We may have been one another's true loves, but who knows. I remembered an old saying, 'when you love someone, set them free.'

She kissed my neck and she whispered in my ear. "Fly away, my love."

I nibbled on her lobe, kissed her on the lips. "You, too. Enjoy the rest of your life. You deserve this more than anyone." We kissed again, and she handed me a package before she walked towards the plane. I'd never see her again. She placed a forty-five-rpm record inside the envelope with songs on both sides.

I put the record on. It started out with some of the greatest fingerpicking I ever heard. Nothing but a girl and her guitar. The record spat out her song, "The Undeniable Shrill of Tallulah Til." The song started out with Miriam talking to me above a single E-chord drone. Her guitar never sounded better. She introduced the ditty in a little poem.

> *Ray and I recorded this song,*
> *In a hayloft right before he died.*
> *It was on a little tape player,*
> *One he carried inside.*
> *Wasn't that fancy, but it will have to do,*
> *Dis da real secret, I wanna share with you.*
> *Here is his last song he ever wrote*
> *He wrote it for me, dat ain't no joke*
> *Now it's all yours, and you can pass it on down*
> *Or we can record it, if you ever get back in town.*

The song kicked in, and with a much clearer tone. She must have gotten hold of some modern technology, and she sang the lead.

It kept the same single chord pattern throughout the song. I loved the single chord drone.

She da devil, She da devil She da devil.

In a man's voice came, "The Undeniable Shrill of Miss Tallulah Til." The voice was unmistakable. It was Ray Wilson's. They sang harmonies about Til, while she sang, "She da Devil."

Soft and Curvy,
Loud and mean.
I can't love ya,
No in between.

She da devil, she da devil, she da devil.
The Undeniable Thrill of Miss Tallulah Till,
She da devil, she da devil, She da devil.

There weren't no deal.
She ain't a witch.
Just angry and mean,
We can't stay hitched.

She da devil, she's da devil, she's da devil.
The undeniable shrill, of Miss Tallulah Til,
She's da devil, she's da devil, she's da devil.

I flipped the record over, and I heard Miriam, with another man singing a little ditty. I made out two guitars. One sounded off beat, while the other masterful. They sang harmonies, and I knew it wasn't Ray singing the male lead. The man sang solo on the lines about him. His voice was off key a bit, but it was haunting, somehow it sounded perfect. In between verses, Miriam took over on the guitar, and played the nastiest slide I ever heard. She should have been famous, but then again maybe the Blues and later rock and roll didn't deserve her.

He Ain't no devil.
He ain't no saint.
I ain't white man's Jesus
I makes demons faint.
I ain't no prophet,
But I got a voice.
Share your smokes—
You got no choice"

It ain't the whiskey.
I don't want your rum.
Don't want you roaming the fields
With a loaded gun
How you live your life,
It's not up to him.
He's not White Man Jesus
And there ain't no sin.

"Miriam Landry was the best musician I'd ever heard, and I was raised in a juke, masquerading as a whorehouse." Sara Barnum, 1963.

www.ingramcontent.com/pod-product-compliance
Lightning Source LLC
Chambersburg PA
CBHW031701170626
46808CB00005B/1553